Evenings at the Claremont

EVENINGS AT THE CLAREMONT

A Novel

Georgia Walkup

For Ann ~~████~~
Love and Peace!
Georgia Walkup

iUniverse, Inc.
New York Lincoln Shanghai

Evenings at the Claremont
A Novel

All Rights Reserved © 2004 by Georgia Walkup

No part of this book may be reproduced or transmitted in any form or by any means, graphic, electronic, or mechanical, including photocopying, recording, taping, or by any information storage retrieval system, without the written permission of the publisher.

, Inc.

For information address:
iUniverse, Inc.
2021 Pine Lake Road, Suite 100
Lincoln, NE 68512
www.iuniverse.com

Evenings at the Claremont is a work of fiction. Names of real places and actual persons have been used to give the story a setting in history. Characters and events depicted in this novel are the product of the author's imagination.

Cover design is taken from details of a painting entitled: *At the Claremont* by the artist, Mary B. Lloyd, and is used with permission of the artist.

Map is reproduced from a drawing by Robert H. Walkup.
Photo of the author was taken by Janet Weil.

ISBN: 0-595-32475-4

Printed in the United States of America

*This book is dedicated
to my husband, RHW, with my love*

Acknowledgments

The inspiration for this novel came from my memories of the Hotel Claremont, especially during the 1950's. Mary B. Lloyd's oil painting of the hotel added impetus for me to finish writing this romance. To all of you listed below, I offer my profound gratitude.

To my adult children for their loving support: Janet, John, Doug, Patty, Rob, and Carol; and to my five grandsons: Josh, Russ, Chris, Joel and Daniel.

To the friendly people of Redding, California for background information: Linda Pepin and Burt Train of the City of Redding Municipal Airport.

To Diane Bateman Muldoon for sending me articles, and to Jack Muldoon and Frank Lloyd for visiting the Claremont in 2003.

To my sister and brother-in-law, Diane and Bert Quint, for their interest.

To the reference librarians at the Beaverton Public Library for directing me to books describing soldiers' accounts of the battle of Monte Cassino and other historical events.

To my excellent editor and consultant, Nancy Osa.

To Steven Lavoie of the Oakland Public Library History Room for providing information about the 1991 fire in the Oakland hills near the Hotel Claremont.

To friends at Christ Church Episcopal Parish for their encouragement.

To my fellow Classic Book Club readers: Sherri, Myrna, Nancy, Kathy and Richard.

To the mermaids and one seahorse of Oswego Pointe: Ann, Erika, Janelle, Judy, Betsey, Donna, Ileen, Pixie, Pat, Bette, Mary, Dianne and Harry.

And finally, special thanks to my daughter, Janet Weil, for taking family pictures at the Claremont, and for sharing ideas and information.

To my husband, Bob, who set me straight on U.S. Forest Service procedures and geographical features of California. You are a fine forester.

Bishop Berkeley 1685–1753

"Westward the course of empire takes its way;
The first four acts already past,
A fifth shall close the drama with the day:
Time's noblest offspring is the last."

**On the Prospect of Planting Arts
and Learning in America**

*The Oxford Dictionary of Quotations
Third Edition, 1980*

The founders named the California city for Bishop Berkeley. In 1868 Berkeley was chosen as the site for a land grant college destined to become one of the great universities of the world.

Locales of
Evenings at the Claremont

Chapter 1

Berkeley, California

Gary Morgan decided that the perfect place to propose marriage to Natalie would be the Garden Room at the Hotel Claremont. He would make a reservation for Saturday dinner, requesting their favorite dance tune from the orchestra leader. Then, leading her onto the balcony, he would slip a ring on her finger. He leaned back in his swivel desk chair, grinning and placing his hands against the back of his head.

"Well, aren't you the romantic?" he congratulated himself. He pictured Natalie's face as he said…what? What words would he say? He had to come up with an original proposal. After all, he was a lawyer, or at least a third-year law student at Boalt Hall. Didn't lawyers have a way with words? He began writing mock legal argumentation on a yellow pad.

"*Whereas,* the Plaintiff has fallen in love with the Defendant; and *Whereas,* named Defendant has reciprocated such affection; *be it known* that Plaintiff offers a proposal of matrimony with all rights and privileges pertaining thereto granted to beloved Defendant…"

In his sparsely furnished apartment, Gary said aloud, "Don't be a nut. Stick with words of love. The ring," he reminded himself, tipping his chair forward with a thud. He grabbed his coat, counted his money, and headed out to shop for a solitaire—the most brilliant diamond he could afford. At least he could put down a hundred-dollar deposit and negotiate the balance. Checking his watch, he saw that he barely had time to reach the jewelry store on Shattuck Avenue before it closed.

For the past five months, Gary had known that Natalie was the only woman he would ever wish to be his wife.

September, 1951

Once, when Gary Morgan was driving with his roommate from their apartment two blocks north of the campus to the Morgans' home in Piedmont, his friend had joked, "You know, Piedmont is a nice place to live, but I wouldn't want to *visit* there."

Berkeley had gained its identity as the site of the University of California after one nineteenth-century editor had tagged the city "the Athens of the Pacific." Its citizens were a complex intermingling of academics and professionals, as well as laborers, craftsmen, and artists who lived in homes extending from the salt flats near San Francisco Bay to the winding streets leading north to Grizzly Peak. Berkeley's ethnically diverse population expanded over the years as the University's enrollment became one of the largest in the nation. On the campus, one could find students of every race and virtually every national origin. Physicists and plumbers and poets all lived in Berkeley.

In contrast, the adjacent community of Piedmont was known for its neighborhoods of affluent families, living in traditional houses with manicured lawns. As the name suggested, Piedmont was located in the gently rolling hills between Berkeley and Oakland, a convenient place for commuting, a desirable location for small shops and apartment buildings. Gary Morgan's maternal grandfather was one of those investors who had bought land in the Piedmont area in the early years of the twentieth century. Grandfather Lundgren had prospered as a result.

Gary had taken his roommate's quip about Piedmont as a typical case of sour grapes. He had long since grown used to stereotypes expressed about privileged Piedmont dwellers.

Gary and Natalie would probably never have met if the Tates had not held an "Open House" the Saturday after Labor Day to celebrate Ed Tate's new position with the Oakland firm of Cobb and Fortis. Gary had received his invitation at his parents' home in Piedmont. His mother, sitting at her French provincial desk, inquired about his mail.

"Is that an invitation?"

"Yes. This is one *BYOB* party I should attend," Gary remarked. "My buddy, Ed Tate, was a year ahead of me at Boalt Hall. I missed his wedding to Beverly this summer, but I'll help him celebrate the kickoff of his career."

Mrs. Morgan replied, "Sounds like fun. Why don't you take a girl along?"

"Mother," Gary growled, knowing what was coming. "You know I don't have a *girl*. I'll bring my favorite brew and stop by to congratulate Ed."

"I was just thinking of my bridge friend, Helen Woodard," his mother said, tapping her fingernail against her front teeth. "Her daughter, Gail, is a junior at Cal this year. Why don't you ask her? She's a Tri Delt," Mrs. Morgan added.

"I don't think Tri Delts drink beer, Mother," Gary answered.

"Oh, you!" Mrs. Morgan laughed, pushing him gently. "It wouldn't hurt you to invite Gail Woodard to the Tates' party. Gail is lively; she's ebullient."

"Ebullient is she? Okay, that cinches it. Give me your friend's phone number and I'll call her daughter. You missed your calling, Mother. You're a born matchmaker."

Gary and his date arrived when the party was already in full swing. Most of the men were older than Gary, many of them now married. Gary left Gail chatting with Beverly Tate as he wandered over to a corner of fellow students from Boalt Hall Law School, including Dave Rosenthal, Reed Houghton, and a second-year student named Paul Sawyer.

"What do you think of our pal Edmund becoming a corporate lawyer?" Gary addressed Dave Rosenthal.

"He's leaving the field of widows and orphans open for us," Dave said. Like Gary, he had served in the Army. He was the friend Gary respected most. They had talked about specializing in civil rights and labor relations cases after they passed the California bar exam.

"Are you two going to save the world and advance democracy while the rest of us earn the big bucks and buy Buicks?" Reed chided Gary and Dave. Everyone at Boalt Hall knew that Reed's father was the senior partner at the prestigious law firm, Houghton and Naylor of San Francisco. Reed had deflected envy of his path being paved for him by joking about his material ambitions. Actually, as both Gary and Dave knew, Reed was more idealistic than he seemed, and bright enough to attract offers from many firms without his father's connections. Reed had minimized his heart condition by saying casually, "My ticker just doesn't keep time accurately."

During Gary and Reed's fraternal joshing, Paul Sawyer sat silent, hesitant to join in their conversations. Gary asked him, "What've you been doing this summer, Paul?"

"I went home to Redding. The only job I could get this summer was working on the Shasta-Trinity National Forest, clearing brush and training to fight fires. Fortunately, we didn't have any big blazes."

Paul reddened slightly as he realized the others had stopped talking and were listening to him with interest.

"Hey, Paul, you can be a tree lawyer!" Reed said loudly.

"At least Paul probably got some physical exercise, which is more than I can say for some of us," Gary commented, pretending to punch Dave in the abdomen.

"Yeah, Morgan, the only bending and lifting you do in Judge Oliver's office is hoisting his law books," razzed Dave.

Gary saw Bev Tate showing the girls around the newlyweds' apartment, displaying her new china. He asked Paul Sawyer, "Who's your date?"

"A good friend," Paul said. "Our families have known each other forever. Nat's father, the district ranger, recommended me for the Forest Service job."

Overhearing these remarks, Reed said to Gary, "I don't recognize your girlfriend."

"She's the bubbly blonde," Gary said. "Stash the comments. Here come the ladies."

Bev introduced everyone, saying, "You fellas have had enough time to gab. We have a good group for a game of Charades."

"To think I married a game organizer," Ed Tate groaned.

Gail was wearing her sorority pin, prominently displayed on her chest. Gary guessed her to be about twenty-one years old. Reed's date, Zoe Chandler, was one of a few women students at Boalt Hall. Zoe excelled in mock trial classes, especially in her cross-examination of witnesses.

"Weren't you in American Lit?" Natalie asked Rhonda Kagan, Dave's fiancée.

"Both of you English majors should be good at Charades," Bev interjected.

"Another beer for anyone? Plenty of sandwiches left," Ed Tate said, gesturing toward the buffet table.

Minutes later, Gary found himself on a team with Paul, Natalie, Gail, and Bev, who announced the rules. The teams huddled to write down titles on slips of paper, with everyone making suggestions that ranged from *Winnie the Pooh* to *War and Peace*.

"Okay, time. We're ready," Ed called out.

Beverly ran her fingers through her curly auburn hair as she held up two fingers for a signal. She rolled her head from side to side as Gary called out, "Head!"

She nodded, pulling on her ear lobe.

"Sounds like *head*," Paul said.

Gary began shouting out, "Bed, dead…"

Natalie said quietly, "*Ed, could it be Oedipus Rex?*"

"Great, partner," Paul said. "Got it in eight seconds!"

Zoe gave Gary a slip of paper reading *Plato's Republic.*

"Oh, come on," he protested.

"No talking, Gary," the other team reminded him. He gestured a circle with his hands, suggesting a plate as he moved toward the buffet table.

"No pointing either," Zoe said.

Gary signaled the second word, then marched up and down rapidly as though holding a flag, acting out the Spirit of '76.

"Plate marching. Plate walking fast," shouted Paul.

Natalie stood up. "*Plato's Republic?*" she asked.

"Hey, no fair. Natalie must have peeked," came the voices from Ed's team.

Gary stuck his hand out to Natalie. "Good job," he said.

Gail looked increasingly ill at ease as she began acting out her title.

After whispered help from Ed, Gail made an angry face, and Bev guessed *The Grapes of Wrath* before Ed had to call time.

"Last chance to determine the winner," announced Bev. "Natalie's turn."

Gary watched her intently as she stood in their midst in her gray jersey dress. He thought that she was more attractive than he had first noticed. With long fluid motions of her hands sliding down her figure, she pantomimed a strip tease with a wicked grin, then fell immediately onto the rug with her arms crossed over her bosom and her eyes closed.

"*The Naked and the Dead!*" yelled Gary.

On the ride home, Gail sat as far away from Gary as possible. Whatever topic he brought up led to a dead end. Finally, as he was about to deposit her at the Tri Delt house, Gail faced him with her parting shot. "I didn't know I was going to be *graded* tonight on my knowledge of literature."

Driving back to his apartment, Gary reflected, "So Gail Woodard considers me a pedantic prig. I'll have to talk to Mother about not arranging my social life."

Two days later, Gary phoned Paul Sawyer.

"Paul. Gary Morgan here."

"Hi, Gary. I have a hunch what you're going to ask, but go ahead."

"Have you been dating Natalie for long? Are you serious about her?"

"I've known Nat since high school, but I've never dated her before. I saw the way you were looking at her."

"What's her sorority and her last name?"

"No sorority. Last name is Perrault. She's working on her master's degree, boarding in a private home on Bancroft Street. Here's her number."

"Thanks, Paul," Gary said. "I must have a weakness for good Charades players."

When he called, the woman who answered told him that Natalie was out.

Gary gave his name and phone number. After two more calls, he reached her.

"This is Gary Morgan, friend of Ed and Beverly Tate."

"Hello, *Plato's Republic*," she said with a hint of laughter in her voice.

"Good old Plato really wrote some page-turners, didn't he? How about a movie Friday night? Your pick."

"Fine. Call me about six-thirty and I'll give you directions to the house."

"Your name sounds familiar. Wasn't there an author named Perrault?"

"Yes, you could call him an author." Her voice was soft and sexy as she said, "Charles Perrault is credited with writing the best-known version of the fairy tale *Cinderella*."

Natalie held the *Berkeley Gazette* movie schedule when she answered the door of the small brick house.

"Would you hate it if my choice is *Henry V*? It's playing at the theater on College Avenue. I missed the movie years ago when it first came out."

Gary sat next to her on the sofa, noticing her green eyes, fringed with dark lashes, and her silky brown hair.

"Are you trying to bone up on your Shakespeare for your classes this fall?"

She laughed. "All right, so we choose another movie."

"How could I turn down Shakespeare? You know, Olivier used the Battle of Agincourt as a metaphor for British soldiers in World War II. That *'Once more into the breach'* oration fit right in with Winston Churchill's speeches."

"No, I didn't know that, but if we don't hurry we'll miss the first show."

Over coffee following the movie, Natalie told him that her favorite teacher at Shasta High had inspired her to enroll at the University instead of a junior college. Gary learned that Natalie's parents would have been happier if she had gone to a college closer to Redding. She sounded apologetic as she added, "Dad and Mother are quite traditional. They speak of Berkeley as if it were a foreign place, and they hardly ever visit me."

She smiled as she spoke, but Gary could see the disappointment in her face.

"Your family's attitude is more common than you might think," he assured her. "Dad is a Cal alum and Mother was a student for two years. But I know many guys have found Berkeley overwhelming. Sink or swim. We're survivors, Natalie."

"You were in the Army, weren't you?" she asked.

"Yes."

"Overseas?"

"The Italian campaign. Fifth Army. Some injuries sent me home early with a medical discharge. Let's not talk about the war."

"Sorry. I didn't mean to pry."

"It's all right. When can I see you again? How about tomorrow?"

Chapter 2

▼

During the next few weeks, Gary and Natalie double-dated with his friends, exploring several jazz combo clubs which were becoming popular in Oakland. Once they went to an old Marx Brothers movie, discovering their mutual enjoyment of the zany comics. Then in October, Gary invited Natalie to dinner at his parents' home on the following Sunday.

"I have a Sam Goldwyn contract with my parents to have dinner with them once a month. Mother thinks I need home cooked meals," Gary explained.

"What's a Sam Goldwyn contract?" Natalie asked.

Gary answered in a raspy voice, "An oral agreement. You know that quote attributed to Sam: 'An oral agreement isn't worth the paper it's written on.'"

"I *had* to ask," Natalie said with a grin. "By the way, you sounded more like you were imitating Groucho Marx just now, not Sam Goldwyn."

"Anyway, I'm due to check in with Mother and Dad this Sunday. I hope you'll come along. They're nice people, if I do say so myself."

"I'd like to meet your parents," Natalie agreed.

The next day Natalie shared her news with her friend Jean Swithin after their Faulkner seminar in Wheeler Hall.

"Gary invited me to dinner with his parents Sunday."

"This is getting serious," Jean said. "Gary must be a fast worker—to coin a phrase," she added sarcastically. "When do I meet this paragon? I suppose he's good looking."

"Gary is handsome," Natalie said, "but when I'm with him I don't really think about his looks. He's funny and smart, about six feet tall. He has deep blue eyes, dark eyebrows and wavy brown hair."

Jean laughed. "Sounds handsome to me."

"But no roguish mustache or cleft chin or movie-star profile," Natalie added.

On Sunday, Natalie spent extra time choosing a green knit dress and arranging her hair, which she held back from her face with a velvet band. She pondered what to bring as a hostess gift. Having heard Gary say that his mother liked gardening, she found a book describing the native flowers and plants of California. As she was wrapping it, she wondered if it seemed presumptuous to bring a gift. Then the doorbell rang and she could hear her landlady, Mrs. Carlyle, saying, "Come in. I'll tell Natalie you're here."

There was Gary, waiting for her in the hallway, his eyes giving her an appreciative once-over. He was wearing a navy blue cashmere sweater over his white shirt, gray flannel slacks, and polished loafers. As he helped her with her coat, he kissed her lightly, whispering, "You look beautiful."

They rode almost in silence, with the little gift resting between them on the seat of his old Plymouth. Gary was full of his own thoughts, hoping this occasion had not been a mistake, worrying about questions his parents might ask. He had promised himself when he entered law school not to "get serious" with any girlfriend until he had earned his *Juris Doctor* diploma. So far he had been able to keep that pledge without much difficulty. Once he had told Dave Rosenthal that he would not allow himself to fall in love until he had *J.D.* after his name.

His friend had hooted at him. "Sure, we all say that, and then along comes that special someone. The next thing we know, we're getting a marriage license, renting a tux, and willingly walking down the aisle. I'll enjoy seeing *you* when you fall."

And Dave had said this even before he had met Rhonda Kagan.

Gary's reverie was interrupted by Natalie's question, "Do you have any brothers or sisters? You've never mentioned any."

"No, I'm the only one," he answered. "I suppose Mother thought I was trouble enough and she didn't want any more." He glanced at her, sidelong.

Natalie smiled back at him, wondering why she felt compelled to make a good impression, as though she was going for a job interview. Until this afternoon, she had been relaxed with Gary, but now she felt tense. She knew his father was an officer at the Port of Oakland, U.C. class of 1922. Just then Gary swung into a broad driveway, announcing, "We're here."

"What a beautiful Tudor house!" Natalie exclaimed. "And what gorgeous chrysanthemums, all golden and bronze."

"The garden is Mother's accomplishment," Gary said, opening the front door.

"Good to see you, darling," his mother greeted him, reaching up to stroke his cheek.

"Mother, this is Natalie Perrault," Gary said.

His mother offered her hand, saying, "How nice to meet you."

Mrs. Morgan led Natalie into a spacious living room where Mr. Morgan rose from a wingback chair to be introduced. Natalie judged him to be in his early fifties, sandy-gray haired, wearing a tan corduroy coat over a blue sports shirt.

Natalie held out her small gift.

"Something for you from the campus book store, Mrs. Morgan."

Gary's mother opened the package, remarking, "How thoughtful of you, Natalie. A gardening book."

"I'm afraid it's like bringing coals to Newcastle," Natalie said.

Mrs. Morgan looked at her blankly.

What an idiotic thing for me to say, Natalie realized, adding, "Your garden is lovely."

"Have a seat by the window for a view of Mrs. Morgan's asters," Mr. Morgan suggested. "Gary tells us you're a student of Shakespeare."

Now there's a conversation stopper, Dad, Gary thought, moving closer to Natalie, raising his eyebrows in amusement, but Natalie wasn't looking his way. Instead, he heard her say earnestly, "My major studies are American novels. I'm writing my master's thesis on Willa Cather."

"My, that sounds ambitious," Mrs. Morgan said, having no idea who Willa Cather was.

"What would you like to drink?" This from Mr. Morgan, standing by a small bar setup in the corner. "Grace, your usual?"

"Yes, dear." Mrs. Morgan leaned back against velvet cushions on the couch, smiling across at Gary.

"Natalie, what may I offer you?"

Her own parents were not teetotalers, but they seldom had liquor in the house.

"I'll have whatever Mrs. Morgan is having," she said airily. *That sounded stupid. I don't even know what her "usual" is.*

"Gin and tonic for two, then."

Mr. Morgan fixed the drinks.

"Any beer in the fridge, Dad?" Gary asked. "I'll get it."

Gary returned from the kitchen just as his father raised his highball, saying, "How about a toast? To the Bears. May their season improve".

While Gary and his father rehashed the football season, Natalie sipped her drink, observing Gary's mother across the room. Mrs. Morgan's light brown hair was styled in soft, feathery curls, framing her narrow face. Her bright blue eyes and pinkish complexion gave her a girlish appearance. She was wearing a plum-colored paisley print blouse and a beige wool skirt. Natalie could not imagine her own mother being so dressed up for a family dinner. Mrs. Morgan looked at her watch, then addressed her husband. "Lloyd, I need you in the kitchen for a few minutes."

"May I help you, Mrs. Morgan?" Natalie offered, but Gary restrained her.

"No, thanks. Dinner's almost ready," Mrs. Morgan answered.

"I was going to offer a toast to Willa Cather, but I was afraid you might hit me," Gary said as his parents left the room. When Natalie didn't laugh, he said, "Relax. Just another hour to go."

In the formal dining room, which was decorated with candles and golden chrysanthemums on the table, Lloyd Morgan sliced the ham, dotted with cloves, as he asked Natalie about her family.

"I understand your father is a forest ranger. Is he an Old Blue?"

It took Natalie a moment to realize that an "Old Blue" was a Cal alum.

"No, my father didn't go to college. He was in the Army during the First World War and began working for the Forest Service afterwards. Dad grew up near Mount Lassen."

"Beautiful country," Mr. Morgan said. "We should go there sometime, Gary."

"A few years ago my father took some courses in forest management at Cal State Humboldt. There was nothing like the G.I. Bill for World War I vets," Natalie said.

"Mr. Perrault is the district ranger," Gary added.

Mrs. Morgan passed Natalie the spiced apples, inquiring, "Do you ski, Natalie? Lloyd and I have some friends who enjoy skiing at Mount Shasta. We keep meaning to visit them over the Christmas holidays."

"No, I'm not very athletic, and skiing is too expensive for me."

Mr. Morgan turned his attention to Gary. "Judge Oliver tells me you did very well clerking for him this summer."

"I learned a lot from the judge. He's a good teacher."

Gary and his father carried on a long conversation about Gary's prospects during the rest of dinner. Finally, over pineapple upside-down cake and coffee, Gary glanced at his watch, commenting, "Wonderful dinner, Mother. Natalie and I should be going soon. Midterms this week."

"Thank you for the lovely dinner, Mrs. Morgan," Natalie said.

"Surely you don't have to leave yet," Gary's mother protested. "Why don't we play some bridge? You do play bridge, don't you, Natalie?"

"Yes, but not very often."

"Perhaps Natalie and Gary don't want to play," Mr. Morgan said, pushing back his chair. He looked at Natalie, adding, "I don't play much either. Would you be willing to be my partner?"

Natalie answered, "Of course."

Mrs. Morgan shuffled the deck with the graceful dexterity of a professional gambler, dealing the cards quickly with her manicured hands. During the bidding, Gary winked at Natalie. He and his mother made their bid on the first two hands, then Gary was surprised to hear his father bid game in hearts. Natalie laid down the dummy hand, saying, "Hope this helps."

"Good work, partner," Mr. Morgan said, adding their points after they won the next two bids.

"Let's call this hand the last. We'll win this one, Mother," Gary said.

But they didn't win. Natalie outbid Mrs. Morgan's three spades with her bid of four diamonds, doubled. She beamed at Mr. Morgan when they won.

"We were lucky in our cards, weren't we?" Natalie said.

"You played that perfectly, Natalie," Gary's mother said coolly. "I didn't see how you could possibly make that bid."

✶   ✶   ✶   ✶

On the ride from Piedmont to Berkeley, Natalie seemed preoccupied, responding to Gary's comments with monosyllables. She roused herself as he parked.

"Thank you, Gary. I enjoyed meeting your folks and…"

"I'll come in with you for a few minutes."

She unlocked the front door, calling out in the hall, "Mrs. Carlyle, it's me."

In the silence she explained, "Mrs. Carlyle often visits her daughter and son-in-law on Sundays." Entering the living room, Natalie added, "I always want to call this room the *parlor*."

"It does have a rather Victorian look," Gary agreed. They sat on a faded mohair sofa covered with lace antimacassars on the arms and headrest.

"Are we unchaperoned now?" he asked with a mock leer.

Natalie smoothed out a flimsy piece of lace on the armrest.

"I…think we'd better not see each other any more."

"No, don't say that. Why? Hear me out, Natalie."

"It's nothing you did. I can't explain how I feel, but I know we're not right for each other."

Gary pulled her chin around. "Look at me. You didn't like my interrogating parents and you think I was arranging some sort of *test*. I should have warned you, but you're so quick-witted I really thought you'd be amused. My father always asked about my friends, their families, and backgrounds. Dad doesn't realize how he sounds."

"Let me tell you about my family," Natalie interrupted. "My father was not an *Old Blue;* he doesn't wear an expensive sports coat from Roos Brothers for Sunday dinner. My mother doesn't belong to a bridge club or go to a beauty parlor to have her nails done. Mother didn't even graduate from high school because she had to support herself. She and Dad met at a logging camp where she cooked for the men."

"What does all this have to do with us?"

"Let me finish. Mother still works as a substitute cook at Shasta High cafeteria to help with expenses. I have a memory of my father working the night shift at the mill to pay the doctor for my sister's emergency appendectomy when she was six years old."

Natalie paused, short of breath from her speech. Her voice was shaky as she continued. "Something else you should know. I earn half of my rent here by doing the housework for Mrs. Carlyle on Saturday mornings so you see…"

"So that's why this place looks neat as a pin! Somehow I still don't see *you* as a heroine out of a nineteenth century novel, struggling along in a state of genteel poverty."

He kissed her then, holding her against his chest so tightly she could hear his heart beating. She wondered why she didn't leave things as they were, but some core of honesty made her assert herself. She pulled away from him.

"Gary, my background is very different from yours."

He bent over, pulling his right trouser leg up as she spoke.

"What are you doing?" Natalie asked.

"Look at my memento from Italy. I was a corporal when we landed at a place south of the Sele River in October of 1943. German shell explosions all around.

We were under heavy fire. Then I got hit with shrapnel from mortar bursts. I was pulling a wounded buddy along the ground, calling for a medic. Suddenly another explosion knocked me down. I felt a burning sensation and saw that my leg was bleeding. I must have gone into shock then."

His leg had a scar like a ragged, deep groove just below his knee, almost to his ankle.

"I was a hell of a lot luckier than some guys. We slugged on through the mud. The Italian campaign was a mess. The U.S. Fifth Army had about ninety miles to go. Supposed to be a quick march north. Then the military got a report that German gunners were sheltered in Monte Cassino. The order was given for our bombers to destroy it. The monastery looked like a fortress on a hill."

Gary paused, a faraway look on his face.

"Supposedly the Army brass asked permission of the priests to destroy Monte Cassino. We warned Italian citizens to clear out. But the bombing was a terrible, tragic mistake because the Germans were miles away, hiding in bunkers. All of us in the infantry still had the endless rain and rubble. Worst of all, the damned Germans kept attacking us—gunners in foxholes, and snipers in the mountains. Four weeks of fighting with terrible losses."

He continued speaking rapidly, as though he had to finish within a certain time period.

"My wounds got re-infected that winter. I was sent to a Red Cross hospital near Rome. According to the doctor, I was in danger of having my leg amputated below the knee."

He faced Natalie without seeming to focus on her.

"I was sent back out on maneuvers, given a field promotion to sergeant. Then I suffered a concussion from a mortar explosion. Finally, the Army decided it wasn't worthwhile trying to patch me up over there."

He sighed, returning to the present.

"I have a partial hearing loss from the explosion. Late in 1944 I was given a medical discharge. I spent the last seven months of the war far from the battlefields. Except for looking ugly, my leg is okay."

He let his pant leg fall back into place. Natalie was white-faced as she met his eyes. "I'm glad you told me, Gary."

"I showed you my scar to convince you that whatever baggage we carry from the past doesn't count now. I want us to be together, Natalie."

She reached up, caressing his face, unconsciously imitating his mother's gesture from earlier that afternoon.

"Hold me," she whispered. "Just hold me."

Chapter 3

▼

That night, for the first time in many years, Gary found his thoughts flashing back to January of 1945.

Telling Natalie my war story brought everything back. Not only the war—Agnes.

"You're progressing well, Sergeant Morgan, but you need to have regular physical therapy to prevent your leg from stiffening," the doctor at Letterman Hospital said before discharging him.

"Since you're living in Piedmont, I'm recommending a physical therapist at a hospital in Oakland for your follow-up treatment."

When Gary didn't respond, but just kept staring into space, the doctor continued. "I'm also referring you to an Army psychiatrist for counseling."

"I don't need a psychiatrist!" Gary snapped. "Sir."

"It's your call. Think it over." The doctor stood up, signaling the end of his examination. Gary shook the doctor's hand with an apologetic nod.

A week later he met Agnes, his physical therapist. Instead of a starchy white nurse's uniform, Agnes wore a pink cotton jumpsuit. She tossed him a pair of khaki shorts with the order, "Put these on. Meet me in the weight room."

She put him through a regimen of lifting weights and pulling on the rings for upper body strength, telling him, "You're too skinny! Need to build up your arms and shoulder muscles, Sergeant."

Later, when he was lying on a table, Agnes said humorously, "Now comes the good part. You get a massage. Roll over on your belly."

He felt her smooth hands applying a cool lotion to his neck and shoulders.

"Relax, you're so tense," she murmured. For the next twenty minutes, all Agnes was to him was a pair of hands and a soothing voice. After the treatment she said, "Next time we'll start the leg lifts."

He looked for Agnes eagerly, not seeing her at first in the cavernous weight room filled with equipment. Then she called out to him, "Over here, Sergeant Morgan."

"What kind of torture do you have planned for me today?" he asked.

"Free weights first. Bicep curls." She wrote notes on a tablet. "Climb on the table now," Agnes said after twenty minutes.

Lying on his back, he watched her face, attentive and professional, as she raised his wounded right leg slowly until he winced.

"Sorry." Her mouth pursed, making a little *moué* of sympathy. "You have thirty degrees angle of movement," she explained. "We're aiming for sixty degrees."

She wrote something on the little tablet, saying, "You'll get there, Sergeant, but don't be afraid to yell when it hurts."

"Okay, but call me *Gary*. I don't feel like a sergeant any more. It was a field promotion in Italy. They handed out promotions when too many noncoms got killed in action. I'm not a real sergeant."

"Is that so? Your chart lists you as Sergeant Morgan. Well, I'm not a real nurse. I have two years training in nursing. I guess you could say I got promoted because of the war, too. Shortage of male therapists."

Gary hoped she would go on talking about herself, but she resumed quietly.

"Now try lifting your left leg as high as you can *slowly* while I press down. Again. Your right leg. That's high enough. Repeat."

He submitted to her ministrations willingly. After his massage, he thought, *I don't need a shrink. I have Agnes.*

At home, he told his parents about his treatments, but he never mentioned Agnes by name. During that spring of 1945, Gary saw his father's worried looks disappear. His mother's inquiries grew less anxious. Then one April evening after dinner she began to cry suddenly, her girlish face contorted.

"Oh, darling, I'm so thankful you're home with us. It's dreadfully selfish of me, I know, when so many men are still fighting."

"Now, Grace," Lloyd Morgan began, but Gary patted his mother's shoulder.

"I'm all right, Mother."

She dabbed at her eyes with a balled-up handkerchief as she spoke.

"When we learned you were being sent home to recover, I was almost *relieved* that you were wounded. Isn't that awful? Then I felt so guilty when I saw your leg. I wondered if you'd ever heal…inside, I mean, as well as outside."

Gary's father exchanged an affectionate look with him as if to say, *She has to get this out.* Aloud he said, "You're looking stronger every week. You've gained some weight back, haven't you?"

"I'm fine, Dad."

"Let's have our coffee on the patio this evening," his father suggested. "I see your crocuses are in full bloom, Grace."

*   *   *   *

"Hi, Handsome," Agnes greeted Gary one afternoon in May.

"Hello, St. Agnes," he responded with a bow.

"I'm not Catholic," she said quickly, and they both laughed.

"You don't have to be Catholic to be a saint," he answered, noticing how pretty she looked when she was flushed with pleasure. Usually her sandy brown hair was pulled back severely, but on this day her hair was loose except for a small barrette worn at her right temple. In the exam room Agnes watched him as he lifted his right leg slowly.

"Good! I'm calling that motion ninety degrees. I pronounce you fit."

As she bent over, writing in her note pad, her hair brushed close to Gary's face and he jumped off the table. He kissed her full lips, clasping her tightly to his body.

"Mmm, mmm, sweet Agnes," he breathed.

She backed away, her brown eyes widening, but her voice playful as she said, "You *are* one hundred percent cured."

"When are you off duty?"

Agnes hesitated before replying, "Nurses can't get involved with patients."

"Who made that rule?" Gary scoffed. "You're not married or engaged, are you?" He had always noticed her smooth, ring-less hands.

"Divorced," she said, her face impassive.

"Well, then?" Gary said, dressing in his street clothes hurriedly. "What?"

Agnes opened the door of the exam room as loud exclamations came from a group of people huddled around a radio. "The war's over in Europe! Truman's on the air," a nurse called out. "Germany surrendered unconditionally."

Celebration in the weight room! Tears and hugs and two G.I.'s crossing themselves. A doctor came running into the room to join those listening to the radio announcements.

"Thank God. Oh, thank God," the doctor kept repeating.

"You'll want to be home with your folks," Agnes said as the hubbub subsided.

"No, I want to be with you."

"I can check out now. You were my last patient for the day. You have a car?"

Gary nodded.

"Then let's go. I live in East Oakland."

Like Agnes, her one bedroom apartment was cheerful and neat. Gary noted her record albums stacked on the bottom shelf of a bookcase filled with popular novels, a dictionary, and some medical texts squeezed between two recent issues of *Readers' Digest*. A walnut table held the record player beside a low couch covered with a green and white checked slipcover. By the open window with its fluttering white curtains were two ladder-backed chairs and a dinette table. A brass lamp with a rosy shade and an old-fashioned ceiling chandelier provided the only light in the living area.

"Help yourself to a beer, Gary," Agnes offered. She pointed to the tiny kitchen, adding, "Bathroom is off there if you need to use it first. I'm going to take a quick shower in a minute."

She reappeared, holding a terry cloth bathrobe and a shampoo bottle.

"Won't be long," she promised.

"Maybe I should phone home," Gary said.

"Sure." Agnes gave him a broad grin. "Phone's in the bedroom."

Gary reached his mother on the first ring.

"Yes, we heard. Great news, isn't it? Thank God for all…yes, Mother. I'm with a friend from the hospital. We're celebrating, probably get something to eat here in Oakland. Go ahead with dinner."

As he hung up, sitting on the narrow bed, he smiled at the ridiculousness of the situation, telephoning his mother so she wouldn't worry about him, thankful she hadn't asked for his friend's name.

When Agnes emerged, clad only in her robe, she was rubbing her hair with a towel. As she sat down on the bed he kissed her, slipping his hand underneath her robe to caress her breasts. He gloried in her warm, firm smoothness, her damp hair smelling of shampoo, her moist lips urging his mouth to respond. He shed his clothes quickly and pressed her to his throbbing body as he entered her. She engulfed him with an overwhelming tenderness. Agnes gave a faint, joyful cry as she arched her body in climax. For a few moments they lay embracing each other wordlessly. Gary murmured her name, tracing his fingers over her face. He wanted to tell her how happy he felt with her, but he couldn't find the right words.

Agnes said calmly, "I'll be right back."

His mind drifted off to faraway scenes of Italy. He had always associated war with dirt, mud, and numbing pain. With Agnes, he felt whole again. She embodied everything good he had yearned for during the war.

"Gary, I hate to wake you, but…"

"Wha…where am I?" he mumbled. "What time is it?"

"You fell asleep. I'm going to call my folks. We're still so worried about my brother in the Pacific. But thank God, the fighting's over in Europe."

"You're beautiful, Agnes," he told her. "The most beautiful person I know."

At that moment he truly believed that this wholesome young woman in her white peasant blouse and flowered print skirt was beauty eternal. As Gary dressed, he joked, "Yeah, I guess I should head for home soon. Mother didn't give me permission to stay overnight."

Both of them began giggling as though that was the funniest thing ever said.

During that summer of 1945, Gary sought out Agnes whenever he could meet her. His therapy at the hospital was complete. He knew he was not in love with Agnes, at least not deeply. From her apparent casualness about their affair, he believed her feelings were the same. She never made demands of him or exacted claims on his time. They were lovers without plans or promises.

One afternoon in June as they were sitting on a bench by Lake Merritt in Oakland, Agnes said, "Must be a great view of the lake from that hotel over there."

"I suppose so. How long have you been divorced?"

"Two years. My divorce was final in 1943. Why?"

"Just curious. You must have been married awfully young."

She stared across the lake for so long that Gary thought she wasn't going to respond. Finally she said tersely, "Mickey was a friend of my younger brother, Art. They liked to work on cars together. Mickey would hang around our garage so much that Mom would invite him for supper. After high school I started my nurse's training. It's all I ever wanted to be: a nurse. That's when Mickey and I began dating. One thing led to another, so we got married."

"What went wrong?" Gary prompted.

"Mickey couldn't keep a job. He'd work as a mechanic, then argue with the boss and get fired. My dad got him a job at the GM factory. One day Mickey got in a fight with a guy over some insult; he lost that job. Then he started drinking, hanging around bars. I had an offer to work as a practical nurse doing home care for patients. Stroke victims, mainly. I was the only one earning a regular paycheck."

Agnes faced Gary, looking vulnerable.

"You see, it takes three years of study to become a registered nurse. I had to give up my last year to support us. I tried to keep us together, but Mickey wouldn't change. Our marriage was over."

"Where is he now?" Gary asked.

"Mickey? He was drafted in 1942 about the time I filed for divorce. I don't know where he is. I don't even care. Art's in the Navy on an aircraft carrier. His wife lives with my folks. Art's the only man I give a damn about."

Wrapping her arms around his neck, she added, "Until you came along, Gary."

Making love to Agnes on her single bed with the summer traffic noises drifting in from the open window, Gary felt a sense of wonder that this woman should be so generous to him. Her apartment became a haven as they prepared simple meals together in her kitchen. He always offered to take her to the neighborhood diner, but she would say, "We have plenty to eat here."

They had formed an unspoken pact not to talk about the war news or their families. Instead, they often sat on the green and white couch, listening to her records: Jo Stafford, Frank Sinatra, and a song Agnes loved, "The Gypsy." Gary flipped through the *Readers' Digests*, smiling to himself as he noticed that Agnes always penciled in her answers to "How To Increase Your Word Power."

One evening Agnes broke their silence, saying, "The hospital is changing my schedule. I'll be working the five to midnight shift beginning next week. No more afternoons off, no more physical therapy patients."

Gary had been uncertain how to bring up his parents' plans for a short vacation with him. He promised to call her in a couple of weeks after she knew about her days off. She looked at him intently, saying, "Call me at this number."

"We'll go someplace special," he added, sensing something ambiguous hanging like a cloud between them.

She was waiting for him in the lobby of the hotel overlooking Lake Merritt. Dressed in a navy blue suit with a white rayon blouse, Agnes appeared more sophisticated than usual. She was wearing a red straw hat, tilted to one side. Gary and Agnes entered the dining room, which was packed with Army and Navy officers and their women, along with well-dressed businessmen. Gary was the only noncom in sight.

"I was lucky. Got a reservation for lunch," he greeted her. "Table by the window, please," he added to the waiter.

"I've never seen you in your uniform before," Agnes said.

"Wore it on impulse. Probably put it away in mothballs soon. You look swell! How's the new schedule working for you?"

They made small talk over their lunch, Gary feeling awkward with her for the first time. He described his trip with his parents, the unreality of hearing about Hiroshima while in the midst of Yosemite's rugged beauty...Agnes interrupted him.

"We've never talked much about our plans, but I've decided to go back to school next month to earn my nursing degree. I've saved enough money and it's time I thought about my future."

He nodded, waiting for whatever else she had to say.

Agnes asked suddenly, "How old are you, Gary?"

"Old enough!" he answered.

"Old enough to know better, but too young to resist," she quoted, adding, "I found out you're only twenty-one years old."

"How do you know?"

"I looked in your file. At the hospital I gave my notes on your therapy to the head nurse on duty, but I never read your complete file until the other day. You were twenty-one years old on May fifth. I'll be twenty-seven in ten days."

"What difference does that make?"

But even as he spoke, his mind was busily doing the arithmetic.

Let's see, Agnes was a senior in high school when I was in sixth grade.

"I don't see what difference our ages make," he repeated, trying to joke. "I am a *veteran*, you know."

She reached across the table for his hands, holding his fingers. "You're a wonderful man, Gary."

Before Agnes could continue, the maitre d'hotel stepped to a microphone at the small bandstand, saying, "Stand by for an announcement." Two waiters carried a Motorola into the restaurant. The words from the radio, "Terms of unconditional surrender...Japanese high command," stilled the customers' voices as they listened. Then a cacophony broke out as people began shouting loudly, "It's over! The war is over!"

Agnes stood up, kissing Gary quickly on the mouth. He tried to embrace her, but she pulled away, saying, "I must go home. I need to be with my family."

Gary threw a ten-dollar bill onto the table, following Agnes to the lobby.

"I'll drive you," he shouted. "Don't leave like this."

"Call me a cab, please."

When he put her into the taxi she smiled brightly, as though they would see each other soon. She said, "You have your whole life ahead of you, handsome!"

Gary walked along Lake Merritt in a daze, not remembering where he had parked his car. He felt leaden. A sailor brushed by him, calling out, "Hi, Sergeant! It's really over!"

Gary heard dozens of horns honking and, somewhere in the distance, church bells tolling. Finally, he found his car and began driving toward the Port of Oakland. Soon he realized he was near his father's office.

Lloyd Morgan beamed at him. "You've heard the news. Unconditional surrender."

His father began introducing him to everyone—his colleagues, and his secretary. Clapping his hand on Gary's shoulder, he kept saying to one and all, "My son, Gary."

Gary wondered why it was so easy to give his father pleasure and why he so seldom bothered to seek out his company.

"Give me a few minutes to clear off my desk and we'll go home." His father sighed. "Thank God, the war's over. Shall we have a drink together? Just the two of us?"

Ten minutes later, as they sat in a booth, Gary heard himself telling his father, "I lost my girl friend today."

"Who? I guess I figured you must have someone, but you never said."

"My physical therapist, Agnes Fielding. She's going back to nursing school."

Gary turned his highball glass around and around, making wet circles on the table. His father's expression was serious.

"You'll be starting Cal in a few weeks. There'll be other girl friends. You have your whole life ahead of you, son." His father echoed the last words Agnes had spoken.

"I cared about her, Dad."

Already he was speaking about Agnes in the past tense. When that historic day was given a name—VJ Day—and people talked about what they felt when they heard that the war was over, Gary reflected wryly that his love affair with Agnes had begun on VE Day and had ended with VJ Day. That's what he would always remember.

Chapter 4

▼

"One of the few hotels in the world with warmth, character and charm…"
Frank Lloyd Wright, describing the Hotel Claremont

Like an elegant Edwardian dowager, the splendid white chateau spread its vast skirts over the twenty-two acres of its wooded setting. The Hotel Claremont seemed a link to an earlier era, when fashionable debutantes languidly strolled the porches overlooking the city, when young men dressed in white sweaters and flannels headed for the tennis courts while string orchestras played gentle musical accompaniment to guests taking afternoon tea. Built in 1915, the grand resort had weathered two world wars by 1951, having been refurbished by a new owner during the Great Depression. Now the famous landmark, located exactly on the borderline between Berkeley and Oakland, had grown in popularity with a new generation. Except for the selection of popular tunes and the style of the dances, the scene in the ballroom was reminiscent of the carefree nineteen-twenties.

As she and Gary entered the Claremont one November evening, Natalie glanced around, remarking, "This place looks like the setting in a Scott Fitzgerald novel, very glamorous and yet old-fashioned. I've never been here before."

Gary took her to the cocktail lounge first to admire the view of San Francisco lights across the bay. Looking out through the wide windows facing west, he gestured toward the tennis court below, saying, "Helen Wills learned to play tennis at the Berkeley Tennis Club when she was fourteen years old. Bill Tilden played there also."

"Who's Bill Tilden?"

"First American to win Wimbledon. Helen Wills Moody was a Cal alumna. She's a tennis legend, too."

Natalie was dressed in the silvery gray jersey dress she had worn the night Gary met her. Her only jewelry was a strand of pearls. As they passed along the hallway leading to the Garden Room, Gary ducked into the florist's shop. "I'll just be a minute. Wait here." He came out, offering her a bunch of violets.

"Now, if you're wearing your glass slippers we'll try a fox trot, *Cinderelly*."

For a moderate cover charge couples could sit at a table near the dance floor the entire evening. Gary thought the Claremont was the ideal place for a romantic date, although on this Saturday evening he and Natalie were one of the few young couples there. The dinner crowd was thinning out as the orchestra struck up at the bandstand. Gary and Natalie danced without speaking, their bodies moving together easily, sitting out only the rumbas and sambas. They sipped their drinks slowly as they held hands at their table, making the evening last. Natalie's violets were beginning to wilt. Before their last dance, she put the small bouquet in her purse, thinking, *I'll press the violets and save them forever because they're the first flowers he ever gave me.*

On Sunday, Natalie wrote to her mother.

Dear Mother,

I shared the peach preserves with Mrs. Carlyle, and she sends her thanks. The more I hear about incompatible roommates in dorms, the more I appreciate having a quiet place to live. I wish you and Dad would visit Berkeley and meet Mrs. Carlyle. I told my advisor, Professor Muller, about Dad's family moving to California from Nebraska. He was interested in your Russian family background, too.

I've been going out with a law student, Gary Morgan. Paul Sawyer introduced us. Gary is a vet in his third year at Boalt Hall. I'd like to ask him to come to Redding over Thanksgiving weekend. Gary could stay at a motel. I haven't asked him yet. Call me after 4:00 p.m. Glad to hear Dad is busy with his workshop projects. Give Dad and Julie my love. I'll make my train reservations for Nov. 21.

Love, Natalie

When Natalie did not hear from her mother, she approached Mrs. Carlyle.

"May I phone Redding collect this afternoon?"

"Of course, Natalie. No trouble at home, I hope."

"No, I just want to check about Thanksgiving plans."

When her mother answered, Natalie asked in a rush, "Did you get my letter, Mother? I need to know about inviting Gary."

"Yes. Daddy and I have been talking it over," she said in her maddeningly slow way.

"What is there to talk over? I'll help with the cooking."

"Oh, it's not that. It's just that we were looking forward to having you to ourselves. Your cousins will be here."

Natalie sighed. "Mother, are you telling me that I can't even invite someone who is very wonderful to meet my own family?"

After a prolonged pause, Natalie's mother said, "I suppose it'll be all right."

Natalie hung up, almost in tears. Feeling a surge of disappointment over her mother's ungracious attitude, she was still standing by the telephone when her landlady entered with Gary, carrying a bag of groceries.

Mrs. Carlyle said, "Gary met me on the sidewalk. I had quite a load."

He grinned at Natalie. "I need a break from tort law and took a chance you'd be here. How about going to Blake's for dinner?"

As she put the groceries away Mrs. Carlyle said, "I have a better idea. Why don't you two have dinner with me? I'm making meat loaf. I hate eating alone," she admitted. Natalie's landlady bustled around, wrapping a towel around Gary for an apron.

Natalie said, "I talked to Mother today, Gary. She asked me to invite you to Redding over Thanksgiving weekend. Could you drive up that Friday or Saturday?"

"Sure. That'd be great. You'll find me a place to stay?" Gary asked.

Mrs. Carlyle was pretending not to listen, but finally burst out, "So many new motel chains are springing up now, aren't they?"

"Yes, even in Redding," Natalie remarked, loving Mrs. Carlyle for her friendliness.

Mrs. Carlyle handed Gary the potato peeler, saying, "You'll need to be at the sink. Natalie will fix salad, and I have the meat loaf ready to bake. We'll eat in the dining room." She left the kitchen. Gary bent to kiss Natalie's neck and put his arms around her.

"I may move in here. How would that suit you?"

For an answer, Natalie turned around and kissed him. "I wish you could move in—only to help with the housework, of course."

Over the meat loaf and mashed potatoes, Gary chatted with Mrs. Carlyle. He had mentioned the word *tort,* causing Mrs. Carlyle to call for a definition. Gary warmed to her interest, explaining that *tort* meant any injury or wrong committed to another person or property.

Mrs. Carlyle began a rambling tale about a walnut tree encroaching on her neighbor's lot. Gary never interrupted the landlady's narrative except to joke, "Ah, but if there were no problems with walnut trees and property lines, there would be no need for lawyers, at least not as many."

"That's true," Mrs. Carlyle replied, continuing her reminiscence of life in Berkeley during the Depression. Natalie took the plates to the kitchen quietly as her landlady recalled her memories.

After Gary left Mrs. Carlyle said, "Your beau is charming. I so enjoy him."

Chapter 5

Redding, California

When Natalie's parents met her at the railroad station the day before Thanksgiving, it struck Natalie that her mother looked much older and her father looked the same, as erect and as serious as ever.

"Let me take your bag," he said brusquely, kissing her cheek.

Natalie wiped her nose with a hankie, explaining, "I'm getting over a miserable cold."

"You probably aren't sleeping enough and not eating right," her mother fussed. "You look like you've lost weight since September."

"No, I don't think so. What about you, Mother? Are you taking medication for your high blood pressure?"

Marie Perrault looked at her husband with a resigned sigh. "I cut down on my salt intake. Ralph's been helping me around the house with the heavy work."

The Perraults' house was a rustic ranch style, built only four years before, but as Natalie viewed it, she thought it seemed smaller than she remembered, the sienna brown paint already fading. Then she realized she was comparing her home with the Morgans' formal house and its well-tended gardens. Inside, the living room looked comfortable with the Early American furniture her mother favored. The red and forest green plaid couch and matching rocking chair, the brass-based hurricane lamps, and the stone fireplace appeared welcoming.

"Notice anything new?" Natalie's father asked.

"The coffee table. Dad, it's beautiful. What kind of wood?"

Natalie ran her fingers over the surface.

"Birch. I copied the design from a cabinetmaker's catalog. Your Uncle Will sold me the wood."

"Ralph's been working for the last month to finish it by Thanksgiving," her mother added.

Just then Julie burst into the room, dropping her textbooks on the new table, throwing her arms around her sister. "Nat, welcome home. I have *oodles* to tell you."

"We can talk while I unpack."

In the bedroom they shared, Natalie listened to her sister's lively chatter about high school activities.

"I made the journalism staff," Julie began. "It's really fun. I get to interview business people for ads. I'm trying out for a play. Guess what, Nat? Johnny Browne asked me to go steady. I haven't told Mama or Daddy yet."

Julie brought out a jewelry box from her vanity table, whispering, "Look. Johnny gave me these earrings for my birthday."

She held one topaz earring up to her face, her dark eyes shining.

"I haven't worn them yet in front of anyone except Johnny. Don't tell!"

As Julie continued her monologue about her romance with Johnny Browne, Natalie reflected on how different her sister's personality was from her own.

Julie's one of the most popular kids in high school. Not like me.

In the kitchen, Natalie showed her mother a recipe for cranberry and orange gelatin salad, saying, "I thought it would be nice to have something different Friday night when Gary comes to dinner."

"We'll have plenty of leftovers with the turkey. No need to fix a special salad," her mother said.

"Well, that's just it. Everybody is always full after Thanksgiving. Why don't we have sliced turkey without all the trimmings? We'll have rolls, the salad, and your pumpkin pie for dessert. I'll prepare everything."

Her mother looked very tired. "All right, Natalie; he's your guest. Fix whatever you want Friday."

Julie had gone out with her boyfriend right after dinner, leaving Natalie and her mother to visit while her father listened to the radio. Natalie had the task of tearing bits of stale bread for sage dressing. Her mother was rolling pie dough at the counter as she spoke.

"I hope Julie don't get too serious about Johnny Browne."

"I wouldn't worry about Julie. She can take care of herself," Natalie commented.

"She's not studious like you. Your dad and I never had a minute's worry about you and boys in high school."

Natalie gave a short laugh. "Yes, because there weren't any boys hanging around me in high school. That's not very flattering, Mother."

"I always knew you'd be a late bloomer. And we're so proud of you, doing fine at the University. Your dad don't say much, but he praises you to the skies to your aunts."

"Julie is having the time of her life at Shasta High, and I couldn't wait to get away from Redding. But I did love Mrs. Livingston."

While the pies were baking, Natalie and her mother relaxed in the living room. Her father turned off the radio with a gruff comment about the news from Korea. He lit his pipe, leaning back in his favorite chair, with his legs stretched out.

"Your mother's probably been worrying you about Julie," he said, pausing as he drew on his pipe. "Johnny Browne is a good kid, but I don't want Julie to get too smitten with him because he's bound to be drafted when he graduates in June."

"Couldn't he enroll in ROTC at college?" suggested Natalie.

Her father shook his head. "Doesn't have the grades. Thinks he doesn't need college. His father manages the Chevrolet franchise in town. Johnny wants to work there selling cars. No ambition."

Marie sat, smoothing out her apron. "I like Johnny. He's a polite boy, Ralph."

Her husband's expression softened. "Yeah, like I said, he's a good kid. That's why I hate to see him going to Korea. Mmm, that's a heavenly aroma, Marie. What kind of pies are you baking?"

"One pumpkin, one mince, like always." She smiled, but her eyes were sad.

Thanksgiving was the one day when the Perrault relatives stopped by to visit. Ralph Perrault's two sisters had six children between them. In earlier years the families took turns hosting Thanksgiving dinner, but as the children grew older the wives decided preparing a huge feast for fourteen people was too much work. This fall the family was in further disarray. Aunt Isabelle's and Uncle Will's son, Wayne Benson, was now stationed at Fort Ord.

Aunt Corinne's divorce had become final in August. Eighteen months beforehand, her husband, Stan Munz, had obtained a bank loan to buy a dilapidated movie theater in Redding. After renovating the building and buying projectors and other equipment, he began an aggressive promotion campaign. He displayed colorful Hollywood posters and persuaded minor show business celebrities to publicize movies. Soon the theater, renamed the Palladium, attracted sizable audiences. People began vying for the opportunity to appear as local movie critics. Stan Munz had found his niche.

Unfortunately for Aunt Corinne, her husband had hired a young woman to handle advertising and bookings for the theater. Stan began an affair with his twenty-eight-year-old assistant. His wife discovered his indiscretions quite easily. Corinne Munz was no fool. After months of covering up for her husband's frequent absences from family gatherings, Corinne had gone to her brother for advice.

"What shall I do, Ralph? I thought he'd get over this infatuation, but Stan is with that tramp all the time. The kids are asking questions I can't answer."

Ralph Perrault had always felt protective toward his younger sisters. He never could abide Stan Munz and his risky business ventures, but Ralph had asked Corinne only one question: "Do you love Stan?"

As Corinne had looked away without responding, Ralph put his arm around her shoulder.

"Get a lawyer, Corinne. I know an attorney who'll safeguard your rights. You should claim your share of Stan's income promptly. He has big debts to repay. His financial success may be blown away."

Corinne's breakup was the first divorce in the family. Corinne was still bitter, but she had resumed her job as a clerk for the Forest Service.

"I can't understand why you cook a big dinner every Thanksgiving, Marie," Corinne commented as soon as she and her children entered the house. "Can't you persuade her to quit her part-time job, Natalie?"

Natalie stifled her irritation, thinking, *Why don't you suggest that your brother take Mother out once in a while, Aunt Corinne?*

After Uncle Will and Aunt Isabelle Benson arrived, the cousins broke into groups. Julie took Jackie Munz off to gossip. Her cousin, Edythe Benson, quizzed Natalie about Gary. Ralph scolded eight-year-old CeeCee Munz for scribbling on the new coffee table. At last Will Benson, always the peacemaker, spoke up.

"I'd like to take some snapshots of the family. How about one of Ralph and Marie sitting on the couch, admiring the new coffee table?"

He proceeded to arrange people in groups, clicking his fancy new instant flash camera.

"That's good. I can fit all the cousins in one shot," Will said.

The boys, Louie Benson and Randy Munz, grated on each other's nerves so much that everyone was relieved when Corinne's family left for dinner at a restaurant.

After breakfast Friday morning Natalie remarked to her mother, "We never seem to have real conversations any more when all of us are together. I hardly had two words with Edythe, and Randy Munz is a real pill."

Her mother replied, "Isabelle and Will are more worried than they let on about Wayne. Isabelle said they're driving to Fort Ord to see Wayne in December when he finishes his basic training. And poor Corinne hates to discipline her kids. Jackie seems to be adjusting to the divorce, but Randy's not doing so—Oh, ooh—"

Marie almost dropped the heavy coffee pot she had been rinsing.

"Mother, what?" Natalie cried out.

Her mother was rubbing her right arm. "I couldn't feel anything. My hand just went numb."

Natalie looked at her mother's hands, thinking, *Her veins look so bulging, so ropey.*

"Let's go into the living room," she suggested.

"Nothing hurt. Just my arm and hand went numb all of a sudden." Her mother's large eyes met Natalie's with an unspoken question.

"You rest, Mother. Remember, I'm doing the cooking today."

In the bedroom she told Julie about the incident in hushed tones. "I'm really worried about Mother. She looks worn out. You clean up the kitchen."

"Okay, don't nag me, Nat. I'll be right out."

Natalie confronted her father in his workshop. "Let's take a ride into town, Dad. I want to tell you about something strange."

"Sounds like a little stroke," he said after Natalie described her mother's episode.

"That's what I thought."

"It may be nothing, but I'll see that she goes to the doctor Monday."

"Why not today?" Natalie argued. "She won't go to the doctor unless you insist."

Later, Julie said defensively, "I told Mama she should lie down, but she won't."

"I'm fine, Ralph," her mother said. "I'll make an appointment with the doctor Monday."

Soon Natalie and Julie were chatting in the kitchen while their mother rested.

In the early afternoon, Natalie kept changing her clothes until Julie suggested, "You can wear my burgundy cashmere sweater. The color looks good on you."

When Natalie answered the doorbell, Gary embraced her, holding up a bottle of wine.

"I made it. Took me four and a half hours. No snow, but some icy spots."

Julie was nearest the doorway, staring at Natalie and Gary. As Mr. Perrault reached out to give him a firm handshake, Gary noted Natalie's resemblance to her father—the same clear green eyes. Natalie even had a smaller, feminine version of her father's aquiline nose. Gary knew Mr. Perrault must be two or three years older than his own father, but he looked younger, like a man who spent much of his time in physical activity. With his dark hair flecked with gray and his erect posture, Natalie's father presented a picture of a vigorous outdoors man.

"Good to meet you, Mr. Perrault," Gary said. Turning to greet Natalie's mother, he added, "Thank you for having me. I hope you like Riesling wine."

He thought that Natalie's mother appeared older than he had expected. She was prematurely gray, her hair worn simply, and her face free of cosmetics. Mrs. Perrault wore a dark cotton dress and white apron. Even if Natalie had not mentioned her mother's Russian background, Gary could have identified her Slavic features, tilting dark eyes, and high cheekbones as being eastern European.

"Ah, what a treat," Mrs. Perrault said, taking the bottle of wine. "We'll use Grandmother Mirov's glasses." She hurried to the dining room.

Gary sat near Julie, thinking how much she looked like her mother. Julie had the same dark eyes and sculpted bones, only her glossy hair was dark brown with glints of auburn, and her face was glowing with youth, and rosy lipstick on her mouth.

"Natalie says you were in the Italian campaign during the war," Mr. Perrault spoke abruptly as Natalie brought out appetizers. Gary smiled, recalling Natalie's whispered comment to him, "Dad has no store of small talk."

Before Gary could respond, Mrs. Perrault carried in a tray with wine glasses.

"Ralph, I think we have a toast now," she said. "My mother's family brought these glasses from Russia to San Francisco in 1891. When my mother married my father, these glasses were her dowry."

Somewhat embarrassed by her own speech, Mrs. Perrault blushed. Natalie came to her rescue, offering wine to everyone.

"What a lovely story, and such delicate crystal," Gary said as he lifted his glass.

"To peace in the world," Ralph Perrault said.

"To peace and to our families," his wife added softly.

Across the room, Natalie raised her glass as if to say, *So far, so good.*

Gary moved toward Natalie's father, following up on his earlier question by remarking,

"I was with the Fifth Army. You may be familiar with the role of the Army Rangers in the Italian campaign."

Natalie motioned Julie to accompany her to the kitchen, glad her mother was sitting for once, enjoying her glass of wine.

"Nat, you didn't tell me Gary was so handsome," Julie said before Natalie could hush her. The sisters began last minute dinner preparations. As they sat down to the table, Natalie's father stared at the molded salad, asking loudly, "What's this?"

"It's cranberry-orange salad, Dad. Try something new for a change," Natalie said, half laughing.

"It's very nice, Ralph. Natalie prepared everything," her mother added.

Gary engaged Julie in conversation, complimented Natalie and Mrs. Perrault profusely on the food, and still gave his attention to Mr. Perrault's pronouncements on politics and the conflict in Korea.

"I suppose, being a veteran, you're hoping Eisenhower runs for President," Natalie's father said to Gary in his direct way.

Gary paused, wondering if this was a litmus test of sorts, before responding, "Actually I don't think a military leader is well qualified to be president, not even Ike."

Mr. Perrault raised his eyebrows in surprise at Gary's response. Natalie's green eyes shone as she said, "Dad doesn't believe in the customary advice to avoid politics at the dinner table."

"These two," Mrs. Perrault said, gesturing toward her husband and Natalie, "they like to talk politics." She patted Julie, seated next to her, "Now me and Julie, we don't pay much attention to politics."

Gary saw Natalie wince so visibly at her mother's grammatical lapses that he wanted to exclaim, *It's all right. Your mother isn't the one earning a master's degree in English.*

He saw a look of relief on Natalie's face when he suggested that they take a drive.

"You can be my tour guide, point out the landmarks of Redding," he joked.

As he said good night to everyone, Gary noticed Mrs. Perrault's worn-looking hands, thinking again how aged she appeared.

"I hope you'll tell me more about your family tomorrow, Mrs. Perrault."

In the car, Natalie kissed him. "You're wonderful. Was it awful?"

"I adore you, therefore I love your family, too. *Post hoc, ergo propter hoc* or some Latin phrase covering my feelings. Let's go where we can make up for lost time."

They ended up in the darkened cocktail lounge of Gary's motel, huddled over their brandy and coffee until a voice interrupted their intimacy.

"Hello." It was Paul Sawyer. "I thought I recognized you two."

Out of politeness, Natalie and Gary invited Paul to join them in the booth, but their intimate mood was spoiled.

As they were leaving on Sunday afternoon Gary said, "Thanks for showing me your forest, and for the loan of your boots, Mr. Perrault. Next time we'll climb Mount Lassen."

"Any time, Gary." The two men had spent Saturday together, hiking in the woods.

Julie, hanging back behind her mother, added, "Nice to meet you, Gary."

"Thanks again for your hospitality, all of you. And Julie, thanks for the tip."

Natalie asked, "What was that all about with Julie? What *tip* was she giving you?"

"Ah, that's for me to know and you to find out."

After a few miles Natalie said, "I forgot to tell you the title for my thesis: *Independent American Women Portrayed in the Novels of Willa Cather.*"

Gary patted her thigh. "Now that *is* a catchy title. Wouldn't be surprised if Hollywood doesn't grab up your thesis for a musical."

"Keep your eyes on the road!" Natalie cried, laughing.

CHAPTER 6

▼

By December, all of their Berkeley friends were including Natalie and Gary as a couple.

"Dave's taking the bar exam in March," Rhonda Kagan confided to Natalie, "and assuming he passes, we'll move up our wedding date to June."

"How exciting," said Natalie.

"When are you and Gary going to make it legal?" Dave Rosenthal asked. Just then Gary joined them, and Natalie was glad he hadn't heard Dave's question.

Ed and Beverly Tate invited Natalie and Gary to their apartment for bridge a few days later. Bev was very keyed up during the game. Finally she put her cards face down.

"Oh, Ed, let's tell them."

"Bev's preggers," Ed announced. "In July we'll be parents."

"We didn't plan it this way, but I can keep working at Breuners' store till May," Bev said happily. She kept chatting in her vivacious way as Natalie questioned her about her symptoms.

"There goes the bridge game," Ed sighed in mock resignation.

As she sat in Mrs. Carlyle's parlor, waiting for Gary, Natalie was asking herself some *what if* questions. *What if I hadn't agreed to go to the Tates' party with Paul Sawyer at the last minute? What if I never saw Gary again in my life?*

She tried to shake off her superstitious doubts as she heard Gary's loud knock at the front door. He was using his "code" knock—thump, thump, THUMP—to alert her.

"Are we alone?" Gary didn't wait for her response before kissing her. "You're still planning on taking the train to Redding tomorrow? You could wait till Sunday."

His plea almost persuaded her to cancel her plans, but that would be foolish. Her parents were expecting her for Christmas.

"I'll be back for New Year's Eve," she replied, putting on her coat for their movie date.

"Just a minute before we go out." He handed her a small jeweler's box, tied with a silver ribbon, saying, "Happy birthday, sweetheart."

"Who told you?"

"Julie. She mentioned your birthday was December twenty-first. You never would have let me know, I suppose."

For a moment Natalie wondered if the box held a ring. She hurriedly tore off the wrappings to find a pair of silver earrings, flower shaped. "Oh, they're lovely."

She went to the mirror in the hall, fastening the earrings. She pulled her hair back, arching her long neck.

Gary came up behind her, pressing his cheek against her face as they faced the mirror.

"This is my happiest birthday," she whispered, all misgivings vanishing.

"Hurry back to me," Gary said.

Chapter 7

Winter, 1952

At the end of the semester, Natalie stayed in Berkeley to work on her thesis research, even though Jean Swithin had invited Natalie to stay at her family's apartment in San Francisco during the break.

"We could see a play together or have lunch at the St. Francis like ladies of leisure," Jean had suggested. When Natalie had declined, pleading her thesis writing, Jean had groaned, "Aah, Nat, don't be such a grind. Thomas Stearns and Willa can wait. Our thesis notes will still be here when we get back."

Lying on the lumpy bed in her dorm room, Jean held up a slim black volume of *Collected Poems*, then tossed it onto her desk.

"Now, Ms. Prufrock, is that any way to show respect for Mr. Eliot?" Natalie inquired. Jean bounced off the bed. Reaching for her cigarettes and lighting up, she squinted at Natalie through the smoke.

"You want to stay in Berkeley to be with Gary. Have you been to bed with him yet?"

Reacting to Natalie's glare, Jean said, "Sorry, none of my business."

"Gary's spending this week with his parents in Piedmont," Natalie said coldly.

Jean apologized, "Hey, don't leave. We were going to Jules for a hamburger today. If you change your mind about coming to the city, give me a call. Here's the apartment phone number."

"Thanks, Jean, maybe I will take a day off."

Natalie watched as Jean hastily combed her short brown hair, dabbing on her lipstick in front of the mirror. "That's good enough," Jean said to her reflection.

Jean had no personal vanity. She always looked as though she had just thrown on the nearest skirt and sweater and had more important things on her mind. And yet, Natalie decided, she had a certain sophistication—a San Francisco flair.

As the two of them headed for College Avenue, Jean asked, "Are you still mad at me, about my prying into your love life? I really do apologize, Natalie. I just thought—you're in love, you're twenty-three years old...Don't you dare to eat a peach?" Her gray eyes were full of mirth.

Natalie laughed. "Maybe *I am* Ms. Prufrock. No, I'm not mad at you."

* * * *

The campus was virtually deserted as the campanile tolled nine o'clock on an overcast Wednesday morning. Natalie's advisor spotted her entering the Doe Library.

"What's Willa Cather's young critic doing here during vacation?"

"Trying to put my notes into some kind of concise prose," Natalie replied.

As they walked up the marble stairs leading to the reading room, Professor Muller suggested a reference work, but then interrupted himself. "But for your thesis you don't need numerous footnotes from literary scholars. Your approach of direct analysis of the characters is perfectly valid."

Natalie mentioned some historical research of Nebraska and the Southwest that she was using as background for her writing on Willa Cather.

"I'll be here for an hour or so if you want to come to my office. I'd be glad to look over what you've written," the professor said.

"Thank you. I may do that."

At eleven-thirty, Natalie saw that Professor Muller's office was open. He was bent over his desk, writing copious notes. She rapped lightly on the doorframe.

"Come on in," he said, pushing his glasses up to his bushy eyebrows. His heavy spectacles always seemed to slide down his nose. Professor Muller was probably only a few years older than Gary, Natalie realized, but he seemed the epitome of the fatherly academic type. He yawned, stretching his arms above his head, motioning her to a chair.

"Here are my notes, if you can make any sense out of them," she said.

For the next twenty minutes they discussed Willa Cather's stories and Natalie's thesis. Then Professor Muller said, "I'm recommending you for a possible summer job. You're well qualified to apply for the position. You'd be assisting a visiting instructor for two American lit courses. Of course you wouldn't have any vacation between earning your M.A. and summer session."

"That wouldn't be a problem for me, having no vacation. I expect to apply for a teaching post, but I haven't sent out my resumé yet. I'm superstitious about making definite plans this early," Natalie said.

Her advisor pulled out his cigarettes, offering one to Natalie as she shook her head.

"I always forget. You don't smoke. Most students do." He lit up, studying her. "What are you superstitious about, Natalie?"

"I don't know, exactly," she said slowly. "Maybe I'll never finish this thesis. I'll just get bogged down and give up. Must sound foolish to you, for me to come this far and..."

To her embarrassment, Natalie found that she was close to tears. Professor Muller was looking at her so sympathetically that his homely face seemed almost saintly. He crushed out his cigarette, flicking a speck of tobacco off his shirt before speaking quietly.

"I don't think you sound foolish at all. It would be unusual if you didn't feel stressed at this stage. You've been in school since kindergarten, and the end is in sight, but you can't help feeling doubts, the closer you come to leaving academia."

"I'm worried about my mother's health, too. My parents expect me to live near them and teach in Redding, but..."

The phone rang shrilly just then. Natalie gathered her books as the professor answered.

"Hi, honey," he said, "Yes, I'll be home for lunch. Hold on a minute." He cupped his hand over the receiver, saying, "My wife."

As she walked away, Natalie wondered why she had felt so emotional in Professor Muller's office. Of course she would finish her thesis. That's what her goal had been for this year. *I can hardly wait to tell Gary about the summer job.*

* * * *

That afternoon, Gary was speaking with his mother about his summer options. "I won't take the bar exam until July. I can't apply for a position with a law firm until after I pass, *if* I pass on the first try."

"You'll pass," his mother interrupted.

"Thanks for the vote of confidence, Mother, but there have been some surprises in the past. Remember my roommate, Bill Allyson? He failed the exam on the first try. His grades were good at Boalt, but he couldn't write clearly under pressure."

Grace Morgan was lounging on the sofa as Gary sat hunched on an ottoman. Now she sat up more alertly, asking, "Are you still seeing Natalie Perrault?"

"If you mean am I dating Natalie, the answer is *Yes*. Natalie is my one and only. As I told you and Dad, I liked her folks very much when I met them at Thanksgiving."

"I just wondered if spending so much time with Natalie isn't a distraction. You've never before doubted that you'd pass the bar exam in July, and now you're talking about flunking."

"Mother! I still feel very confident that I'll pass the bar exam."

He stood up, his deep blue eyes so much like his mother's, flashing with indignation.

"Far from being a *distraction* to me, Natalie is my inspiration," he said.

"Don't be angry." His mother reached out for his hand.

At dinner that evening, Lloyd Morgan seemed unaware of the tension between his wife and son. Grace Morgan was unusually silent during the meal as her husband recounted some labor disputes at the Port of Oakland.

"I'm going to call in an arbitrator, Gary. I've tried negotiating with the union representatives in informal sessions before the contract comes up for renewal, but we're not making any progress." He paused, taking a bite. "I know the union reps feel like I'm in the enemy camp, being an officer of the Port, no matter how much I try to see their point-of-view. Still, I'd like to keep the talks going."

"What is your exact role in this, Dad?" Gary asked.

"I'm chairman and mediator of labor relations. Long-winded title, huh? The president of the board told me I was a good listener. Bunch of bullshit, but…"

"Lloyd!" his wife interrupted sharply.

"Sorry, Grace," he apologized, resuming his talk. "Anyway, he said I was fair in evaluating personnel." Gary's father raised his palms upward as though in prayer. "I'm doing my best to bring both sides together. So far my sympathies are with the longshoremen."

"I'm sure you're fair. And Grandfather Morgan would be proud of you," Gary said.

He knew the family history. Lloyd's father, Griffith Morgan, had been a miner in Wales who migrated to the United States as a young man in 1890, with his older brother, Ivor. The two men traveled west until they reached California, and there they earned their bread on the docks by the Bay. Ivor and Griffith Morgan had vowed never to work beneath the earth again. They were drawn to the outdoor life on the busy port. Although the work was as physically demanding as mining, their prospects in California were infinitely brighter than in the slag-filled pits of their birthplace in Wales.

Grace rose, putting her hand on her husband's shoulder. "I wish your father could have lived to see what you've made of your life, dear."

"I wish I could have known him, too, Dad," Gary added.

After his mother left the room, Gary told his father he was returning to Berkeley the next day. "I need to get back to the grindstone. Mother is spoiling me here."

"Come with me to what your mother calls our 'recreation room.' We've moved the television to my study, rather than have it dominate the living room."

Gary saw that his father's desk had been shoved to one corner to allow for a couch facing the television set his mother had ordered at Christmas.

"How am I going to get any work done with this thing in here? The only reason I agreed to buy the damn television was to watch the local news and the political conventions this summer," his father grumbled.

Gary was studying the photos on the wall of his Grandfather Morgan and Great-uncle Ivor, taken in 1896 when they were starting up their own salvage operations on the waterfront.

"How old was Grandfather in this photo?" Gary asked.

"He must have been twenty-six. He and Mother were married two years later."

Gary's father sat down, continuing. "But I didn't bring you in here to revisit the past. What about your plans for this summer?"

"I'll talk to Judge Oliver next week," Gary said. "I'd like to clerk for him again while I prepare for the bar exam."

"You'll be keeping your apartment then? You could save money by living at home."

"Thanks to the G.I. bill and my trust fund, I can afford my apartment."

Gary pointed to his grandfather's photograph. "Look at Grandfather Morgan and look at Grandmother Gwen Lloyd, about to become Mrs. Griffith Morgan." He traced his fingers over another photograph of a young woman dressed in white, masses of hair piled on top of her head. "They were quite a pair, weren't they, Dad"?

Lloyd Morgan studied the photographs for a minute before replying. "Did I ever tell you about my first spring at Cal, after I pledged SAE? I took your grandmother to dinner at the Hotel Claremont. That was in 1919. Mother had rarely set foot in Berkeley. She still lived in our old house near the docks, but I told her I wanted to show her the elegant hotel in Berkeley. I remember she said to me coquettishly, 'You mean I'll be going in style with a fraternity man?' She dressed up for the occasion, looking almost as young and pretty as she does in that photograph, and we had a fine time."

Gary had rarely heard his father reminisce in this way.

"She had been a widow for three years and she still mourned my father, but she appreciated any little outing. Did I imagine some discord between you and your mother this evening, Gary?"

So your antennae are working just fine. No wonder you're given mediation duties at the Port of Oakland, Gary thought before answering.

"I was just expressing my concerns about passing the bar exam, and Mother overreacted. I wonder how Mother thinks I made it in the Army without her by my side," Gary added. To his surprise his father looked at him severely.

"No need to be sarcastic. Your mother loves you more than you can guess. Just remember, our mothers are our first loves and deserve our respect above all others."

I wonder whether Freud would agree with that, Dad. But aloud Gary merely asked, "Did you have an ulterior motive in telling me your story about taking Grandmother Morgan to the Claremont?"

"What if I did?"

"Then I'll go and make my peace with Mother now," Gary said.

Chapter 8

"I haven't seen this dress before, have I?" Gary asked as Natalie opened the front door of Mrs. Carlyle's house one Saturday evening in early February. He whistled as she twirled, showing off the ice-blue moiré taffeta skirt.

"Christmas money I've been saving for something special. I splurged at the Sather Gate Apparel shop."

She unbuttoned the matching jacket, saying, "Without the jacket, the dress can be worn as a formal. The sales clerk said short formals are fashionable."

"Very elegant," Gary said. "Three guesses where we're going for dinner tonight."

"San Francisco?"

"No. I made reservations at the Claremont."

"Gary, I don't know why I thought we were going to San Francisco." She kissed him lightly. "Don't look that way. I love the Claremont."

Later, at the hotel, Natalie was summing up her conversation with Professor Muller. "I'm keeping my fingers crossed about this position. I could stay in Berkeley all summer and…"

"Are you finished, Miss?" their waiter interrupted, hovering over the table.

"You've hardly touched your steak," Gary said, motioning the waiter away.

"I've been talking instead of eating," Natalie replied. "The steak is perfect, even better than Mrs. Carlyle's famous meat loaf. Tell me about your talk with Judge Oliver."

"The learned judge said he'd keep me busy as his clerk. I want to introduce you to him soon. We'll both be gainfully employed if you have an inside track with the English department," Gary said. "Dessert? I see our waiter approaching again."

Natalie shook her head. "Couldn't eat another bite."

"Then let's dance."

After the third dance, Gary led her onto the balcony outside the ballroom. Natalie had removed her jacket for dancing, but now she shivered in the February chill.

"Goose-bumps," she murmured.

Gary rubbed her arms and kissed her, oblivious to couples passing by. "Marry me, darling, and I'll keep you warm forever," he whispered. "I love you, Natalie. Marry me," he repeated between kisses. He fumbled in his coat pocket for the ring, slipping it on her finger.

Natalie drew in her breath, "Oh!" Peering in the darkness at the ring, she was trembling from the sharp winter air.

"You can exchange the ring for another style," Gary said. "It's a little loose on your finger, isn't it?"

"It's perfect. Beautiful!" She stretched out her hand, admiring the solitaire.

"Then your answer is *Yes*, I take it." Gary resumed his casual manner of speaking. "You're freezing out here." He hurried her along the balcony. Just inside the doorway, she kissed him again.

At their table, Gary signaled their waiter. "Bring us champagne, please—California champagne. The lady just agreed to become my wife."

As the waiter hurried off, the orchestra leader raised his baton to lead a rendition of Hoagy Carmichael's "Stardust."

"Let's dance to this one," Gary said as Natalie twisted her ring, remarking on how the diamond reflected the lights around them.

"You do realize that I come with the ring, Natalie. You have to take me, too."

Natalie rose, giving a mock sigh, "Guess I can manage to put up with you for the next forty years or so."

As they finished the dance, Gary handed the orchestra leader a piece of paper. The conductor grinned at Gary. Turning to his band, he called out, "A drum roll, please."

As the drummer energetically did his stuff, the leader spoke into the microphone.

"The Dick Jurgens Orchestra, coming to our listeners from the beautiful Hotel Claremont, announces the engagement of Miss Natalie Perrault to Mr. Gary Morgan…" Cheers and applause from the crowd temporarily drowned his voice out. Dick Jurgens leaned over to Natalie, covering the microphone. "Do you have a favorite song for us to play in your honor?"

When Natalie hesitated, Gary looked at the pearl necklace she was wearing and suggested, "What about the Glenn Miller classic, 'A String of Pearls'?"

Forever afterwards, Natalie linked the strains of sweet swing music playing that familiar melody with friendly strangers smiling as she and Gary danced around the ballroom. The hotel photographer, a bustling young woman, was waiting at their table to arrange several poses of Natalie and Gary with their cheeks pressed together as they gazed self-consciously toward the flashbulbs.

In the days after Gary's proposal, the following correspondence took place.

Sunday, Feb. 10, '52

Dear Mother and Dad,

I'm glad you didn't mind being awakened so early last Sunday morning by my phone call. Just had to tell you how happy I was right away. Gary keeps saying how much he likes both of you. I'm enclosing the Morgans' address.

Please write a note inviting the Morgans to Redding. It might be easier if we host a dinner at the inn where Gary stayed. I suggest the weekend of Feb. 23–24.

All my love,

Natalie

Grace Morgan received a letter, written on flimsy notepaper, decorated with a pink rose at the heading.

Dear Mrs. Morgan,

Natalie's father and I invite you and Mr. Morgan to come to Redding the weekend of February 23–24 for a family dinner to celebrate Natalie's and Gary's engagement. We look forward to meeting both of you.

Very truly yours,

Marie Perrault

Marie received the reply from Grace Morgan on cream-colored bond stationery.

February 16, 1952

Dear Mrs. Perrault,

Thank you so much for your kind invitation to come to Redding. Lloyd and I have another commitment, and must ask for a "rain check." Since Gary and Natalie have not set a wedding date, perhaps we can postpone the formal announcement of their betrothal.

Sincerely yours,

Grace Morgan

"What commitment can be more important than their son's engagement?" Ralph Perrault asked when his wife showed him Grace Morgan's message.

"Well, she does suggest a later date." Marie's voice trailed off. "We'll put an announcement in the Redding paper. That's the correct way of doing things. I'll call Natalie this evening."

Gary was with Natalie when her mother called at Mrs. Carlyle's home.

"Yes, Mother, send the announcement to the newspaper. Something short—just Mr. and Mrs. Ralph Perrault are pleased to announce the engagement of their daughter, Natalie, to Mr. Gary Morgan. Hold on, I'm putting Gary on the line."

"Hi, Mrs. Perrault. I should tell you my *legal* name is Gareth Lloyd Mor— that's right G A R E T H. Mother will be in touch with you about rescheduling the family dinner."

"So your real name is *Gareth?* Sounds like one of the Knights of the Round Table. Wasn't Sir Gawain's brother named Gareth?" Natalie asked.

Lloyd Morgan was looking at the note from Natalie's mother. "What do we have on the calendar for the last weekend in February?"

"You're on the Cal Reunion Committee, Class of '22, thirtieth anniversary. Remember? The committee meets at the Claremont on February twenty-third," his wife reminded him.

He pulled off his reading glasses to see his wife more clearly. "I'm one of about twenty members of my class on that committee. I wouldn't be missed, especially since the reunion isn't until November. Suggest another date soon, Grace. We don't want to offend Natalie's parents."

But the weeks slipped by without any further communications between Grace Morgan and Marie Perrault.

Chapter 9

▼

"I'm not in favor of long engagements," Gary repeated as he was driving home from his fraternity formal dance. They had been arguing about their marriage date. Natalie had suggested August.

"Let's elope tonight. We're even properly dressed for a wedding," Gary said.

"I know you're joking," she began.

"No, I'm not," he interrupted. "But let's get married in June."

"It's not that I have my heart set on a formal wedding with trailing bridesmaids, but I expect to be married just once. I don't want some furtive elopement," Natalie said.

"What do you have in mind?" he asked. Returning from the dance held in Walnut Creek, they were following Fish Ranch Road, the street lined with eucalyptus trees winding toward the Hotel Claremont.

"Watch out!" Natalie shouted as a speeding car overtook them.

"You're skittish tonight," Gary said.

"I hate this road. Slow down." Natalie tensed up at every hairpin turn. "How much did you have to drink?" she asked.

"I'm okay, Natalie. We're over the worst part. See the lights of the Claremont?"

She breathed more easily then, as though the floodlights illuminating the palm trees surrounding the hotel were welcoming them home.

"Relax," Gary said. "We're almost to my place. We can talk there."

Without speaking, they entered Gary's apartment and he switched on a dim light. Pulling off his tuxedo jacket and shirt, he threw them on his couch.

"There! I always feel like a waiter in a tux. That damn collar is too tight."

Natalie collapsed in a low club chair, still huddled in her evening wrap. Her face in the semidarkness was closed in, her body taut.

"You're still angry," Gary said. "Our first fight over my driving. What a cliché."

"I can't help being nervous when you drive so fast, especially at night."

Natalie averted her head, speaking so softly he could barely hear the words. To perceive her better, he turned on the gooseneck lamp. A soft glow spread from the corner of the room. Her light green eyes widened as he approached her.

"Sweetheart, I'm sorry for upsetting you. Let's kiss and make up."

He knelt down before her, resting his head in her lap. She began stroking his hair, caressing his face half-buried in the folds of her taffeta gown. She bent down to kiss him, warming to his mouth on hers. His hands slipped under her wrap. Then he removed her dancing shoes, stroking the arch of one foot.

"You're wearing your glass slippers tonight," he whispered.

"Plastic," she replied. "Clear plastic with rhinestones. The latest in footwear."

A few minutes later they lay on top of his bed, caressing each other. Natalie's pale blue formal, garter belt and stockings were draped over a chair next to Gary's tuxedo pants. She was still wearing her strapless bra, her panties, and her pearls.

"My sweet love," he whispered.

"I'll have to leave soon."

He kissed her deeply as he caressed her, then as he pressed her to him, her body suddenly grew tense and she pushed him away.

"No." Natalie sat up straight. "I can't. I have to leave."

She reached for her clothing as he rubbed his forehead, avoiding her eyes.

"I'm a virgin," she said. "Am I bragging or complaining? I don't know."

He dressed quickly in jeans and a sweater. They turned their backs on each other.

"I misread your signals, that's all," he remarked.

He drove her to Mrs. Carlyle's house with exaggerated caution, saying as he pulled into the driveway, "You'll notice I didn't break any speed limits."

On the porch she lifted her chin, looking into his eyes as she whispered good night. His kiss brushed her lips and he was gone.

For a long time that night she lay on her narrow bed, dry-eyed, but shivering as though she would never find warmth again. Her last conscious thought before sleep overtook her was that her romance had been ill fated from the beginning and now was spiraling downhill.

Probably because he had consumed more highballs than usual at the dance, Gary fell asleep almost immediately. But when he awakened on Sunday morning, he pondered his actions of the previous evening. Had he behaved badly? He excused himself from boorishness; at worst, he had been careless in his driving and selfish in his desire. His tuxedo jacket and shirt thrown over the couch, and his black tie and carnation boutonniere dropped on the carpet reminded him of his ardor for Natalie. He felt there was something false in their unconsummated romance. She now seemed tentative with him, reining back her emotions. Until they became bonded in flesh, they were becoming more critical of each other, more elusive and superficial with every encounter.

After his shower and shave, he felt his dull headache receding. As he gulped tomato juice, waiting for the coffee to boil, he resolved to see Natalie without calling first. A creature of habit, he washed his dishes and stuffed his soiled laundry into a pillowcase.

By eleven o'clock he was knocking on Mrs. Carlyle's kitchen door, where he could see Natalie through the window. Her look of sudden joy changed to one of wariness as she opened the door. Gary heard himself saying in a rush, "Whatever is wrong between us, I want to make it right. You looked happy to see me, but now you seem distant."

She backed away, twirling her loose ring around her finger. "We could break it off right now, Gary, if you're having second thoughts."

He reached for her hands, leading her to a small table before speaking. "Yours is the only vote that counts, Natalie. The only reason to get married is because we love each other. I knew I loved you very early on, maybe even that first time we met. I've never stopped loving you."

"Then we mustn't hurt each other or let little quarrels come between us."

He kissed the palms of her hands, baffled still by her reserve, saying, "Let's make our wedding plans. Have you had breakfast?"

"As much as I want."

"Where's your landlady this morning?"

"At church. That's where I met her—at the Presbyterian Church on College Avenue. It seems so long ago. I told Mrs. Carlyle I was looking for a place to live near the campus."

"So your Perrault ancestors were French Huguenots?" Gary asked playfully.

"I doubt if they were calling themselves Huguenots by the time they settled in Nebraska. Just plain Protestants, American Presbyterians. I was glad I went to church that Sunday. Mrs. Carlyle invited me to her house, and we struck up our arrangement."

"Would you like us to be married in that church? What's the name of it?"

"St. John's. Yes, and I think you'll like the minister, Reverend Hutchinson."

"Then we'll go together next Sunday. See how easy I am?"

A few minutes later they heard Mrs. Carlyle drive into the garage. Natalie opened the kitchen door, calling out, "Gary and I are in here. Sorry I missed going to church with you," she added as her landlady entered.

Mrs. Carlyle removed her straw hat as she remarked, "Mr. Hutchinson asked about you, Natalie. I told him you and Gary are engaged." She looked inquiringly from one to the other. "It's not a secret, is it?"

"Of course not," Natalie said. "Gary and I expect to be married at St. John's. We'll set the date soon."

"June, right after graduation," Gary said. "We'll be in church next Sunday. Now I have to do my laundry. Cleanliness is next to godliness, I've heard."

"I'll come with you to the ÿaundromat." Natalie followed him.

Outside Gary asked, "What happened to Mrs. Carlyle's hair? It's blue."

"Once a month she goes to the hairdresser for a 'rinse,' to keep her gray hair from getting that yellow look," Natalie informed him. "When the hairdresser uses too much of the stuff, it turns the hair a violet-blue. Like the Blue Fairy in *Pinocchio*."

Gary saw that Natalie was herself again. Her aloofness had vanished.

"We've made big decisions," he said. "I'll see you in church and you'll see me in court or at least in the office of Judge Oliver. I could say the judge is my spiritual advisor."

True to his promise, Gary introduced Natalie to Judge Oliver in late April. As he had anticipated, she and his mentor warmed to each other from the start. With her customary quickness, Natalie noticed two quotations framed near his desk:

"The axis of the earth sticks out visibly through the center of each and every town or city." and "It is the province of knowledge to speak and it is the privilege of wisdom to listen."

"Oliver Wendell Holmes?" she guessed, adding, "The father, I mean."

"Yes. The elder Holmes was the poet, not the Supreme Court justice," Joaquin Oliver said as he clasped Natalie's hand in his own broad one. "Delighted to meet you. This lady is sharp, Gary. Please be seated."

"I've just survived my oral exams, including a great many questions about Ralph Waldo Emerson, the Transcendentalists, and the Boston Brahmins, so the senior Holmes has been on my mind lately," Natalie explained.

Judge Oliver exerted his charm on Natalie, bending his massive silver-haired head toward her as he spoke. "My mother named me *Joaquin* after the poet Joaquin Miller. I suppose she hoped that I would become a dashing poet of the West, although as I learned later, Joaquin Miller was something of a rascal. Gary tells me you'll be married in June. What foresight to choose a wife who can help you write your briefs," the judge said.

"That's my intention, sir," Gary said, grinning.

"Mrs. Oliver and I look forward to inviting you to our home after your honeymoon. She can enlighten you on techniques for keeping a lawyer husband from spending too much time buried in musty legal papers."

"Show off!" Gary exclaimed after they said good-bye to the judge. "Joaquin Oliver is one of Boalt Hall's alumni of 1913—a brilliant mind. You held your own with him."

"The judge looks like someone from MGM central casting," Natalie replied. "He's the only person I've ever met in real life who could be described as *leonine.*"

Chapter 10

▼

A few days later, Natalie opened a letter from the English department to read that she had been selected for the summer position as a graduate assistant with a stipend of two hundred dollars a month. Hurriedly, she placed a call to Redding, eager to share the good news with her family. She listened to the phone ring seven times before telling the operator she would try again later. Gary was in a class, but on impulse she dialed the Morgans' home.

"Hello," Grace Morgan answered.

"Mrs. Morgan, it's Natalie. I just received notice that I have that summer job."

"Congratulations. I know how much you wanted the position. Have you told Gary?"

"Not yet. He's in class now. I just couldn't wait to tell someone."

"I'm glad you called. Your mother wrote to me suggesting a family dinner the evening before graduation. Since the wedding will be two days later, she thought that would take the place of a rehearsal dinner. Lloyd and I would like to co-host with your parents."

"That sounds lovely, Mrs. Morgan."

"Don't you think you could call me 'Grace'? Since the dinner will also serve as a graduation party, we can kill two birds with one stone. Well, *that's* not an appropriate way of putting it, but you know what I mean."

"Thank you, Grace. That does make it easy for everyone. No need for you and Mr. Morgan to drive to Redding to meet my family, since they'll be here so soon."

Hanging up, Natalie let out a deep sigh of relief. It seemed that her worries about Gary's mother disliking her had been unfounded. Since their engagement, Natalie had been to the Morgans' home only once to meet Nelson and Elinor Lundgren. Gary intended to ask his cousin, Eric Lundgren, to be an usher. She recalled Gary saying, "Uncle Nelson is the son of my Grandfather Lundgren's first wife. I don't see Eric very often. He's a trader with Uncle Nelson's securities firm, still a bachelor at thirty-one."

Eric had not been present at the Morgans' home when Natalie had met the Lundgrens, but she had felt quite reassured by the welcome given her by Gary's relatives.

"About time you got married," Nelson Lundgren had bantered. Natalie observed that Gary, his mother, and his uncle resembled each other, especially their deep blue eyes and high foreheads. Gary's voice and black eyebrows were like his father's, but his good looks came from the Lundgren genes.

"Now maybe you can get Eric off the stick," Nelson Lundgren had said.

"You act as though Gary has just been frittering his time away instead of going to law school," his wife had rejoined. To Natalie and Gary, she had added, "We're delighted for you two. And Grace tells me you're a very good bridge player, Natalie,"

Natalie thought Elinor Lundgren was the sort of woman often described as "well preserved". Her ample figure was encased in a dark blue skirt and blouse with a jabot, her faded blonde hair artfully styled, and her smooth face rosy with top-of-the-line cosmetics.

"Natalie and I were quite a success at the bridge table, weren't we, partner?" Lloyd Morgan had remarked.

Grace Morgan had excused herself to "discuss business matters with Nelson."

Gary's aunt and his father had entered into a spirited conversation about the candidacy of Robert Taft against General Eisenhower. Natalie had sat by, a polite smile fixed on her face until Gary said good-naturedly, "Taft doesn't have a chance against Ike, Aunt Elinor, and you know it! Natalie and I are voting the Democratic ticket this election."

When she was still unable to reach anyone in Redding, Natalie telephoned the chairman of the English department.

"I'm grateful to you and Professor Muller for sponsoring me," she began.

"We had several fine candidates this spring," the chairman replied, "but all of us on the selection committee felt you were the best qualified. Jean Swithin is our alternate choice in the event you declined. John Muller thought you should know that. I understand you and Jean are good friends."

"Yes. Thank you for telling me. I'll be seeing Jean this afternoon."

She found Jean smoking, seated on a stone bench by the campanile as the bells tolled three o'clock.

"Where would you like to go for dinner, Jean?" Natalie asked. They had made a bet with each other. Whoever was selected for the position would treat the other one to dinner.

Jean shrugged, replying, "As long as I didn't get the position, I'm glad it was you. I thought it would be one of us."

"You're bound to get excellent letters of recommendation," Natalie said.

"I'm applying for a teaching post at my old school in the city: Katherine Wylie Academy. Here comes Gary."

He bent over to kiss Natalie. "Congratulations, honey. Mrs. Carlyle found the note you left with your news."

"We're taking Jean to dinner to celebrate," Natalie told him.

"Name the place, Maid-of-Honor," Gary teased.

"How about Bertoli's? I'm fond of ravioli and vino. Though I must say I feel like a Miss America runner-up right now. Am I supposed to grab you and cry, Natalie?" Jean rose, pushing up her sweater sleeves.

Gary mimicked a violin player, rasping, "Ah, you're breakin' my heart, kid."

At dinner, Jean kept up a steady patter in her rapid style. She had a way of mocking Natalie's seriousness that amused Gary. He noticed that Jean had dressed up for the evening in a black linen sheath, decorated with an artificial red carnation at the neckline.

"Jean, we need to pick out your dress for the wedding. I want you to choose first. Then I'll select the bridesmaid dresses for Julie and my cousin Edy," Natalie suggested.

"Let's go shopping in the city," Jean said. "Just so I don't get stuck looking like Little Bo Peep. By the way, Gary, who's your best man? An eligible bachelor for me?"

"I wish it could be Dave Rosenthal, but I've asked Reed Houghton, a fraternity brother. Yes, I believe he is still unattached, Miss Swithin."

"Why isn't Dave your best man?" Jean questioned.

"He's Jewish. I'm afraid his rabbi wouldn't permit him to take part in a Calvinist ceremony. Anyway, Dave and Rhonda will be married a week later. They're full of their own plans," Gary explained.

"Dave's uncle and aunt have a catering business. We're hiring them for our reception, too," Natalie chimed in happily. She and Jean giggled over their glasses of Chianti as Jean imitated some of their professors. Gary had ordered plain tonic water for himself, inserting a comment now and then, but mostly being an audience of one for Natalie and Jean. Bertoli's had long been a popular restaurant with Berkeley students because of its low-priced Italian bill of fare, coupled with a good wine list. Even on this Tuesday evening the place was filling up fast. Gary surveyed customers crowding in the doorway.

"Ed! Bev Tate," he called suddenly. "Come on over. Join our table."

"It's been ages," Natalie said, introducing Jean to the Tates.

"How are you feeling, Bev?"

"Fine, I just can't keep awake past nine o'clock every night," Bev grinned. "I've also heard too many jokes about swallowing a basketball. Two and a half months to go. I'm on a strict salt-free diet, but Ed had a hankering for veal parmigiana."

Ed signaled the waiter for menus and ordered a liter of wine.

"What's this? Are you on the wagon?" Ed asked, pointing to Gary's glass.

"I'm being good, drinking tonic water tonight," Gary explained.

"That's what I'll have, too," Bev said. "And minestrone soup and bread."

Natalie hunted up their waiter to pay the bill before Gary offered to pick up the tab for the Tates as well. Jean whispered, "Let's go to the *loo.*" She liked using British expressions. In the ladies' room Jean said, "I was dying for a cig, but I didn't think I should light up when your friends sat down with us. I feel like a fifth wheel."

"Don't be silly. By the way, you look very San Francisco tonight."

"Mother surprised me with this dress last week. I. Magnin sale. Since we both wear the same size, we share clothes."

Jean twirled her hair behind her ears. "Gary is something,. How many guys would put themselves out for their fiancée's friend?"

"You could have invited a date tonight, Jean."

"My social life has been on hold while I finished writing my thesis. T. S. Eliot is the only man in my life right now."

"But you *have* finished your thesis. I'm still trying to find someone to do the final typing. We should be getting back."

"Right," Jean agreed, crushing her cigarette in the ashtray. As the two of them threaded their way through the crowded restaurant, Jean recited, "In the room the women come and go, talking of Michelangelo."

Natalie and Jean were laughing as they joined the others, leading Gary to comment, "Looks like we'll have to cut off the vino for these two. What's so funny?"

"Just an English major's jest," Jean said. "Nat and I are getting rummy on Willa Cather and T. S. Eliot."

"We'll watch Ed and Bev eat their dinners now," Gary said.

"Bev's eating for two, but I'm eating for *three*," Ed said, diving into his food.

Driving Natalie home, Gary remarked, "I asked Ed to be an usher. Since we met at the Tates' party, Ed should be part of legalizing our marriage contract."

"That was lucky the Tates showed up at Bertoli's. We need to order the invitations next week. If only Mother lived here to take care of these things."

"You sound bossy already, just like a wife," Gary sighed.

"I just remembered that my folks don't know about my summer job. Would you do me a favor?"

"Probably. Especially if you kiss me like you mean it."

She did so, several times.

"Would you arrange a blind date for Jean to meet Reed Houghton? Jean hasn't had much fun lately. We've both been such grinds."

"I'll do one better. I'll invite my cousin Eric for Jean. I think they'd hit it off. We'll double date at the Claremont. How would that suit you?"

"We're too happy, darling. Sometimes I think we're tempting the *Eumenides*."

"You're very sexy when you say something in Greek."

Chapter 11

▼

"You're sure you don't mind shortening my dress, Mrs. Carlyle?" Jean asked, holding a large glossy box.

"No, dear; try it on. I'll get my tape measure."

"You're an angel, Mrs. Carlyle," Natalie said. "Gary and his cousin will be here to pick us up. This is the only time Jean can model her dress."

"Ta-dah!" Jean exclaimed, pirouetting across Mrs. Carlyle's parlor in a swirl of shimmering aquamarine taffeta.

"What a lovely color. Now stand still, dear. Are these heels the same height as the ones you'll be wearing in the wedding?" Mrs. Carlyle asked.

"Yes. I think the dress should be an inch and a half shorter to be the same length as her bridal gown."

Natalie sat by, handing Mrs. Carlyle pins as her landlady measured.

"I liked the ballerina length for my gown. The bridesmaid dresses are a pale peach."

As Felicia Carlyle finished measuring, she flexed her fingers, saying, "I have some happy news. My daughter Sarah and her husband are expecting a baby in November, so after your wedding I expect I'll be sewing baby clothes."

"How exciting," Natalie said. "You'll be such a wonderful grandmother."

"I can see you're thrilled about the baby," Jean added. "I'll change now."

"Be sure to give me Sarah's address. I want to write her a note, telling her how much I've appreciated having you as a second mother. Let me pay you for the sewing."

"No, the hemming is nothing. Call it a little gift. I'm looking forward to meeting your family. Why don't you try on your wedding gown now? I can compare the length with Jean's dress."

* * * *

Eric Lundgren arrived to find his cousin fixing himself a sandwich in the apartment.

"You're early," Gary remarked. "Ham and cheese okay? We'll call this dinner, save some money."

"Sure. I was going to treat us to dinner, but a sandwich is fine. So your bachelor days are numbered," Eric said, slathering mustard on his bread.

"It's been a long time since we've seen each other," Gary commented. "You still enjoy your wheeling and dealing?"

As Eric removed his coat, draping it over a chair, Gary observed that his cousin was developing a slight paunch already.

"I like being a trader, everything except the hours. Rising at four-thirty is not fun. Have to be at work when the markets open in New York."

Eric munched on his sandwich. His light gray eyes behind wire-rimmed glasses darted around the room, assessing everything.

"You're bringing your bride to this dump to live?" Eric inquired suddenly. "What about a G.I. loan for a house? It's pretty much a buyer's market now."

Gary shook his head, saying, "You and Uncle Nelson. You're both always selling or promoting something, aren't you? My lease on this apartment isn't up till September. I take the bar exam in July, remember? Natalie has a summer job on campus, so this place will have to do until fall. But thanks for your advice, Eric," he added with a grin.

"No fee," Eric laughed. "I'll come to you for legal counsel with the expectation you'll do your investing through me. Now tell me about my date...Jean?"

Promptly at seven o'clock Gary knocked at Mrs. Carlyle's door and the men entered to glimpse Natalie in her white lace wedding gown. Her silky dark hair tumbled to her shoulders as she smiled before disappearing down the hallway.

Eric was thinking, *Natalie is a vision.*

Mrs. Carlyle called out in alarm, "Oh, Gary! You shouldn't come in yet!"

"Shall we go back outside?" Gary asked.

"No, of course not. It's just an old superstition," Mrs. Carlyle replied. "The groom isn't supposed to see the bride's dress before the wedding."

"I didn't see a thing, Mrs. Carlyle, just a white blur," Gary assured her.

Eric Lundgren faced a young woman whose deep gray eyes mirrored his own with an amused expression. "You must be Jean. I'm Eric Lundgren."

Natalie entered, smoothing her hair as Gary said, "Natalie, meet my cousin."

"How do you do, Natalie?" Eric said, brushing her cheek with his lips.

"We're going in Eric's car. It's newer, bigger, and a lot cleaner than mine," Gary explained as they left Mrs. Carlyle.

The May evening was unusually balmy, and the girls wore only light woolen shawls over their spring dresses. Elinor Lundgren had described Natalie as "a quiet, serious girl, not a beauty, by any means," but now Eric thought that description was wrong. Perhaps because Natalie glowed with happiness, she looked especially radiant that evening. Eric thought her silvery voice and classic features were very appealing.

"I've never been to the Claremont," Eric remarked to Jean.

"Neither have I, but it's the East Bay's answer to the Fairmont," Jean added. "Gary tells me you went to San Francisco State. My kid brother plans to enroll there."

"It was a good college for me, right after the war. I wanted to major in economics and go into business. Since I was an *old* freshman, I didn't have time to waste. Say, this is quite a setting—palm trees and gigantic eucalyptus trees. Looks like a castle on the hillside," Eric interrupted himself to admire the hotel gleaming in the twilight as he swung his car into the parking lot.

As Gary and Natalie watched their friends dancing a rumba, he said, "I had a hunch Eric and Jean would hit it off."

Natalie was thinking how easily Jean had engaged Eric in conversation without trying too hard. She remarked, "They have San Francisco in common, even though Eric's family is wealthy, whereas poor Jean…"

"Why *poor* Jean?" Gary asked, frowning as he always did when Natalie mentioned money.

"Jean's parents were divorced about five years ago. Apparently Mr. Swithin was the manager of a restaurant that folded. They had been living way beyond their means, but the divorce was a big shock to Jean and Hal, her brother. Mrs. Swithin works as a bank secretary."

Eric Lundgren couldn't remember when he had enjoyed himself as much as he did that evening. He thought Jean Swithin was witty, as well as attractive. Her keen gray eyes and her generous smile captivated him. He noticed that the blue dress Jean was wearing was of good quality, with an ivory lace collar framing her face. As they talked while smoking on the balcony of the Claremont, Eric learned that Jean's mother's apartment was near his own place on Green Street.

"If you're spending tomorrow in San Francisco, why don't I drive you home tonight?" Eric offered. "Do you think we've left the lovers alone long enough?"

As Eric and Jean made their way back to the table, Natalie whispered to Gary, "I like your cousin, even though he's not as handsome as you."

"You think not? Look who else is coming our way." It was the assertive woman who had taken their engagement photograph, asking, "Wouldn't you like a souvenir photo of your evening at the Claremont?"

Caught by the flash bulbs, Natalie appeared startled. Eric squinted behind his glasses, but Gary and Jean looked their best in the finished photograph.

"We'll take two copies," Eric told the photographer, pulling out his wallet.

In the ladies' lounge, Natalie asked Jean her impressions of Eric. Reading Natalie's thoughts, Jean said, "You're so up in the clouds, you want everyone else to be happy, too. But this is one of the few blind dates that turned out well. Arranging a date for a friend is like recommending a movie."

Jean paused before the mirror, adjusting her wrap before turning directly to Natalie. "You know how you resent it when someone says, 'Oh, you'll *love* this movie,' and then you just hate it? But tonight was fun. Eric Lundgren's hair may be thinning already, and his body needs some exercise, but I like Gary's cousin very much. He looks quite *prosperous*," Jean declared.

Chapter 12

After Memorial Day, the chairman of the department called the five honors candidates for master's degrees to his office for a briefing. "I'm very pleased with your theses," the professor began, "and don't they look impressive in their black bindings?"

He handed the booklets to the students, telling his small audience, "I hope you'll read each other's work. Mr. Grassi, you must travel to Italy some day and pay homage to Dante since you have put so much effort in your interpretation of the *Inferno,*" the chairman stated in his formal way.

"I'd like that, but I just got my draft notice so I'm probably headed for Korea," the student replied. Natalie and Jean exchanged glances with Vincent Grassi, whom they referred to privately as their "Renaissance Man." His thesis was titled *The Circles of Hell Revisited through a Twentieth Century Perspective.*

"Somehow Dante doesn't seem very relevant right now," Vince said.

The tall chairman said, "Everything in literature is relevant."

The professor reviewed the schedule for the reception following graduation. He then remarked to Natalie, "Your parents will appreciate your thesis dedication and your tribute to those Nebraska pioneers that Willa Cather immortalized."

The others turned to Natalie, as she was about to frame an answer when the secretary opened the door, passing a message to the professor.

"Natalie, you have a phone call," he said quietly.

Natalie lifted the phone, thinking of her wedding plans. Perhaps the caterer was trying to reach her. *No, Mrs. Carlyle wouldn't interrupt unless…*

"Hello, Mrs. Carlyle," she said.

"Your father just called. Your mother suffered a stroke. She's in the hospital."

"*No, oh, no,*" Natalie felt her heart pounding. "I'm coming at once. I'll..."

"I have the hospital number for you, dear."

"*Mother...*" Natalie sobbed as the secretary stared at her.

On the five-hour train ride home to Redding, she did not yet realize that her life was changing forever. Her mind was still too preoccupied with the myriad tasks she had left undone, all the actions necessary to cancel arrangements for her wedding. The first thing she had said to Gary was "We must call off the wedding."

"We'll *postpone* the wedding if we must, but maybe we can still be married on the fifteenth. You don't know your mother's condition yet," he said.

"Please let everyone know what's happened."

"If only I could drive you home, but I can't get out of my final session with the dean," Gary explained.

"You can't miss graduation and receiving your law degree. You can't disappoint your parents, Gary. Your mother can help with the phone calls. I hope your family isn't stuck with those deposit fees."

"Natalie, for God's sake, don't worry about bills. Just tell your father how sorry we are."

Still, with every rhythmic turning of the wheels on her tedious journey, she avoided thinking of her mother in the hospital by asking herself endless trivial questions: Would Jean retrieve her graduation robe from Mrs. Carlyle? Would Dave Rosenthal's uncle give a refund? Would Gary call the florist to cancel the order?

She had expected her father and Julie to meet her train. As she disembarked, she looked around frantically for them. Carrying her suitcase into the station, she saw her Aunt Isabelle hurrying forward. They embraced wordlessly. Isabelle said, "Thank God, you were able to come so soon. Your father is staying at the hospital. Julie is home by the phone."

Natalie nodded. "How is Mother?"

"No change. Still in a deep coma. I guess that's what you call it. Shall I drive you right to the hospital, or do you want to go home first?"

"To the hospital, please."

Her father was talking to the doctor—a cardiovascular specialist. His face was drawn as he muttered an introduction, "My daughter, Natalie. Mama has regained consciousness. We can see her in a few minutes."

"She'll live! Oh, thank God!" Natalie gasped. "I was so afraid, Daddy."

"Let's sit down," the doctor said. "I want to tell you about your mother's condition before you and your father see her. Strokes are caused by *thrombosis*, a narrowing of the blood vessel from the heart to the brain, or an *embolus*, a clot breaking off…"

To Natalie, the physician seemed too young to be droning on in this pedantic way. She struggled to pay attention, interrupting him to ask, "So you're saying Mother's stroke was caused by both thrombosis and an embolism?"

The doctor looked annoyed. "Yes, technically that's known as a cerebral infarction."

Her father appeared dazed. "Marie put her hand to her head and said, 'My head hurts.' The only warning I had."

Natalie reached out to him.

The doctor's tone softened. "Often that's the only symptom, Mr. Perrault. There was no way you could have foreseen a sudden collapse. The left side of Mrs. Perrault's brain has been affected. We won't know for a while how her motor skills or speech may be impaired, but she has survived the critical first hours."

"We want to see her now. I want my wife to know I'm here."

Marie Perrault was lying flat on the hospital bed, her arms and hands inert outside the white sheet. Her dark eyes sought her husband's face, and she struggled to form words, but the only sound that came from her mouth was a low moaning.

"Raah, whaa?"

He kissed her forehead. "Don't try to speak," he whispered. "I'm staying right with you, Marie. Natalie is here, too."

Natalie gently pressed her mother's right hand, hoping her own expression was more reassuring than her reaction to those frightened dark eyes and slack mouth. After a few minutes, Natalie left her father alone with her mother.

Julie leaped up from the couch as Natalie and her father entered the house.

"Mama regained consciousness, Julie. We won't know much more until morning."

"Daddy, take off your shoes, get more comfortable while Julie and I fix us something to eat," Natalie said. "He's exhausted," she whispered to her sister.

"I took phone messages. Gary called twice and Jean Swithin," Julie's voice trembled.

It was ten o'clock before Natalie called Gary, repeating to him in flat tones the doctor's description of her mother's stroke.

"Hang in there, sweetheart," Gary spoke reassuringly. "I called Reverend Hutchinson first. He sends his prayers to you and your family. He's ready to marry us whenever we wish. We're taking care of everything from the Berkeley end about notifying people."

"I'll call you tomorrow. Thank Jean for me, will you? And Mrs. Carlyle."

"I love you," Gary said. "You have my Piedmont number?"

Chapter 13

▼

A week later Gary's mother told him, "We're going ahead with dinner at the Claremont the evening before graduation."

"But Natalie won't be here. I tried to persuade her to come back to Berkeley for graduation at least, but she feels she can't leave her family."

"I'm sure Natalie wants you to go ahead with our family plans. If Mrs. Perrault improves, Natalie can always stay with us. That's what I told her when we talked on the phone. She urged us not to cancel the dinner," his mother said, studying her list of names.

"I had made the deposit to the Claremont already. It's nonrefundable. I've invited Judge Oliver and his wife, Nelson and Elinor, to take the place of Natalie's family, so we'll still have twelve—the three of us, the three Lundgrens, the Olivers, Jean Swithin, your friend Reed Houghton, plus Ed and Beverly Tate. Let's see that makes seven men and five women, a good balance."

"Fine, Mother. Whatever you want to do," Gary agreed.

* * * *

In San Francisco, Frances Swithin was treating Jean to lunch at a fashionable restaurant in Maiden Lane. Frances kept glancing around at the other tables, hoping to spot a celebrity.

"We were lucky to get a table. For once the boss didn't have last minute typing for me so I could meet you early. He's gone all this afternoon, too. This place is really popular, Jean," she said as the waiter brought their menus. Leaning forward, Frances whispered, "Isn't that Joan Crawford?"

"Where?" Jean asked.

"Don't look. The table by the window. She just sat down."

Jean smiled indulgently at her mother. "I'll peek in a minute. I'll tell you my news."

"About Natalie's canceled wedding, you mean?" Frances asked.

"Indirectly. The chairman of the department told me he'll have to notify Natalie that I'll be given the summer appointment unless Nat can return to Berkeley right away. It's been ten days since her mother's stroke. He checked to see if I still wanted the position. Of course I told him *yes.*"

"Good thing you hadn't committed yourself to another job."

"It's ironic, isn't it? Poor Nat. I don't like to benefit from her misfortune, although she may be on her way back to Berkeley."

"So you'll know tomorrow one way or other about the job? What are you having to eat? The shrimp and avocado salad is scrumptious."

"Sounds wonderful."

Frances Swithin ordered, adding, "I'll have a Gibson, very dry with two onions. Jean?"

"Iced tea for me," Jean said, following her mother's gaze across the room where two waiters were hovering over an attractive brunette who was wearing a broad-brimmed black straw hat.

"It *is* Joan Crawford," Frances Swithin breathed. "Isn't her suit stunning? And that hat looks like a Lilly Daché."

"I'm taking Natalie's gift for Gary to the dinner tomorrow," Jean said.

Now giving her attention equally to Jean and the shrimp salad, Frances asked, "How are *you* getting to the dinner? Not on the Key System F train, I hope."

"No. Eric Lundgren's picking me up—Gary's cousin. He asked me to meet him at his office at four o'clock today. We're still calling people to explain about the wedding being postponed. He has one list of names, I have another."

Frances, who began bombarding Jean with questions, now ignored Joan Crawford. "You have a date this afternoon? Do you want to wear my black linen sheath? Tell me about Eric."

"He has an apartment here in the city. His parents' home is down the peninsula in Atherton."

"Atherton!" Frances interrupted, as if to say *The Riviera.*

"Yes, Mother. I agreed to collaborate with Eric Lundgren to help notify everybody about the wedding being off." Her expression grew serious as she said, "I should be home by sixish, but if Nat calls before I get home, don't mention the summer job."

"I won't, but don't you feel guilty, either. You deserve that job as much as Natalie does. I'm proud of you."

Inside the building, with the gold lettering proclaiming *Lundgren Investments: International Traders,* Jean found Eric Lundgren. His shirtsleeves were rolled up as he scrutinized a pile of paper slips on his desk.

"How's the market?" she asked.

He rolled his eyes, replying, "The market today is 'mixed,' as we say. Highly technical term '*mixed.*' You found me in this warren of a work place." He smiled broadly. "I asked the receptionist to announce you so I could usher you in."

"I think the receptionist has left for the day," Jean said.

Eric poked some papers onto a spindle and pulled out an extra chair.

"Let me get these confirms out of the way, then we'll get to our task."

For the next fifteen minutes they sat with their heads together, deciding who still needed to be called.

Finally Eric said, "I'll phone these six people and you can check with Natalie about the others. All the family members have been notified." He paused, frowning. "It's a damn shame, isn't it? The wedding being off, I mean. Gary's pretty low. We'll have to cheer him up at the dinner. It does seem funny Natalie can't come back to Berkeley."

Jean stood up, taking her cue from Eric, who was putting on his suit coat and straightening his tie.

"How about a drink before I take you home?" he suggested.

"No thanks, really. I just appreciate the ride for tomorrow."

"Come on, no arguments." Eric took her arm, leading her onto Montgomery Street.

Frances Swithin was stretched out on her new modular couch from Gumps, her high heels kicked off onto the floor, when she heard the apartment door open and Jean's voice calling out, "Mother, I'm home."

"Hi, how was your date?" Frances said just before Jean walked in with Eric.

"Oh, excuse me," Frances sat up quickly, touching her hair.

"Mother, this is Eric Lundgren," Jean's said, noticing Eric's amusement.

"How do you do, Eric," Frances extended her hand, slipping into her shoes.

"Didn't mean to disturb you," Eric said smoothly. "I'll pick you up at five-thirty tomorrow, Jean. A pleasure meeting you, Mrs. Swithin."

Jean hurried toward her bedroom to change her clothes as she said, "I see you wearing that 'cat that swallowed the canary look,' *Mother!*"

"I was just thinking that Eric is better-looking than I expected him to be from your description," Frances protested, saucer-eyed.

Chapter 14

"I was counting on Eric to give directions to the Claremont," Nelson Lundgren said as he drove toward the Bay Bridge.

"He's picking up Jean Swithin, Natalie's friend," his wife explained.

"I thought this was to be a family dinner for Gary."

"Originally Grace and Lloyd were hosting a rehearsal dinner, but when the wedding was postponed, they couldn't very well *disinvite* guests. Eric gave me directions to the Claremont. I have them here." Elinor Lundgren fished through her capacious purse.

"I set up an account in Gary's name with our company," her husband said. "I bought shares in a select mix of American companies trading internationally, adds up to five-thousand dollars for our family graduation gift."

"Nelson," Elinor breathed. "You surprise me!"

"You think that's appropriate, don't you? Always helps to have a lawyer in the family," he said briskly.

"I think it's very fine of you. I had no idea you intended to be so generous."

As he turned off the Bay Bridge onto Bayshore Drive, Nelson Lundgren remarked, "The way I see it, the success of Lundgren Investments comes from Father's estate invested over the years. Grace's son certainly deserves his share while he's starting his career, just as we helped launch Eric."

"I agree with you, but not every uncle would be as generous as you are."

"Well, I'll be pleased to present our gift to Gary. I just hope to hell Grace doesn't expect me to make a speech. You know how she can be at social affairs."

His wife smiled to herself, saying, "Yes, Grace will be in her element tonight."

Privately, Elinor was glad she had splurged on her elegant mauve lace dress from Ransohoff's. The color was flattering to her fairness. Nelson looked impressive in his perfectly tailored dark blue suit. Elinor Lundgren liked her sister-in-law well enough, but she was not to be outshone by Grace Morgan this evening.

"Lloyd and I hope we can count on you to be our ally, Judge. Perhaps you can convince Gary that postponing his wedding may help him concentrate on preparing for the bar exam," Grace Morgan spoke earnestly. Greeting Mrs. Oliver, Lloyd Morgan overheard his wife's remark.

"Everyone is here except Gary," Grace added.

"I hardly think we should involve Judge Oliver in raising Gary's morale. Our table is over here," Lloyd Morgan said, escorting the Olivers into the Garden Room.

"How festive, with blue and gold streamers on the table," Mrs. Oliver commented.

"It isn't that I feel reluctant to get *involved* with Gary's emotional state, but it would be a hard sell for me to argue that boning up for the bar exam is preferable to an anticipated honeymoon with a beautiful young bride," Judge Oliver's sonorous voice carried enough to be heard by the guests already seated.

Bev Tate nudged Ed as Lloyd Morgan began the introductions. "So that's the great Judge Oliver you've told me about," Bev whispered.

"Class of 1913, scholar and legend. Probably looks down on the likes of me grubbing away at Cobb and Fortis," Ed replied.

"My father sends his regards," Reed Houghton said, shaking hands with Judge Oliver.

"I expect you'll be joining his firm soon," the judge remarked.

"As a very junior member. I still have a great deal to learn about the real world," Reed responded with uncharacteristic modesty.

At the far end of the table, Elinor Lundgren was beckoning Eric and Jean toward her.

"Grace seated Nelson next to herself, but I want to get acquainted with you, Jean," she said. "We're so sorry about Natalie's mother's stroke. Eric tells me you've been a trouper, calling people."

"It's the least I can do. Natalie sounded worried last night. Where can I put this gift?" Jean held a flat package on her lap. "It's Natalie's present to Gary."

"I'll take it to Aunt Grace," Eric offered. "Here's Gary now."

Everyone looked up expectantly as Gary bent to kiss his mother. His eyes showed a certain weariness, but he smiled at the guests, saying, "Thank you for being here. I just spoke to Natalie, who sends her best. Well, Mother, looks like we're here to celebrate."

Gary couldn't rid himself of his malaise, although his good manners concealed his feelings. *Surely Natalie could have been here,* he thought. "What about your aunts?" he had demanded in his frequent phone calls to Redding. "Doesn't your father want to see you receive your master's degree after your hard work?" Really, he couldn't understand the Perrault family. With an effort, Gary chuckled at Judge Oliver's congratulations, sprinkled with Latin legalisms, and thanked his uncle Nelson for his generosity. Finally, he hugged his father after opening the handsome leather briefcase with his initials *GLM* embossed in gold letters. Ed Tate read aloud irreverent lawyer jokes.

"This gift is from Natalie," Grace informed everyone as Gary unwrapped the package.

He said, "She knew I would like this," holding up a framed print of the signing of the Declaration of Independence.

"I happened to be with Natalie when she spotted the picture at a little bookstore off campus a month ago," Jean told Elinor Lundgren.

"Say, I think I recognize one of my law professors in the picture," Reed Houghton said, peering at the Founding Fathers. His comment lightened the sentimentality of the moment. To Grace Morgan's relief, everyone engaged in lively conversation. She felt proud of Gary, despite his abstraction and the strained look on his face.

On their ride back to San Francisco, Eric told Jean about his family.

"Gary is something of a hero to Dad," he disclosed. "His tour of duty in Italy was certainly more eventful than my assignments with ordnance officers. Astigmatism determined my lot in the Army," he explained. "Tried to enlist right after Pearl Harbor, turned down because of poor eyesight. I finally was accepted in the Army, but deemed unfit for overseas duty, so I spent the war as a paper shuffler at the Presidio."

"Those days seem so far away now," Jean replied.

Eric continued, "My sister died of leukemia in 1943. I'd never heard of the disease until Annette was stricken."

"I'm so sorry," Jean murmured.

As Eric parked his car before the Swithins' apartment building, he removed his glasses carefully, laying them on the dashboard.

"Would you like to come in?" Jean suggested.

Eric kissed her several times before replying, "Let's stay here. You're not cold, are you?"

Jean kissed him back. "No, I'm not cold," she whispered between kisses.

Chapter 15

Redding

Natalie's days fell into a never-varying pattern. At dawn she would rise and prepare her father's breakfast while he showered. Then, careful to smile, she would look in on her mother, dozing. Natalie wondered if her mother was aware of how bare her sewing room looked, now that all personal accents and furnishings had been cleared to make room for the walker where the sewing machine had been. No more cascades of colorful fabric tumbled across the Singer, ready to be fashioned into a dress for Julie or bright new curtains for the kitchen. Instead of spools of thread of every hue and delicate trimmings arranged on the shelves, there now stood bottles of pills, clean washcloths, and a plastic basin.

Every morning Natalie vowed to bring a vase of flowers to the room, to tack up an artistic calendar, anything to bring life to the surroundings. And every day she got so caught up in the routine of bathing, dressing, cooking, feeding, bed making, vacuuming, and caring for her mother that she forgot about aesthetics until the next day.

At first Natalie had put all her efforts into communicating with her mother, reading her local newspaper articles, trying to induce her to talk, but those dark eyes would become troubled, gazing intently into Natalie's face. Her mother would sink back onto her pillows, closing her eyes in resignation as if to say, *Don't force me to talk.*

Each evening, when her father returned home from work, Natalie would rush up to him with a litany of her complaints: Julie was not helping with the housework, her aunts had stopped coming to visit, the doctor was not returning her calls…

Ralph Perrault would suck in his breath, shutting off Natalie's grievances until she would gradually cease talking, and he would say, "I'll sit with her, Natalie. You rest."

That was another thing. Ralph Perrault had begun to speak of his wife as a pronoun, *she* or *her* instead of *Marie*. This was the state of the household barely three weeks after her stroke. Julie was her usual self, the only one talking at the dinner table while her father and Natalie barely spoke, preoccupied with their own thoughts. In the evenings Julie would sit by her mother's bed, recounting her activities. Ralph and Natalie could hear Julie laughing occasionally as she carried on a nearly one-sided conversation. Julie told her father, "Mama understands everything. She even smiled today."

Then one afternoon in July, Natalie came home from the grocery store to find Julie lying on her bed, sobbing quietly into a pillow.

"It's so hard, isn't it? Day after day not seeing any improvement in Mother. I know you try to amuse her, Julie," Natalie said, standing in the doorway to their bedroom.

Julie raised her head. "I wasn't crying about Mama," she said. "Johnny got his orders. We don't have any more time together. He leaves for Fort Ord tomorrow."

"I'm sorry, Julie. I've got to put these groceries away."

Julie followed. "I'll help you, Nat. Mrs. Browne invited me to their house for dinner tonight. Do you think I should try to explain to Mama?"

"No, but look in on her now, since you won't be here later," Natalie answered, "and wash your face first so Mother won't see that you've been crying," she added.

Ralph was buried in the newspaper while Natalie cleared their dishes from the table when the doorbell rang.

"Now who can that be?" he said irritably, answering the door.

"I hope this isn't a bad time, Mr. Perrault," said Paul Sawyer.

"No. Come in, Paul. Have a seat."

Natalie came forward, offering a cup of coffee. Paul shook his head, "No thanks, Natalie. I was so sorry to hear about Mrs. Perrault's stroke. Dad and Mother, too. We didn't want to bother you right away, but is there anything we can do for you now?"

"Natalie's taken on her mother's care. She's doing a good job," Ralph said. "There is one thing you might do. Take this girl out of the house, give her a break from her nursing."

"Dad!" Natalie burst out.

Paul's face reddened. "I was just going to do that. Gary called me before I left Berkeley. I promised him I'd be checking in with you folks."

"Say hello to Mother, Paul," Natalie suggested. Her mother recognized Paul, who was quite easy and relaxed in his manner.

Natalie whispered, "Most people avoid Mother. Nobody visits us."

Paul squeezed her hand. He was more disturbed by Natalie's wan look than by her mother's contorted face.

"Let's take a drive, Nat. You need to get out."

She glanced down at her cotton blouse, which was sprinkled with food stains. "You talk to Dad. I'll be with you in a minute."

Paul told Ralph Perrault about his work in his father's insurance office. "I can't give any legal advice yet, officially, but I do explain California compensation law to Dad in plain English, and I can do some research. So many cases are coming up involving workers at the lumber mills."

"I thought you might want to work for the Forest Service again," Ralph said, "but working in your father's insurance office is better preparation for your law career."

"My allergies flared up again this spring. I was bothered a little last year, but I still enjoyed working in the woods. I've had reactions to pollens over the years, bad enough to give me a deferment from the military. Say, is Julie around?"

"No, she's at her boyfriend's house. Johnny Browne."

Natalie entered the room to hear Paul say, "I was going to ask Julie if she'd like a summer job in Dad's office. One of his agents got drafted, and his secretary is leaving soon to join her husband in San Diego, We need someone to do typing, filing, and answering the phone."

"That might be the best thing in the world for her," Ralph said eagerly. "Call Julie tomorrow and talk it over."

"So now I won't even have Julie to help me around the house this summer?" Natalie snapped as they got into Paul's car.

"If I was out of line to bring up the job offer for Julie, just say so. I can tell her Dad hired someone else. The last thing I wanted to do was make things tougher for you."

"No. You were just being nice. I'm the ungrateful wretch." Natalie smiled at him.

"I know a place where nobody knows us," Paul said, casting a glance at Natalie with her eyes closed, her head thrown back against the car seat.

The roadhouse was virtually deserted except for a few loggers drinking beer at the bar. Paul and Natalie sat in a booth.

"Cheeseburgers, fries, and a beer sound okay to you? I haven't had dinner."

"No, thanks. I just finished dinner, but I'll have a beer," Natalie said. "I wasn't exaggerating when I said no one comes to visit Mother," she continued. "Not even Aunt Corinne or Aunt Isabelle. It's as though people think having a stroke is contagious. Then to make matters worse, Dad keeps telling everyone how well I'm managing, and he refuses to face up to reality. We need a practical nurse to care for Mother."

Paul allowed her to vent her frustrations while he ate his cheeseburger. Natalie had always been so proud, even in high school, that he had found her intimidating. Now, as she poured out her feelings, he sensed her vulnerability. She interrupted herself abruptly to ask, "Could I have another beer? I didn't realize how thirsty I was."

"Sure." He signaled the bartender. "Have some fries, too. Look, Natalie, there's a very simple solution to your problem."

"What?" Her green eyes brightened with such hope that he hesitated before replying. "Get married. Make a phone call and Gary will be here to rescue you. Your father will get along. People always do."

Instantly, her eyes glazed over and she averted her head. "I promised Daddy I'd stay through the summer. Now that Gary's so close to taking the bar exam, it's really better for him to be studying and clerking for Judge Oliver. Gary and I always end up agreeing that we'll just wait until August to get married. I didn't mean to burden you."

"Hey, no *burden*, Natalie. I told you I wanted to help you and your family."

"You do. You were generous to think of Julie for the office job. We owe you, Paul."

The next morning, Ralph Perrault drove his Forest Service pickup to a building with the sign *Western Life & Casualty Co., Gilbert Sawyer, Insurance Broker.*

He told Julie, "If Gil Sawyer decides not to hire you, just give me a call at my office. I'll give you a ride home."

"Thanks, Daddy. I hope it will be Paul who interviews me."

"Well, honey, I doubt it, but you'll do fine." He grinned at her, adding, "You look very secretarial."

Mr. Sawyer waved at Ralph through the window as he beckoned Julie into his office. He was an older version of Paul, with the same fair complexion, curly light hair and quizzical expression. Gilbert Sawyer got right down to business, firing away questions.

"How many words per minute can you type, Julie?"

"I've tested at seventy with no errors."

"Ever worked in an office before?"

"I've answered the phone for the journalism department at school. Here's my transcript showing the business courses I've taken."

Julie thought Mr. Sawyer's expression softened as he studied her high school record.

"Let's see how this works out. The main thing for you to remember is to ask questions if you don't understand something. Don't guess. Be accurate with people's names, phone numbers and the like. Pay is two hundred dollars a month. Think you can handle the job?"

"Yes, sir. I enjoy office work. Thank you for the opportunity," Julie was brimming over with enthusiasm as she shook Mr. Sawyer's hand.

"I'll turn you over to my secretary, Muriel Barry."

By ten o'clock, Julie felt as though she had been saying the words "Western Life and Casualty, how may I help you?" all her life. She kept a list of Mr. Sawyer's clients handy, and took a deep breath before answering the phone. Just when Julie thought her bladder would give out, Muriel Barry said, "You can take a break any time, you know."

With relief she headed for the bathroom. Back at the file cabinets, Muriel showed her the numbering system for the cases, saying, "You'll catch on. Here's Dick Turlington."

Julie was introduced to the sales agent who kept telling Muriel Barry how much she would be missed.

"Gil and I are taking Muriel to lunch. Today's her last day," Dick Turlington explained.

Mr. Sawyer emerged from his office, asking, "Can you mind the store alone, Julie?"

"Yes, sir."

At noon Paul Sawyer found Julie eating a sandwich at her desk.

"What's this? Is Dad such a tyrant that you don't even get off for lunch?"

"I'd rather eat here until I learn my job better," Julie answered.

Paul thought she looked even younger than seventeen in this setting.

"I've been on an errand for Dad this morning. I didn't get a chance to welcome you." He pulled some papers from his briefcase. "Type these notes for me when you have time," he said, dropping his report on her desk. She swiveled to the typewriter immediately.

"Not this minute!" Paul exclaimed. "Finish eating. This afternoon will be fine."

He disappeared into his private office.

Julie had to retype Paul's report because she accidentally put the carbon paper facing the wrong way. The back of the first page was a messy blur. She was just finishing the new version when Mr. Sawyer and Mr. Turlington returned. The men gave her puzzled looks.

"Muriel won't be back this afternoon," Mr. Sawyer said. He seemed about to add something else to Julie, but just headed back toward Paul's office instead.

In a minute Paul came out. "Is my report ready?"

"Right here. And the file copy." Julie handed him the neatly typed pages.

Paul squinted at her, laughing. "Did you have a problem?"

Julie thought he saw the crumpled papers with the carbon smears in the wastebasket. "I did spoil some paper, but I'll pay for it," she said worriedly, her dark eyes larger than ever. Paul bent toward her.

"No, no. Julie, look at yourself in the mirror. I'll answer the phone for you."

In the bathroom Julie saw that she must have wiped her cheeks with her carbon-stained fingers. She had black streaks on her face. Quickly, she washed her face and hands.

Paul and his father smiled at her sympathetically when she returned to her desk with as much dignity as she could command. By the end of the day Julie had chewed off her lipstick, and broken her right thumbnail, but all the papers were filed correctly, her desk cleared, and reminders for the next day noted on her steno pad.

At four-thirty Gil Sawyer began lockup procedures as he told her, "First day on a new job is always tough. It's quitting time for all of us today. Last one out always locks up, but we can show you that routine tomorrow."

"I'll drive you home," Paul offered.

Marie Perrault was using her walker in the living room when Paul and Julie entered.

"I love my job, Mama," Julie said, beginning to chatter eagerly as her mother nodded and murmured responses.

"How did she do?" Natalie questioned Paul off to one side.

"She learned quickly. Answered the phones without leaving anyone on hold, even typed a report for me," Paul said loudly.

Julie looked at him gratefully, "Thanks, Paul, for the ride home and for everything."

"See you tomorrow, *Miss* Perrault."

Chapter 16

▼

By June, Gary had resigned himself to telephone calls to Redding, reassuring Natalie of his love, but a month later her comments were terse, almost as if his calls were a nuisance.

"I don't have much time to talk, Gary," she would say.

"How about if I drive up to see you next weekend?"

"Maybe later this summer if Mother's improving," she replied.

"What about your aunts? Can't they spell you?"

"No! I've told you before. I'm sorry, but Dad depends on me."

Finally, after one painful conversation with Natalie in tears, Gary had agreed not to call so often, realizing his pleas were simply adding to her stress.

"I'll write to you," he had promised. "My nose is raw from the grindstone."

July 12, 1952

Dearest Sweetheart,

Just got an announcement from the Tates. It's a boy, Edmund, Jr., weight 7 lbs. 2 oz. born July 1. Will give Ed a call next week, maybe visit the family.

Judge Oliver advises me that getting plenty of sleep is the best preparation for the bar exam. I spent July 4th with Mother and Dad. Dad is voting for Ike. When I told him why I'm supporting Stevenson, he barked, "Are you an egghead?"

Somehow we'll get through these next weeks.

I love you,

Gary

When she read the news of Ed and Bev Tate's baby, Natalie remembered the evening at Gary's apartment when she had thought it so momentous to preserve her virginity.

"How *quaint* I was," she mused. "What if I had become pregnant? Would that have been so tragic?"

She recalled reading a Victorian novel in which the lovers were described as being married "in nature." Gary and I would have been married *in nature*, too, she thought. People always accept a *fait accompli.*

She answered his letter with a lively account of her political discussions with her father.

Isn't it funny how fearful Americans are of an intellectual occupying the White House? I'm madly for Adlai, but longing for Gary.

Love,

Natalie

Julie was stretched out on her bed, writing a letter to Johnny Browne. Her bold, flowing style of writing was punctuated with hearts, the words *LOVE and KISSES* in capital letters. She concluded:

Will you have leave at the end of basic training? I can hardly wait till your arms are around me again. I miss you terribly and kiss your picture every night. When I tear a sheet from my desk calendar, I think I'm one day closer to seeing my Johnny again.

I was using the calculator to figure the HOURS until September 24 when your basic training will be over. Mr. Sawyer asked me what I was doing. Was I embarrassed!!! I told him I was figuring my earnings for the summer. Mr. S. looked like he didn't believe me. When it's slow at work I straighten up Paul Sawyer's desk.

Your arms must be getting even more muscular, Private Browne. The better to HUG me when you come home. LOVE and more LOVE, Julie

"What will happen to Mrs. Schmidt? Won't she get any benefits?" Julie asked Paul Sawyer as he drove her home from the office one afternoon.

"You must have read the summary I prepared for Dad when you typed it," Paul said.

"I still don't understand why Mrs. Schmidt didn't receive money from insurance after Mr. Schmidt was killed in that logging accident," Julie remarked.

"Because Mrs. Schmidt wasn't really *Mrs. Schmidt*, at least not in the eyes of the law. That's what I to checked out for Dad. She wasn't entitled to death benefits, even though Herman Schmidt was covered by the company insurance plan."

"That's so unfair!" Julie exclaimed. "Isn't there common-law marriage? I read that the Schmidts had been living as man and wife in Redding for over fifteen years."

Paul parked the car, facing her youthful indignation. "That's a misconception many people have. Only a few states recognize common-law marriages, and California isn't one of them. Unfortunately, Herman Schmidt never bothered to obtain a divorce from his wife in Idaho. The couple lived here as Mr. and Mrs. Schmidt, but Rose couldn't produce a marriage certificate. It's a damn shame she didn't insist that Herman Schmidt get a divorce. They could have been married someplace out of Redding for privacy."

"You'd think the insurance company could make an exception," Julie argued.

Paul smiled, saying, "Marriage is more than a promise of love. It's a legal contract. One more thing. Don't ever discuss the cases outside the office. I hope you will ask me questions. Just don't gossip about office business even at home."

"I won't. My Office Procedures teacher told us to remember that the first letters in *secretary* spell *secret.*"

"And as far as Western Casualty and Life making an exception, that would just make the rates much higher for all the other policy holders. No room for sentiment in the law, Julie. I'll stop in for a minute to see your mother and Natalie."

Chapter 17

▼

San Francisco

Jean Swithin raced for the F train to San Francisco, hoisting a portfolio of students' papers as she boarded the crowded car. Holding on to a strap, she pushed the packet into a corner with her toe. When several passengers got off at Ashby Avenue, she sat down gratefully. Her hose caught on a loose piece of woven cane sticking out of the seat.

"Oh, dammit!" Jean muttered, seeing the run in her stocking spreading down her right leg. An elderly woman gave her a censorious look.

Sorry, lady, but this has been a long week. Now I'm down to my last pair of nylons.

She retrieved her portfolio from the floor, brushing the dust from her skirt. Closing her eyes, she almost fell asleep as the train jiggled and swayed its way across the Bay Bridge.

"We have a visitor," Frances Swithin announced as Jean entered the apartment. Her brother Hal said, "Yeah, I just got the catalog the other day. Maybe you can tell me about some of the courses. Oh, hi," Hal broke off as Jean walked into the living room where Eric Lundgren was seated, looking very much at home. Hal had been working as a "runner" at Lundgren Investments for the past month.

"I called with some good news. Your mother invited me to tell you in person," Eric said. "Gary passed the bar exam. He said they'll set the wedding date for late August."

"Isn't that wonderful news? What happened to your skirt?" Jean's mother asked.

"Filthy train. Where's the wedding to be?"

"In Redding. Same cast of characters, smaller version."

Eric smiled at Jean's utter lack of self-consciousness about her rumpled appearance.

As Hal returned, bringing the San Francisco State catalog, he said, "Eric's helping me pick out my courses." Hal's deep gray eyes darted from Eric to his sister.

"We're just having pot luck tonight, Eric, but won't you stay? You'll have time to change, Jean," Frances suggested.

Jean raised her eyebrows. "All right, *Mother*," she replied in mock meekness.

Frances Swithin's potluck turned out to be salmon loaf with hollandaise sauce, steamed rice, avocado salad and raspberry tarts from her favorite bakery.

"You're spoiling me, Mrs. Swithin," Eric grinned. "Hal, you and I can do the dishes tonight."

"I can't believe this visiting professor from Pennsylvania," Jean said to her mother. "The man assigns the students a paper a week, one page, typed. Then he barely skims the papers, gives them to *me* to grade each weekend. I told him *nicely*, Mother, that I thought he should be writing the criticisms. He's doing research for a book he's writing. The upshot is that I'm stuck with the papers. My sympathy is with the students, natch."

"Isn't this your last week of summer school?" Frances asked.

"Yes, thank God. I need some references for my job search so I'm biting my tongue until this instructor heads back to Pennsylvania."

Hal and Eric were stacking dishes in the kitchen when the apartment buzzer sounded. Jean was stretched out on the couch, bare feet dangling.

"That's probably Skip. He said he'd be over," Hal shouted to his mother.

Frances pressed the button to open the street entrance. In a minute Jean heard her mother say, "Oh, it's you."

Hal and Eric walked into the living room just as Jean sat up to receive a kiss on her cheek from a freckle-faced man of fifty. "Hello, Dad," Jean said, "This is Eric Lundgren."

"Harry Swithin," Jean's father introduced himself, shaking Eric's hand. "Glad to find all of you home," he continued jovially. "I'm in the city on business. Ordering some special wines for the opening of a new restaurant."

"You're too late for dinner, Harry," Frances said coolly. "Would you like coffee?"

"No thanks," he waved his hand. "I just stopped by to check in with the kids. Didn't mean to interrupt anything." He looked significantly from Jean to Eric.

"Eric is a San Francisco State grad, Dad," Hal said. "I've been working at his father's company this summer."

"Lundgren," Harry muttered, half to himself. "Would that be Lundgren Investments? Yes, I know the firm." He sat down in the armchair, saying, "Bring me that catalog of yours, Hal. Let's take a look at it."

Harry Swithin's pale blue eyes scanned the pages while Hal pointed out the courses he expected to take.

"Guess I will take a cuppa coffee," Harry said. "Nice couch, Frances. New, isn't it?"

"I'll get Dad's coffee," Jean said, seeing the grim look on her mother's face as she replied tersely, "I bought the couch after my raise this spring."

In the kitchen, Jean made a fresh pot of coffee. As she measured, she felt the tension of the week coming over her. Why did her father show up unexpectedly—and never at appropriate times? True, he had flown from Los Angeles in June just in time to see her receive her master's degree at the Greek Theater. He had even treated the family to dinner afterwards. But then several weeks later Jean had learned that he was late with the alimony payment again. Jean handed over her summer check each month for household expenses.

"I hate having to dip into your earnings, Jean," Frances had said. "I don't like to criticize Harry in front of Hal, but you know how your father is…so undependable."

"Hal knows that, too. We'll make out, somehow," Jean replied.

Eric interrupted her reverie.

"You all right?" he asked, wrapping his arms around her waist from behind.

"Just tired. Coffee's perking." Her hand shook slightly as she poured a cup. "I'm glad you're here tonight," Jean whispered to Eric.

"Hey, you're never going to get rid of me. I'm the original man who came to dinner and stayed and stayed."

Chapter 18

Oakland

"So how's life in the D.A.'s office? I never imagined you as a law and order man, Dave," Gary needled his friend. They met for lunch in Oakland near the Alameda County Courthouse, where Dave Rosenthal had been working since June, following his marriage to Rhonda Kagan.

"Surprisingly, I like it. My workload is heavy, though not very stimulating, but I like being part of the whole judicial system."

Dave munched on his pastrami sandwich. "Only drawback is I can't work on the Stevenson campaign," he added meditatively.

"Yeah, I haven't been as active as I expected to be either," Gary said. "Going on interviews has taken all my time."

"Rhonda's doing enough telephoning and envelope stuffing for both of us," Dave said. "How's the job search going?"

"Looks like my best opportunity might be Cobb and Fortis," Gary answered. "I just came from an interview with Mr. Fortis himself."

Dave's jaw dropped. "You're razzing me! After all you and I said about Ed Tate selling out? I mean that firm is respectable enough, God knows, but is that what you really want to do? Be an advocate for insurance companies with deep pockets?"

"I lost my idealism some time after I realized that most of the law firms in the Bay Area were not crying out for my cerebral outlook. I'm afraid I put too much confidence in Judge Oliver's recommendation, and some nice letters from colleagues of my father, executives at the Port." Gary shoved his plate aside.

"Can I have that pickle if you don't want it?" Dave asked, reaching across the table as Gary laughed at him. He munched before saying, "Listen, Morgan, come back to my office. I have a wild idea."

Ten minutes later Dave was rummaging through a file cabinet, his sleeves rolled up, his dark eyes snapping with excitement.

"The only firm I considered before I got the offer to work for the D.A. was with Murphy and Gallagher. Union lawyers. Look at their firm's background; here are some notes I kept."

Gary scanned the details quickly. Apparently Murphy and Gallagher had an opening for a research attorney as support for their trial lawyers.

"They have the courtroom hot shots," Dave explained, "but they need a brainy consultant to do the spade work—proper citations."

"Why didn't you take the job?" Gary asked, his mind already weighing possibilities.

Dave grinned. "Because I *do* like being part of the courtroom drama, even as second banana or as *third* banana for the D.A."

"I admit grunt work seems to be my specialty," Gary stated, "and I have honed my research skills under Judge Oliver's mentoring. But maybe you have to be Irish Catholic to work for Murphy and Gallagher," he joked.

"As a matter of fact, I think one reason M and G wanted to hire me is that I'm Jewish. Remember? Besides, you're Welsh—a Celtic brother," Dave asserted.

"And it occurred to you that it might be a *coup* for Murphy and Gallagher to have the son of a Port of Oakland officer as a junior member of the firm," Gary suggested.

"The thought did pass my mind. Do you have your resumé with you? Okay, here's what I propose. I'm going to call Jack Gallagher, suggest an interview, if you're game."

He gave a glowing recital of Gary's qualifications over the phone, then circled his thumb and forefinger.

"Jack Gallagher will see you at three o'clock today. Here's the address. Fifth floor. Now I gotta get busy, keep Alameda County free of crime, give the taxpayers their money's worth."

"Will you and Rhonda come to the wedding?" Gary inquired. "Later this month?"

"Sure. The wedding in Redding? Very poetic. We'll be there with bells on. Let me know how the interview goes," Dave said, waving away Gary's thanks.

Chapter 19

Murphy and Gallagher had offices on the fourth and fifth floors of one of the oldest buildings along Broadway, in the heart of downtown Oakland. Gary thought that it looked as though the partners wanted their offices and utilitarian furniture to reflect their blue-collar image. He rode to the fifth floor in an old-fashioned cage elevator occupied by a gum chewing operator who told him, "Mr. Gallagher's office is straight ahead," as she opened the brass accordion door.

A middle-aged secretary showed Gary into the junior partner's office where a muscular, red-haired man in his late thirties greeted him with a deep voice. "Jack Gallagher. Glad to meet you. Have a seat."

"Thank *you* for seeing me on such short notice, Mr. Gallagher."

"Dave Rosenthal sang your praises to me."

"Well, what are friends for?" Gary replied lightly, even as he noted that Gallagher's grey-green eyes were meeting his, sizing him up coolly. No jolly Irish giant here.

"I brought my resumé," Gary continued. "Most of my experience has been clerking for Judge Joaquin Oliver."

Jack Gallagher studied the sheaf of papers Gary presented to him, remarking with apparent casualness, "Your father is Lloyd Morgan, I believe."

"Yes." *This guy does his homework.*

"I'm sure you must have some lucrative offers, including working with the Port's counsel."

Gallagher waited patiently for Gary's response, his blank expression worthy of a good poker player. Gary kept eye contact with him as he spoke fervently.

"I'd like to work for a law firm directly related to the people of the community. My grandfather and great-uncle found their way from Wales to the Port of Oakland with a little change in their pockets. By hard labor they made a good deal of money from the salvage company they founded. I'm the beneficiary of their energy, but my father never let me forget that nothing is produced without labor—physical labor as well as mental effort…" Gary broke off. *What the hell am I doing, making a speech?*

Gallagher's eyes glinted with amusement. The suggestion of a smile played around his mouth as he said briskly, "I'll review your background with Mr. Murphy. As senior partner, he will meet with you before any decision is made. You'll be hearing from us within a day or so."

Jack Gallagher concluded the interview.

"What's your take on Gary Morgan?" Leo Murphy asked an hour later.

"He came off as rather pompous, takes himself very seriously." Jack Gallagher added, "Morgan seems so damn *young*. I was surprised to learn he was a veteran, awarded the Purple Heart."

"You think he wouldn't fit in? The rich kid from Piedmont?"

Gallagher hunched his shoulders and said, "I just don't know, Leo. I don't think you'd be wasting your time meeting him. We need another attorney. Work is increasing with the longshoremen's contract coming up for renewal."

Murphy glanced at the clock. "I'll call Morgan right now. The only time I have free tomorrow is nine o'clock. Do you want to sit in, Jack?"

"No, it's your decision. I do think Gary Morgan really wants this position!"

In his apartment, Gary answered on the second ring, his excitement mounting as he told Leo Murphy that he would be there in the morning. He paced in a state of mental tumult. He must have impressed Gallagher more favorably than he had thought. If the senior partner made him an offer, would he take it? As he started to phone his father, he drew back. No, Gary knew all too well that his father would try to dissuade him from joining this firm.

He ate his solitary dinner, laid out his best suit, laundered shirt, and a tie Natalie had given him for his birthday in May. At that time he had remarked that the royal blue and gold chevron pattern was too gaudy for him. Natalie had retorted, "Oh, don't be such a stuffed shirt. Wear it for me."

Now he was tempted to call Natalie right away, but he would wait until tomorrow. Setting his alarm for seven o'clock, he willed himself to fall asleep.

The senior partner's office was only marginally larger than Jack Gallagher's, one wall adorned with Leo Murphy's diploma from Gonzaga University, and some photographs. A cartoon from the *Oakland Tribune* depicted Murphy with catlike whiskers and paws placed on the shoulders of two laboring men. The caption read "Leo, the Longshoremen's Lion."

"My wife and daughters don't think I'm that fierce," Murphy said quietly, shaking Gary's outstretched hand and motioning for him to be seated.

Gary thought that the senior partner looked more dog-like than feline. With his solemn brown eyes and vertical creases running along his short nose, the lawyer resembled the Gonzaga University mascot: a bulldog.

Leo Murphy began describing the specialized work of the firm in his surprisingly soft voice. He pointed to a photograph behind his desk of himself, some ten years younger, and slimmer, standing next to a smiling bald man whose face was vaguely familiar to Gary.

"Henry Kaiser," Murphy said, as if reading a question in Gary's mind. "Great man," he added pontifically. "He was a motivator as well as a genius at shipbuilding. While you were fighting with the Fifth Army in Europe, men and women, too, were building liberty ships in the Port of Richmond at a rate no one could have imagined possible. Sometimes Kaiser launched one ship a month. Those steelworkers, welders, and riveters were our home front heroes."

Looking directly at Gary, the lawyer paused to let his words sink in.

"Nowadays," Murphy raised his inverted v-shaped eyebrows as he spoke, "these workers and others are not always treated fairly. Members of this firm must be advocates for these people. Here at Murphy and Gallagher we require a commitment of a different order than you'll find from a firm practicing corporate law. Even if you're just looking up case law or digging into arcane legislation, you must believe that you're doing your job for all those workers out there. Think you can make that pledge?"

"I do," Gary said, as if reciting his marriage vow. Instantly, he wondered if Leo Murphy was offering him the position or just speaking rhetorically.

"I'd be interested in knowing who your heroes are," Murphy queried.

Gary recalled bull sessions when he and Dave Rosenthal had argued the merits of various legal legends. Dave's hero was Clarence Darrow, but Gary had always been a supporter of Fighting Bob LaFollette, the progressive Republican.

Now he answered, "The jurist I admire most is Oliver Wendell Holmes. He fought the good fight. A room at the Berkeley Public Library is named for him."

The senior partner beamed, shaking Gary's hand, saying, "Good choice."

Murphy called Jack Gallagher into his office telling him, "I'm offering Gary a position with us. Please introduce him to everyone on the fourth floor, Jack."

"Welcome aboard, Gary," Gallagher said as Leo Murphy buzzed for his secretary, Josephine Pennington, giving her instructions about papers for Gary to sign. Leo Murphy explained, "I'm due in court in twenty minutes. I'm turning Mr. Morgan over to you, Josephine." To Gary he added, "Mrs. Pennington is one of those people who keeps the world turning."

"Thank you, Mr. Murphy. I'm proud to be joining your firm," Gary said, still reeling from the speed with which he had been propelled into this new sphere.

"You'll be assisting Bob Wessell. We're preparing for negotiations of the new longshoremen's contract," Jack Gallagher said as they entered the elevator. "Bob will be meeting with the union officials. He'll fill you in."

"Uh-oh," Gary interrupted. "I'm planning on being married August twenty-fourth. I expected to start work right after Labor Day."

When the elevator operator stopped on the fourth floor, Jack Gallagher stalled, asking Gary, "Have you met Thelma? Mr. Morgan, Thelma Kline."

The operator and Gary exchanged nods as Gallagher hurried ahead. Bob Wessell's shirtsleeves were rolled up, his desk strewn with papers and splayed legal tomes. Following the introductions, Bob asked Gary eagerly, "Are you ready to wade through this with me? I'm afraid my wife and kids won't recognize me when I show up at home. Been camping out here."

"Gary has marriage plans. He won't be available for two weeks," Gallagher stated.

"I'd be glad to spend today having you brief me," Gary offered, knowing that he was postponing telling his family and Natalie his big news.

"Good enough," Wessell agreed. "I'll introduce Gary to everyone, Jack."

As Gary read the labor contracts, listening intently to Bob Wessell's explanations, he thought, *Ready or not, I'm earning my salary.*

At noon he met the other attorney, Constanz Nicharios, called Nick, whose swarthy complexion and olive black eyes contrasted with Bob Wessell's crew cut and scholarly appearance.

"Nick and I are both San Francisco State alums, class of 1942, followed by the draft. The war delayed our careers. I've been with M and G for three years now," Bob said.

"I joined the firm a year later," Nick added, "but we have one other Boalt Hall alum. Sabina," he called after a woman just preparing to leave the outer office.

"Sabina, this is Gary Morgan, newest member of Murphy and Gallagher. Sabina Black, best friend of the food handlers' union," Nick explained.

Sabina could have been a fashion model or an athlete with her tall, sinuous body and perfect posture, Gary thought.

"Glad to meet you, Gary. We can use all the help we can get. Bye for now."

Exotic was the word that came to mind to describe Sabina Black. She could have been any age from her late twenties to forty. Gary knew she must be several years ahead of him, because he surely would have noticed her around Boalt Hall.

"All of us think Sabina gives us class when we go to court. Don't let that glamorous exterior fool you. Sabina is one tough litigator," Nick told him.

Chapter 20

▼

That evening Gary steeled himself for his parents' reaction to his news.

"Murphy and Gallagher!" Lloyd Morgan exclaimed. "Sounds like a Vaudeville act." He shook his head, frowning.

"They're a very respected firm, Dad," Gary began, but his father interrupted angrily. "Respected? Respected by whom? By union bosses with their hands in the till?"

"Isn't this decision awfully hasty, darling?" his mother interposed. "I thought you were considering Cobb and Fortis."

He had anticipated that his parents would not be overjoyed by his decision, but Gary was unprepared for his father's outburst.

"Cobb and Fortis were possibly, just *possibly* considering me, Mother. So far I've had six interviews over the past ten days and no other firm has offered me a position or even a follow-up interview. Mr. Murphy has given me an opportunity to become part of a vital law practice. I'm *needed* right away. I'm sorry to disappoint both of you, but I believe I've made the right decision."

"Stay for dinner," his mother said. "You can tell us more about this firm."

"Not tonight, thanks. I'll phone Natalie from my apartment."

His father did not urge him to remain.

"Gary, I've been trying to phone you with my news," Natalie began.

"Okay. Your news first."

"You remember me telling you about my teacher, Mrs. Livingston?"

"Uh, yes," Gary responded slowly. He had been sure Natalie was about to say that her father had finally hired a practical nurse.

"Mrs. Livingston is having major surgery later this month, a tumor to be removed. She has two months' leave time coming. Anyway she recommended me to the principal. He wants me to take Mrs. Livingston's classes while she's recovering. Substitute teachers are in short supply."

"That's impossible! We're getting married on the twenty-fourth."

"Gary, it'll be fine. Dad says he'll find a practical nurse for Mother while I'm teaching. I'll be earning my dowry," she said gaily, "just like in a Victorian novel."

"What kind of marriage would that be with you in Redding and me here?"

"Why can't you be here, too? We can rent a motel cottage. You could follow up on interviews, wait for an offer. It will only be till early November." Her voice trailed away.

"Aren't you interested in my news, Natalie?"

"Of course. What?"

"I joined Murphy and Gallagher law firm. Started work today."

He heard her give a nervous little laugh. "Gary, that's wonderful. Leo Murphy is famous in Oakland. The longshoremen's lawyer. What did your folks say?"

"They were less than thrilled, as you can imagine." Gary relaxed, enjoying Natalie's enthusiasm. "So you'll tell the principal why you can't substitute?"

After a prolonged silence, Natalie said, "No, I promised. Signed a short-term contract. I tried to call you all afternoon. This is like 'The Gift of the Magi', isn't it? Both of us getting jobs on the very same day, thinking our jobs will make everything easier, only it's turning out the *reverse*, making more problems."

"I don't know what the hell you're talking about, Natalie. Will you marry me or not?"

"I promised to teach for two months. I thought you'd understand."

"And I thought you promised to be my wife." He hung up.

In a few moments the phone rang. Natalie calling back, of course. He flung himself on his lumpy bed, staring at the ceiling as he counted seven rings without answering.

By 8:30 a.m. Gary was arranging the desk assigned to him by the fourth floor lead secretary, Mrs. Ryan. His obviously new monogrammed brief case was at his feet when Bob Wessell entered.

"Thought we weren't going to see you till after Labor Day," Bob said.

"Change in plans," Gary answered without glancing up. "I'm here to work."

"What about your wedding?" Bob asked, looking owlish behind his round glasses. "Nothing bad, I hope."

"A postponement," Gary said so brusquely that Bob did not press him further.

"Then we can pick up where we left off yesterday," Bob suggested.

Gary reached Dave Rosenthal just as he was leaving for lunch.

"I've joined Murphy and Gallagher."

As he listened to Dave's congratulations, he thought, *at least someone's glad for me.*

"Let's meet for a brew at five o'clock. I owe you, Dave."

Chapter 21

Frances Swithin could hardly avoid hearing Jean's outbursts on the telephone. Cries of "You've got to be kidding" and "No, I don't understand" punctuated Jean's conversation with Natalie. Finally Jean moaned, "Nat, at least talk everything over with Gary in person."

"What?" Frances inquired as Jean walked into the living room.

"Can you believe it? Natalie's postponed the wedding again. She made a commitment to substitute at the high school in Redding. It's ironic isn't it, Mother? I called to share my news about being hired at my former school, thinking she'd be full of last minute details about her wedding. Then she started crying, saying the wedding was off. Gary's starting his job with an Oakland firm, and Natalie won't leave her family yet."

Frances said, "Sounds like she just got cold feet. She must not love Gary."

"She's crazy about him, but I'm afraid she's misjudged Gary. He's not going to cool his heels forever. There's such a thing as being *too* hard to get. I never did tell Natalie I got the teaching post at Katherine Wylie, but Eric was most impressed. He said he thought I'd make an excellent instructor for snooty young women. We're celebrating at the St. Francis tomorrow night."

"You'll be a terrific teacher precisely because you were *not* a snooty young woman, even when you were a student at the Academy," Frances said piously. "What are you wearing tomorrow?"

Looking through Jean's closet, Frances held up the pale aqua dress Jean had put aside to wear for Natalie's wedding.

"Is it bad luck to wear a maid-of-honor dress on a date?" Jean asked.

"Of course not," her mother said. "The color is very flattering to you."

"This color is flattering to anyone."

"Jean! It's lovely on you. Also it's definitely summery, so you might as well wear it tomorrow because you won't have any other occasion before fall."

"My mother, the fashion maven."

Frances had fallen asleep over her best-selling novel. The television screen was showing test patterns when Jean entered the apartment at 1:35 a.m.

"Mother," Jean whispered, shaking her mother's shoulder.

"What time is it? This couch is too comfortable."

Jean turned off the television and switched on a soft light.

Frances was wide awake now. "Did you have a good time?"

"Yes. Notice anything?" Jean placed her left hand on her mother's knee.

"Ahhhh, darling. What a gorgeous ring. A solitaire and sapphires!"

"Eric would have come in with me, but he was afraid you'd be asleep."

"Which I was," Frances laughed. "Are you wildly happy?"

"Wildly. We love each other deeply. Forever and ever."

"Now, tell me *everything*—how Eric proposed and…"

"Not everything," Jean mimicked her mother. "Eric wishes we could marry immediately, but we're thinking right after Christmas. Grace Cathedral, a thousand or so of our closest friends, reception at the Top of the Mark…"

Frances giggled, her face mirroring her daughter's happiness.

Chapter 22

▼

Gary was verifying citations in Murphy and Gallagher's library on the fifth floor when he caught sight of a young woman hurrying past the open doorway. When he peered into the hall, he saw her entering Leo Murphy's office.

"Who's the blonde secretary on the fifth floor?" Gary asked Bob Wessell. "I thought I'd met everybody by now."

"That's Dona Dailey, spelled with one *n,*" Bob answered. "She's been on vacation. She works for both Jack and Leo. Josephine has seniority, but Dona is the best-qualified legal secretary in the firm."

Bob uttered his last statement so quietly that Gary strained to hear him.

"A little jealousy among our more matronly secretaries when Dona was hired, but she's proven herself to be very capable," Bob explained.

Later, Gary was browsing the library shelves when he heard a feminine voice say, "Hello, you must be Gary Morgan."

Her lovely face was framed by curly marmalade blonde hair and animated by sparkling hazel eyes. Dona introduced herself, adding, "Mr. Murphy said how pleased he is that you have joined the firm."

"Thanks to Bob Wessell, I'm learning as fast as I can."

"Let me know if I can help you find what you need in the library. Research is my specialty," she said briskly.

At noon Dona stopped by Sabina Black's desk, asking, "Time for lunch, counselor?"

"Sure, and you can tell me about your Tahoe vacation, you lucky girl."

Bob Wessell motioned toward the departing women. "Best friends, those two," he said. "Maybe in another couple of weeks you and I can take a real lunch break. Today it's another ham sandwich and apple for me."

Gary reached for his own brown bag. Next Wednesday he and Bob were meeting with the union officials to present the final longshoremen's contract. For Gary, the pressure of the past ten days' work had been a blessed distraction. He had an excuse to avoid his mother's dinner invitations, his father's sharp questions about Murphy and Gallagher, and Natalie's telephone calls imploring him to accept her decision to teach in Redding.

"All I'm asking is for you to show sweet reasonableness," Natalie had entreated him the night before. He had broken off their conversation. Then Eric had called with the opening words, "I'm lovely, I'm engaged, and I use Palmolive soap."

His cousin's banter only dampened Gary's spirits further. He was hard pressed to offer his congratulations to Eric.

"Take my advice. Bundle Jean up and steal away to Reno tonight," he advised Eric.

Dona Dailey stood in the elevator when Gary entered on the fourth floor. Thelma, the elevator operator, remarked, "You two just made it. I was about to lock up."

Dona said, "You never need to wait past five-thirty, Thelma."

Outside, she remarked to Gary, "Thelma likes playing the role of our office martyr. If she's not on duty, we use the stairs. The street door locks automatically at five-thirty."

"Thanks, I'll remember that," Gary said as they walked along Broadway.

"Thelma's also something of a gossip. I found that out my first month. One Friday I was transcribing some dictation, finishing some work for Mr. Murphy, and didn't notice how late it was. Jack Gallagher and I got on the elevator together. I hadn't even known Jack was still in the building. Thelma said something arch about the two of us working late on a Friday. Jack spoke to Thelma sharply, reminding her we couldn't be clock watchers."

Dona stopped, facing Gary. "I remember feeling embarrassed, but Jack told me not to worry about Thelma."

"Thanks for the warning," Gary said.

"Here comes my bus. See you tomorrow," Dona said, running down Broadway before Gary could offer her a ride.

He hated going back to his apartment, eating alone.

Chapter 23

Redding

"I can't believe how fast this first week has gone," Natalie said at supper.

Ralph Perrault relaxed, thinking that Natalie seemed more animated than she had been in months. He believed that he should have protested her taking the substitute teaching position, certain that she would not wish to postpone her marriage any longer, but she had convinced him that her decision was freely made.

"It's my chance to see if I like teaching, Dad. My last hurrah for Shasta High. Gary and I have waited this long, a few more weeks won't matter."

Ralph had hired a practical nurse to care for his wife. At dinner, Marie was making more sustained efforts to join in their conversations. As Natalie talked about her students, her mother said, "I ahways thought you'd be good teacher, Nathawie." She still had trouble with her *l*'s, but she was practicing her speech more regularly now.

Julie told her family that Mr. Sawyer said she could work in his office on Saturday mornings. She could hardly wait for Johnny Browne's leave later in September.

"Having a part-time job will make my senior year *bearable*," Julie sighed.

"What about journalism staff? Senior class play?" Natalie asked.

"Journalism class is okay. But with Johnny gone, I won't be going to any dances."

"Why not?" her father asked. "You shouldn't moon around all year, Julie."

"Well, I'm certainly not going out with any other boy while Johnny's overseas."

"Johnny Browne will be in Korea for a long time," he began, but her mother said hoarsely, "Don't bothah her, Raaph".

Changing the subject, her father asked Natalie, "Have you talked to Gary this week?"

"I tried to reach him before dinner, but there was no answer at his apartment. He's been working late this week. I'll try again in another hour."

Jack Gallagher had invited Gary to join him and Bob Wessell for a drink after work that Friday. Jack praised Gary for his help in drawing up the union contract, saying, "You had a hell of an initiation to Murphy and Gallagher."

"Yeah, it's not always this hectic," Bob chimed in, "just ninety percent of the time. You'll get used to it, Gary."

The cocktail lounge was dimly lit, becoming noisy with businessmen crowding into the booths.

"Well, look who's here! Make room for us," Sabina Black said, sliding in beside Gary as Dona seated herself beside Bob.

"I've had a triumphant day in court," Sabina announced, "so I coaxed Dona to celebrate my victory over that asinine blockhead representing the hospital. You know the man I mean, Jack."

"Congratulations, counselor." Jack raised his highball glass in salute.

"A Manhattan for me," Sabina said to the waiter. "What are you having, Dona?"

"I'll have an old-fashioned," Dona answered. "I wish I could have been a fly on the wall in the courtroom. Sabina has been telling me about this unworthy adversary."

"No names, please. These walls have ears!" Jack joked.

A few minutes later, Bob left for home. Sabina finished her drink, saying, "I'll be trotting along, need to hear about my son's first week in fourth grade. Miles promised to take us out to dinner tonight."

"Excuse me, gentlemen," Dona said, heading for the ladies' room.

Jack Gallagher watched her weaving her way between male customers.

"Sometimes Dona likes to be one of the boys, imbibing with us after hours. Look. Every man in the place is staring at her," Jack observed.

"You can't blame them. She's gorgeous," Gary said.

"Right out of a Technicolor movie, isn't she? But she's also good at her job. Very professional."

Jack downed the last of his drink. When Dona returned to the booth, Gary offered to buy another round, but Jack declined, picking up the tab.

"No thanks. Marilyn's expecting me."

"There goes a happily married man," Dona remarked, popping a maraschino cherry into her mouth. Gary stared at her across the table.

"I'm not being sarcastic. Jack and Marilyn Gallagher really are a happy couple. I've been to their home many times."

"I didn't doubt you for a moment," Gary assured her. "Does this place serve real food, or just peanuts?"

"Yes, I think so. Steak sandwiches, fried prawns, things like that."

Dona glanced around, stirring the dregs of her drink with a plastic swizzle stick.

"I'd really like it if you'd have dinner with me. It would be just terrific if you'd keep me company, Dona."

She hesitated perhaps a full minute, not meeting his eyes.

"All right, Gary," she said finally, returning his gaze.

"I hear you went to Tahoe on vacation," Gary said.

"My brother and sister-in-law invited me along to help with their kids, ages five and three. We did some water skiing and playing on the beach at South Tahoe."

"That's it?" Gary knew he sounded incredulous. He had pictured Dona Dailey at Tahoe with a man. "You spent your vacation as a baby-sitter?"

Dona laughed. "Well, yes. I'm a doting aunt. With me there, Brian and Ginny could go out in the evening. But I had fun, too."

They talked quite easily with each other. She filled him in on Sabina Black, whom she described as a tigress fighting for working women's rights.

"Take this case today. Sabina brought a woman into court—a cook for the culinary workers' union. During the war this woman worked at the GM factory, making the same wages as the men. When the men took back those jobs, this woman worked as a union cook. She's been employed at a hospital, but found out recently that the male cooks, doing the exact same work, are being paid thirty cents more an hour."

Dona paused briefly, dipping a prawn into hot sauce, before continuing.

"The woman went right to Sabina, spilled the beans, so to speak, on the union. The hospital hired an attorney to fight this woman's claim for back wages."

"But wouldn't that be a conflict of interest for Sabina to represent this woman if Murphy and Gallagher represent the culinary workers' union?"

Munching on a prawn, Dona shook her golden head. "No, our firm enforces the terms of the contract, the wages of the union members," she explained. "The union was violating its own agreement by having a double standard in its pay scale. Our firm would hurt its reputation if this discrepancy in pay continued."

Dona was enjoying Gary's close attention.

"The opposing lawyer argued that the male cooks were working harder, lifting heavier pots or some idiotic line. But when Sabina put Florence, the cook, on the stand, the judge could see that this woman was a very competent worker. She has excellent job evaluations from her supervisor. Sabina said Florence was one tough cookie, a great witness. Other female cooks have been suffering from the same wage discrimination, but Sabina wanted to make her points by individualizing the problem with just one witness."

"I can see why you admire Sabina," Gary said.

They exchanged opinions about members of the firm, with Gary praising Bob Wessell for his patience. Dona mentioned that Nick Nicharios, who lived in San Francisco, didn't socialize much. Gary confided his preconceived idea that everyone at the firm would be Irish Catholics. Dona ticked off some names. "Bob Wessell is Catholic, but not Irish, same for Josephine. Nick is Greek Orthodox. Sabina is half-Jewish; her father was British. I'm Irish, but not Catholic; so is Mae Ryan. Come to think of it, Leo Murphy and Jack Gallagher are the only attorneys who fit your stereotype," she stated.

When Gary could prolong the evening no longer, he asked to drive her home.

"Gosh, I didn't realize it was so late. You're sure you don't mind giving me a ride? I live in San Leandro with my father," Dona informed him.

That evening the phone kept ringing in Gary's apartment.

Chapter 24

▼

One Thursday evening Gary received an unexpected phone call at his apartment.

"It's Felicia Carlyle," a familiar voice said. "I found some things Natalie left in a chest of drawers. I wouldn't bother you about this, but I have a new boarder who wants to move in tomorrow."

"I'll be right over, Mrs. Carlyle."

He followed Natalie's landlady upstairs, feeling oddly nostalgic about this house.

"These were stuck in the back of the drawer," Mrs. Carlyle explained, handing him a thick University catalog. As he flipped through the pages, a paper napkin printed with gold lettering, *Hotel Claremont,* fluttered to the floor. Pressed in the catalog, he found a bouquet of dead violets. Within a stiff cover was the photo taken at the Claremont the night Jean and Eric met. *Was that only four months ago?*

"Thanks so much, Mrs. Carlyle," Gary said. "I'll take these things to Natalie when I go to Redding this weekend."

"And what about your wedding plans?"

"We expect to be married in November," he replied.

"Give Natalie my love."

Intending to surprise Natalie with a visit to Redding over the weekend, Gary had not mentioned his plan during a recent telephone conversation, but the next day Jack Gallagher invited him to his home for a poker game on Saturday.

"If you have no other plans," Jack added.

"I'll be there. Hope the betting doesn't get too rich for my blood," Gary said, telling himself it would benefit him to know Jack better, glad he had not promised to see Natalie.

The Gallaghers' house in an old neighborhood was a typical Victorian monstrosity, painted white with dark green trim, complete with gingerbread details and even a cupola. A sprawling oak tree in the front yard spread its branches near a children's swing set. On this warm September evening Gary could hear the sounds of laughter and a child's high-pitched voice coming from the open windows. Gary knocked on the ornate front door that was decorated with leaded glass.

"Come in. I'm Marilyn," Jack's wife welcomed him. She had dishwater blond hair, a trim figure, and a pajama-clad boy clinging to her skirt. "And this is Dennis, who is about to have a story and go to bed."

Jack Gallagher greeted Gary, introducing him to his neighbor, Mel Talbot, and his brother, Andy, who was talking to Bob Wessell.

"Andy will try to sell you a Chevy if you don't watch out," Jack said, handing Gary a can of beer.

"You fellows aren't going to take advantage of me, I hope," Gary said, shaking hands with Mel and Andy. "Bridge is my game. I'm pretty rusty at poker."

Mel rubbed his hands together in mock glee, saying, "Just what we're looking for. A tenderfoot. We need to get our money back from Jack, the highwayman."

"I thought only ladies played bridge," Andy said.

Gary pretended not to pick up on Andy Gallagher's implication that bridge was an effete game, whereas poker was *macho*.

Jack ushered the men into his den, furnished with a round table, a captain's chair, and sturdy side chairs. A buffet table was laden with cold beer and bowls of potato chips. The walls were covered with photographs of Jack in his football uniform, wearing an Oakland Tech jersey. One picture showed him kneeling, his hand placed on a football, with two St. Mary's College teammates. Marilyn was wearing his letter sweater in another photo.

"I played center for St. Mary's," Jack explained.

"Are we gonna play poker or not?" Andy Gallagher jibed.

The men removed their jackets, loosened their ties, and the game began. After the third round and his second beer, Gary went hunting for the bathroom.

"Down the hall, to your left," Jack called out.

On his way back, Gary heard Marilyn's voice coming from the living room.

"Okay, Matt, you're next. You need to take your bath. Deirdre, you can take the magazine to your room and read in bed," Marilyn added.

"Mama, I want to show Dona this dress in the magazine," a young girl replied.

"Oh, that's very *chic*, Deirdre. Green is your color." Dona deliberately mispronounced *chic* as "chick" with a wink at Marilyn.

"Hi, Dona," Gary greeted her. She was wearing a maroon rayon blouse, setting off her tousled blonde hair and fair complexion. She sat on the sofa with her legs tucked under a full skirt. The red-haired girl seated beside Dona grew suddenly shy when her mother introduced her. "This is our oldest, Deirdre—a fifth grader. Matt is in second grade."

"Mama, I want to play poker. Daddy's been teaching me." Deirdre said.

Marilyn turned to Gary with an appealing look. "Some fathers tutor their children in history or geography. Jack uses poker hands to teach strategy! Honey, Daddy wouldn't like you kibitzing when he has guests."

"I'm not a kibitzer," Deirdre protested so vehemently that Gary laughed.

"We'll see if your Daddy will let us play one hand together," Dona suggested.

"One hand only," Marilyn reminded the girl as she led Matt upstairs.

Back at the poker table, Dona and Deirdre huddled together, with much whispering and Dona pointing to the cards. Andy and Mel ceased their banter. Dona had that effect on men, Gary noticed.

"We're not giving you any special consideration, you know," Jack said with mock sternness to his daughter. "Five-card stud is the game."

Gary could not take his eyes off Dona as he played his hand. At the office she always dressed in tailored suits with high-necked blouses. Even the mannish suits did nothing to hide her curves. But tonight she seemed a provocative combination of youthfulness and sensuality. Dona's eyes met his as Deirdre said, "I'm in and raise you one" to her uncle Andy, pushing a nickel from her pile across the table. Deirdre's expression was as blank as her father could wish. When she raked in her winnings, she giggled, revealing that she had only a pair of tens to Andy Gallagher's pair of queens.

"What a bluff! Off you go now," Jack ordered.

Dona stayed at the table. "I'll see if I can increase Deirdre's winnings," she said.

Gary noticed her small star-like hands as she picked up her cards. They were quite different from Natalie's strong, tapering hands. Dona's were soft with pink nails. He wondered how she could type so well with such delicate hands. Very seriously, she studied the cards she was dealt. Gary found it hard to concentrate on the game.

After a while Dona got up, saying, "I'll quit before I lose Deirdre's stack of chips."

Gary won the next pot. "My lucky night," he said, dealing the next hand.

Marilyn and Dona were chatting in the kitchen when the game broke up, shortly after ten o'clock. Marilyn was smoking a cigarette, leaning against a counter as Gary entered. Dona stopped in the middle of something she was saying.

"Thanks for your hospitality, Marilyn," Gary said. Turning to Dona he offered, "Can I give you a lift home?"

Marilyn stubbed out her cigarette. "I was just about to drive Dona home."

"It's no trouble," Gary added.

"All right, I'll get my jacket." Dona answered. "I invited myself here. Pop drove me."

In the car he could smell her light, spicy cologne and something else, the scent of her skin and hair. He felt desire overwhelming him now that they were alone. He knew why he had accepted the invitation to play poker at the Gallaghers. In the back of his mind he had hoped Dona would be there. She probably guessed that. He knew why she had invited herself, too. For a full minute neither of them spoke. Then, just as he was about to say something to break through the artificial barrier between them, Dona began talking about Marilyn Gallagher, who had gone to a Catholic women's college but had never completed her education.

"Marilyn's very bright, but her only topic of conversation is the kids," Dona said.

"What about you? What made you decide to be a legal secretary?"

"I always hoped to go to Cal. Why go any place else if you live in the Bay Area? I had good grades, too. When I was a junior in high school, Mom was diagnosed with stomach cancer. She lasted a year. Pop was working a full shift at GM. We had a tough time of it, seeing Mom in pain but feeling helpless."

All this Dona said in a matter-of-fact tone.

"When I graduated from high school Pop thought I should train for a job. I enrolled in a six-week course in business-college. I did well," she said lightly, "especially in taking dictation. I filled in for stenographers on vacation."

Dona paused. "Even after I became a legal secretary, I always intended to go to college and earn a degree in business administration."

"Surely it's not too late for you to do that," Gary answered.

"Theoretically, you're right. Practically speaking, I'd be foolish to give up my good position now. But it's hard for me to understand why Marilyn Gallagher didn't finish college. I suppose my reaction is like kids who don't get to take piano lessons envy the kids who do."

    Lights were blazing inside the Daileys' yellow stucco house as Gary pulled into the driveway.
    "Pop's home," Dona said, turning toward Gary. "Would you like to…"
    He kissed her then, tasting her lips, caressing her cheek.
    "Sweet, sweet," he murmured between kisses.
    She pulled away from him suddenly, sliding out of the car. Gary's last sight as he drove off was her bright aureole of hair as she opened her front door.

Chapter 25

Leo Murphy convened a rare meeting on Monday morning. As the attorneys gathered around the conference table, Dona entered, carrying a heavy stack of folders. She balanced them awkwardly.

"Here, let me take those." Gary lifted the files from her arms. She avoided eye contact. The senior partner sat at the head of the table, Jack Gallagher at his right hand.

"Where's Nick?" Jack asked.

"In court. The cannery workers' case in Monterey," Bob Wessell answered.

"Dona, keep Nick's file. Distribute the others. This won't take long," Murphy began.

Dona was taking notes as the senior partner explained that the firm was considering investing in mutual funds, giving the attorneys the option of setting aside a percentage of their fees. He concluded, "Dona will give you the brochures and information about a couple of companies. Talk things over with your wives—or husband in your case, Sabina."

Murphy glanced at his watch. "After you've reviewed the information, let Dona know if you're interested or if you have any recommendations for other funds."

As everyone else left the library, the senior partner said, "Gary, I want to talk to you."

Hoping his face didn't reveal his anxiety, Gary remained seated as Leo Murphy spoke.

"I wanted to sound you out about taking on some clients who come to us from time to time, mainly widows of union workers. The firm has never sought individual clients. As you know, we don't practice family law. But often the unions recommend us to someone who has a personal legal problem. It seems hardhearted to turn away a widow who needs a lawyer to help settle an estate, for instance. I think you'd be an ideal attorney for such clients."

Gary exhaled. Absurdly, he had imagined that Leo Murphy was going to interrogate him about Dona. Could Jack Gallagher have speculated to the senior partner about Gary driving Dona home from the poker party?

Why are you paying attention to Dona? Aren't you engaged to another woman?

He had imagined Murphy posing such questions. Now Gary responded to the senior partner, "I'll be glad to meet with any clients you send my way."

Murphy described briefly the legal complications facing a certain Mrs. Rafferty. "You can pick up the file on Mrs. Rafferty from Dona," he concluded.

In the outer office, Gary deliberately held onto Dona's hand as she gave him the file. Her eyes darted around the now deserted room.

"Josephine's not here," Gary whispered. "We won't be sent to the principal's office for talking or passing notes in class. How about lunch in an hour?"

"I'm having lunch with Sabina."

She swiveled to her typewriter and began typing at a furious pace.

"You'll never guess what I thought this morning's meeting might be about, egotist that I am," Sabina said as she and Dona were seated for lunch.

"What?" Dona said abstractedly.

"I thought Leo was going to announce my partnership in the firm. He's been calling me in for informal chats recently, handing out compliments like Halloween treats. And why do I get the feeling that you're a thousand miles away?"

"Oh, sorry. I can't imagine the boss being that impulsive about a partnership. He'd tell you first, Sabina."

"After five years with M and G, I'm becoming impatient. Now you tell me what's making you so moody and absent-minded today," Sabina said.

She wondered if Dona was still dejected over the end of her love affair from last spring. Sabina had upbraided her husband for inviting the man in question to their tenth wedding anniversary party in March. "If you knew he was a louse, Miles, why on earth were you pals with him?" she railed later. Miles responded predictably that he knew no such thing. His friend had told Miles he was legally separated from his wife.

"He was not a *louse* or a wolf to my knowledge," Miles argued. "Just a congenial guy who had been helpful to me."

"You were friendly with him because he's an editor of the magazine publishing your articles," Sabina retorted.

Miles shrugged. "We're hardly responsible for our guests' romances."

Dona and the editor were the only single people at the party.

"What's your editor friend's name?" Sabina asked Miles.

"Trent Shelby, the man with two surnames."

"The Douglas Fairbanks, Jr. look-alike. I'll introduce him to Dona."

And Sabina had taken Dona by the arm over to the movie-star handsome man with a pencil-thin mustache who looked like a fish out of water among all the lawyer types. Sabina had seen the immediate attraction between Dona and Trent Shelby. Miles's friend had charmed Dona, relating his adventures as a journalist in Europe. Now, as the editor of a travel magazine in Menlo Park, he mingled with the country club set.

"Do you play tennis?" Trent asked Dona, suggesting lessons for her at his club.

The week following the Blacks' party, Dona bought herself a tennis outfit, shoes, and a racket. At the office she was very excited, quizzing Sabina about Trent Shelby.

"How old is he? How did Miles meet him?"

"He must be over forty. He was a reporter in Paris when World War II broke out."

What Sabina hadn't said, and what she later regretted not telling Dona, was that the man was still married with three young children. But what good would a warning have done? Dona had found out his marital status soon enough.

Almost every weekend from April through June, Dona rented a car to drive twenty-five miles to San Mateo County, where she played tennis with Trent Shelby at his country club. She couldn't borrow her father's car, and her expenses were mounting. Once Dona borrowed money from Sabina. Although she had repaid the loan promptly from her next paycheck, Sabina had asked sharply, "Why doesn't Trent ever take you out in the East Bay? What is his status exactly? Has his wife filed for divorce?"

Dona said, "He's working out terms with his lawyer. He asked me to be patient."

Every Monday morning Dona glowed with suppressed excitement.

"She's head over heels in love with the guy," Sabina said to her husband one Saturday. They were watching their son, Adam, and his friend play croquet in their back yard. Miles said, "Bad business. Since my article was published, I haven't had any reason to contact Trent. I ran into him in the city yesterday when I was picking up our theater tickets. He looked flustered, then said something about Dona being 'a sweet little thing.' Trent told me that a divorce would be too expensive, too hard on his kids."

Miles frowned. "Obviously Trent was never serious about Dona."

Sabina muttered, "Damn that man! Dona is so naive. Just because she's gorgeous, you men think she's wise in the ways of the world."

A few days later, while Sabina was having lunch with her, Dona said suddenly, "It's over between Trent and me. His wife won't give him a divorce."

Before Sabina could respond, Dona added, "I was a fool. All his promises were lies. Why is it the good guys are always taken?"

"In Trent's case, the *bad guy* was already taken. Good riddance," Sabina stated.

Now Sabina asked Dona, "You're not carrying the torch for that *louse*, are you?" She never called Trent Shelby by his name any more.

"No. I'm over him. I don't wake up thinking about him every day. I go whole *weeks* not even thinking about him." Dona spoke softly. "I did love him. Nobody else ever made me feel the way Trent did, like I belonged to that country club set. Like I was one of them."

Chapter 26

That Monday Gary read Natalie's latest letter, full of anecdotes about her students, ending with the words, "When will you be coming to Redding? I miss you dreadfully. Glad you asked Eric to be your best man since Reed Houghton will be away on his trip to Europe. Just think, Jean will be our cousin-in-law."

Gary phoned to tell her about his first real client, Mrs. Rafferty. He concluded, "I won't be in Redding until the first weekend in November. We can get the marriage license then."

He tried to ignore the disappointment in her voice by inquiring about her teaching, laughing at the student gaffes Natalie had quoted.

It was almost six o'clock on Friday when Gary finished hanging his framed diplomas and his print of "The Signing of the Declaration of Independence" in his office. He surveyed his polished desk with pride.

"All settled?" Dona asked, standing in the doorway.

"Does it look like a real lawyer works here?"

"Absolutely. Nice touch," she waved toward the picture.

Gary put on his coat, saying, "I invited Mae Ryan to dinner as a reward for her extra help in organizing things, but she turned me down. How about you?"

"All right." Dona surprised him by accepting.

They were overlooking Lake Merritt, enjoying their cocktails.

"I've never been to this hotel before. Have you?" Dona asked.

It was only then that Gary remembered being in that very dining room on VJ Day with Agnes. Repressing that bittersweet memory, he answered curtly, "Just once, a long time ago. Why have you been avoiding me all week?"

His sudden intensity was daring her to be honest with him.

"That's a leading question, counselor," Dona parried.

"I think the judge will allow it," Gary replied.

"Rule number one in becoming a secretary is this: never allow any emotional entanglements to distract you. I quote my first teacher in business college as my citation."

"I've never seen you violate that rule at the office. You're always very professional." Gary was amused by her seriousness. "I really don't think we're breaking any laws recognized by the California Code by having dinner together. *Relax*," he urged.

Just then the waiter arrived, taking their orders. Dona was reflecting that Gary's kiss when he took her home from the poker party probably meant nothing to him. He was lonely, that's all. As Dona's mood lightened, Gary could feel himself unwinding. He studied the wine list, splurging on a liter of burgundy to accompany their filet mignon, even though Dona protested that she did not drink wine.

When she clicked her glass to his, Gary offered a toast: "To crime!"

Dona did not become worried about Gary's condition until half an hour later when she realized that he had literally consumed almost all of the wine and was now unusually garrulous. Her own wine glass was still half full.

"Shh," she whispered, bending toward him as his voice became louder. People nearby were turning to stare at him. He was rambling incoherently, something about never being able to please his parents.

"They gimme the third degree when I go home," he slurred. "Wha' do they expect?"

"You're upset. You've had too much to drink. Something hit you," she said quietly.

"I feel sick. Where's our waiter?"

He fumbled for his wallet. Dona took charge, signaled for the bill, and they left the hotel, with Gary leaning on her. Walking toward Gary's car, she told him firmly, "I'll drive."

"Gawd, I feel awful," he moaned as she drove along Telegraph Avenue. "You'll never forgive me for this, Dona."

"Don't be silly. Just give me directions to your place. I don't know Berkeley."

Finally, in his apartment, he staggered to the bathroom, where she could hear his violent retching. She took a dampened kitchen towel to him. He buried his face in the towel, mumbling, "Sorry, Dona, never had this happen to me before. What the hell did I say in the restaurant?"

"Nothing to worry about. I'll take your coat and tie."

"Must have been the onion rings," he said so solemnly that she laughed.

"Okay, so blame it on the onion rings. Plus the two Manhattans you chug-a-lugged before dinner, not to mention the expensive French wine."

"Flushed away, down the toilet." He sat down by his desk, holding his head as he spoke. "I'm still woozy. Are you mad at me?"

"No. You didn't make much sense. You kept saying you couldn't please your father."

Gary headed back to the bathroom, calling out, "I'm just gonna brush my teeth. Make yourself at home."

She hung his coat on a rack and curled up in the club chair. No photographs on display, nothing to reveal his personality. A wrinkled issue of *The Berkeley Gazette* was the only sign someone lived here. As if he could guess that she was noticing the barrenness of the room, Gary announced, "Since I took my books and pictures to the office, this place really looks drab."

He sat down gingerly on the worn sofa, patting the cushion beside him, inviting her to join him.

"You look much better," Dona said, noting that his healthy color was now restored, but his deep blue eyes still looked sad in a way that tore at her insides.

"I just may live. You're way too far away," he pleaded. "Come over here and keep me company. I think I'm fit to be near you now."

He embraced her then, kissing her tentatively at first. She could feel desire stealing over her as he whispered words into her hair. She heard him say, "I have this ache for you that won't go away and now I've ruined everything. Stay here. Don't leave, honey."

She disengaged herself, going to the phone on his desk. Moments later she said, "Pop, I'm staying at Sabina's tonight. Uh-huh. Yes, I'll see you tomorrow."

"Don't you need to call Sabina to make sure she'll cover for you?" he asked.

"No. I've never given Pop reason to check up on me. Why would he?"

She walked back to him in her stocking feet, looking small and trustful. He embraced her as she returned his kisses, stroking the back of his neck. They clung to each other wordlessly for a time. Then, as his need for her became more urgent, she surrendered to her own hunger.

So long without tenderness, so long without passion…

Dona's thoughts swirled about as Gary pressed his body against hers. *And here was this man who desired her in his own loneliness.*

He smelled the aroma of percolating coffee, and for a blurry moment between sleep and wakefulness, he couldn't imagine who was moving around in his apartment. Then he remembered everything. He checked his watch—8:56 a.m. on a bright September morning.

"I don't know about you, but I always need some coffee first thing. I found some tomato juice in your fridge; it's supposed to be a hangover remedy," Dona called out.

"My shirt looks better on you than it does on me," he remarked, coming up behind her. She was wearing his faded blue denim shirt, which barely reached her thighs.

"It looked like it was ready for the laundry. I borrowed it for my breakfast attire."

"Are you always this cheerful in the morning?" He relaxed because of her casual attitude. Without answering, she drank her juice, peering at him over the rim of the glass.

"How're you feeling, Gary?"

"Fine. What would you like to do today?" he asked warily.

"I'll be off soon. You can drive me to my bus stop near the office."

Within a few minutes she emerged from the bathroom, showered, dressed in her beige gabardine suit, and made up to face the world. He felt profoundly relieved as he told her, "I don't want you to be in trouble at home."

"No, we don't want any complications at the office either. Are my seams straight?" She pivoted on her high heels, showing off her shapely legs.

"Perfect," he assured her, pondering the complications that could follow if she confided in anyone—Sabina Black, for instance.

As he watched Dona board her bus in Oakland, Gary realized he was near Dave Rosenthal's apartment. Gary felt ravenous. He had hurried through juice and coffee with Dona, grateful that she seemed impatient to leave. Thank God she hadn't wanted to *talk,* to analyze what had happened between them. He subdued his own guilty feelings by convincing himself that Dona was able to take care of herself. After enjoying an omelet at a coffee shop, Gary ordered Danish rolls to bring to the Rosenthals. Five minutes later, when Dave, looking rumpled and unshaven, opened the door, it occurred to Gary that he should have phoned first. But Dave was cordial, thanking him for the rolls.

"Rhonda's in the shower," Dave explained. "We're finished with the *Chronicle*. Here's the sports section. What are you up to, Gary?"

"Nothing special. Just checking in with you two."

Dave looked as though he didn't quite believe him. Gary admitted to himself that lately he was visiting Dave and Rhonda to assuage his own loneliness.

He said abruptly, "You must be a hell of a cross-examiner," laughing to conceal his nervousness. "Such a penetrating stare you have, counselor."

"How's everything going at Murphy and Gallagher?" Dave asked.

"I'm happy with my decision, even if my father is disappointed." Gary was about to divulge his feelings, but Rhonda entered, telling about her volunteer work for the Stevenson campaign. Gary's opportunity for confiding in Dave passed.

Chapter 27

"You'll probably want to make some changes," Eric told Jean as they entered his apartment on Green Street. "Most of my stuff comes from my parents' house. Shall we go shopping soon or wait until after the wedding?"

"You'd better not mention the words *furniture* and *shopping* in front of Mother or she'll go on a binge at Gumps the likes of which this city has never seen," Jean replied.

She was astonished at Eric's offhand description of the mahogany coffee table and antique wingback chair as *stuff*. Was the Persian rug underneath her feet also a cast-off from the Lundgrens' mansion, she wondered.

"Unlike Mother, I'm not a frustrated interior decorator. I love your view from the balcony." She opened the sliding doors, stepping onto the narrow ledge, squinting in the bright October sunshine.

"Just room enough for some plants. Geraniums, perhaps," Jean mused.

"Then you shall have geraniums." He hugged her. "Too breezy to be out here long."

"Your family furniture is beautiful. After we've plighted our troth, we'll decide about any additions."

"Sure you don't want to try out my bed today?" Eric suggested.

"You're incorrigible." She laughed. "Will you be sorry if I give up teaching after this year?"

"Are the young ladies of K. W. Academy throwing spitballs at you?" he joked.

"I'm just not meant to be a teacher. Every time I talk to Natalie, she's upbeat about teaching. She said even her worries about her mother and her separation from Gary vanish when she's in the classroom. Natalie quotes her students constantly. Seems the kids are reading *The Scarlet Letter*. During a class discussion, one boy thought the word 'adultery' simply meant reaching adulthood."

"Hey, that's what I always thought," Eric exclaimed, wide-eyed behind his spectacles.

Jean continued, "My students, world-weary adolescents, never give me any laughs or even any feedback. These future debutantes sit in front of me with politely bored expressions as I seek to enthrall them with *Le Morte D'Arthur*. I imagined these girls would warm up to the Arthurian legend, romance, knights, and ladies fair. Nothing. Last week we read medieval ballads. They didn't even respond to *Lord Randall, My Son* or the cruelty of *Barbara Allen*," she added.

"You're probably being too hard on yourself," Eric said.

"My ego is battered, and I can't bear to fail at my post. I want to *earn* my salary."

"Read *The Canterbury Tales* in the original to me if it'll make you happy," Eric offered.

Later, Jean repeated Eric's words to her mother, adding, "Wait till you see his elegant apartment. I can hardly believe I'll be the mistress of such fancy digs."

"I planned to invite the Lundgrens to dinner here for an engagement party, but maybe our apartment isn't suitable," her mother said uncertainly. "I could reserve a table at the St. Francis."

"No. Eric raves about your cooking. He probably thinks I'm a gourmet cook, too. What a disillusionment is in store for him. Our apartment is fine, Mother. It's homey."

Chapter 28

▼

To his surprise Gary found he enjoyed his individual clients more than he had expected. They presented few legal challenges, but he became sympathetic to their need for someone to guide them over the hurdles as they settled estates, disposed of property, and struggled to put their families' financial affairs in order. Gary had a growing realization that he was not combative enough to relish courtroom pyrotechnics. Bob Wessell took up the adversarial role more eagerly than he ever could. Gary had some litigation under his belt by late October, but he admitted that he had no flair for drama.

Following one case that they won handily, involving the machine and die workers union versus a manufacturing company, Gary caught Bob eying him strangely as they packed their briefcases.

"What?" Gary asked his colleague. "Did I miss a point in summation?"

"No, not at all. You were very cool. That's it, I guess. You puzzle me. You know, Gary, when a case comes to court, somebody wins and somebody loses. We won, but you act completely neutral. When we win, I get a rush, a feeling like beating the neighborhood bully."

"You're saying I don't have the fire in the belly," Gary remarked as he and Bob left the courthouse.

Bob looked embarrassed. "Don't misunderstand me. I'm not criticizing you. Sometimes too much emotion can get in the way of argumentation or distract a jury. We need your level-headedness and logical approach."

Still, Gary knew he was most comfortable drawing up Mrs. Rafferty's agreement to sell her husband's woodworking equipment, or advising a young brother and sister about tax consequences after they received compensation from their father's fatal industrial accident. His professional fulfillment came from the expressions of relief he saw in his clients' faces as he relieved them of some nagging worry. Whenever he heard Mrs. Rafferty in the outer office announce to Mae Ryan, "I have a two o'clock appointment with Mr. Morgan," Gary smiled, knowing he was giving a sense of importance and dignity to that widow.

Once Gary treated Dona to lunch. A "working lunch," he told her briskly. He needed her help in researching a case. Dona had spent her own lunch hours finding references in the law library for Gary, giving him timely reminders about motions to be filed. He kept their conversations friendly, but always professional. Several times, as he thumbed through the various citations or scribbled notations for his brief, he caught her looking at him with a questioning expression on her face. To relieve his guilt over becoming involved with her, he had presented a small package to Dona following the favorable verdict in the machine workers' case.

Her face was glowing as she accepted the gift.

"What's this?" she exclaimed, childlike. They were alone in the law library.

"Just something to thank you for your patience, guiding me through this labyrinth," Gary said, pointing to the stacks of references.

"You shouldn't have bought me anything," she demurred before slipping the ribbon off the gift with her polished nails, opening a costly pen and pencil set.

"How elegant," she said. "Much too fine for taking dictation."

"I hope this *is* something you can use at the office."

Gary picked up his briefcase, heading toward the elevator because Dona had moved closer. She accompanied him, the wrapping paper still crushed in her palm as they rode in the elevator.

"Is it your birthday or something?" Thelma, the operator, asked Dona.

"We won a big case," Gary announced firmly. Dona smiled at him flirtatiously behind Thelma's back. On the fourth floor, Dona entered Sabina's office, leaving the door open. Bob Wessell and Nick Nicharios were huddling over a calendar at Mae Ryan's desk.

"Hey, Gary," Nick called out, "We were just wondering, have you and your fiancée set a date yet? We need to plan the court schedule for November."

Gary conferred with them quietly for a minute, then walked down the hall. Sabina came out of her office saying, "I didn't know Gary was engaged."

"He told us back in August," Bob explained. "I think you were on vacation when Gary joined the firm, Sabina."

"No," Dona said sharply, "*I* was the one on vacation."

Chapter 29

Gary spent election night with the Rosenthals, watching the returns on television, with a sense of inevitability about the outcome. Dave said, "If you were with your Murphy and Gallagher colleagues, you could be holding a wake tonight."

The three of them watched Adlai Stevenson make his concession speech with the wit that had endeared him to his supporters. As he stood up to leave, Gary said, "I've run out of excuses for snacking in front of your television set, Rhonda. I must owe you about five dinners by now."

"We're planning to bill you, Gary," Rhonda retorted, "so you won't make Natalie do all the cooking for *us* once you're married."

Now, on this Wednesday morning, Gary arrived at work, feeling downcast. The offices seemed strangely quiet. Gary was writing a bench memorandum for one of Jack Gallagher's cases when Dona entered, closing the door behind her.

"Hi, you're the only bright face around here this morning," Gary said, thinking she looked especially alluring. Dona leaned against his door, her face luminous. Instead of one of her tailored suits, she was wearing a black jersey dress, emphasizing her blondness and her pallor. When she didn't speak right away, Gary commented, "Well, cheers for Ike. Looks like we're in for an administration of charm mixed with golf."

"I'm pregnant," Dona said.

Until that moment Gary had believed that to describe one's head as swimming was only a figure of speech. But he was reeling. His reaction was to stand, pressing his palms hard on his desk, urging Dona to sit down. He really was afraid he was going to faint. Seated, she gazed up at him intently, trying to read his expression.

"Are you sure, Dona? Are you absolutely sure?" His voice sounded harsh.

"Oh, yes. You can check with my doctor if you don't believe me. The gynecologist gave me the news late yesterday."

He scanned her face, locked his eyes with her hazel ones as though they were having a staring contest.

"Have you told anyone else?"

She uttered a short sound, something between a cough and a laugh. "No, of course not. I thought you should be the first to know."

Just then Mae Ryan knocked, opening his door. "Excuse me, Mr. Morgan. I didn't realize anyone was with you. Here are those files you asked for."

Mae glanced from Gary to Dona quizzically.

"I need to get back to my desk," Dona said quickly.

He waited until he was sure everyone on the fourth floor had gone to lunch or had left the building before phoning Dona.

"We need to talk. Can you come to my office right now?"

She calmly repeated the details of her medical report, supplied her doctor's name and address, and answered Gary's questions with a serenity he found difficult to fathom. Dona smiled ruefully. "You must have known this could happen, Gary, that night you asked me to stay with you."

"It must have been then," he said in a low voice. "I'll help you. I care about you." Even as he spoke, a part of him was thinking like a lawyer.

Don't commit yourself to anything binding. Don't admit culpability.

When Dona left his office, with nothing resolved between them, he ran down the four flights of stairs to the street. He was suffocating. He needed fresh air, breathing space.

Christ. Jesus Christ, what have I done? His pace quickened as he strode along Broadway, heedless of people passing by on this dull November day. At last, when he returned to the office building, he fancied that Thelma gave him an odd look as he entered the elevator. He dialed Dona's extension number. On the fourth ring Josephine Pennington answered impatiently. "Dona's gone for the afternoon. Anything I can do for you?"

"No, no thanks. It can wait."

Dona did not return to the office Thursday. No explanations for her absence were given and Gary was afraid to ask questions of anyone on the fifth floor.

"Is this Gary Morgan?" An unfamiliar male voice asked over the phone late that day.

"Yes."

"This is Hugh Dailey, Dona's father. I'd like you to come to my house tonight. I think you know where Dona lives."

"Yes, Mr. Dailey. I can be there by five-thirty."

"I'll see you then."

As though he had been watching through the window, Mr. Dailey opened the front door before Gary had time to knock. Gary glanced around the living room questioningly.

Dona's father stated, "Dona's at her brother's house. Have a seat."

"Mr. Dailey, I want you to know how much I care about Dona."

"Hold on...you just hold on until I've said my piece."

Hugh Dailey glared at Gary with probing brown eyes, sitting up very straight in his chair. He was a ruddy-faced man, with a shock of curly white hair; he was wearing a blue dress shirt without a tie, khaki slacks, and white socks with well-worn soft slippers. Gary eased himself into a rocking chair.

"As I understand it, you've been to this house twice, bringing Dona home, but you never once came inside to introduce yourself," Mr. Dailey began.

"I would have..."

"No, you listen!" The older man took a deep breath before continuing. "I've always told Dona, any man who doesn't want to meet your family isn't worth knowing. Her mother died when she was in high school, so I've done my best to protect her. She had to grow up in a hurry, go to work. But she's still my own darling child."

He passed his work-roughened right hand over his eyes.

"You say you care about her? What do you plan to do now that you've got her in trouble?"

"Whatever Dona wishes me to do," Gary said solemnly, standing up. "But Dona and I must make our decisions together, sir."

A glint of respect shone in Hugh Dailey's eyes, as though Gary was a clever pupil who had given the correct answer to a difficult question. For the first time, Dona's father's expression relaxed as he pushed himself up from his chair, then winced in pain.

"My *dogs* are killing me. Standing all day at the plant. Can't wait to get into my slippers as soon as I get home."

It had been a long time since Gary had heard a man refer to his feet as *dogs*.

"Dona will be home soon. How 'bout a beer?" Hugh Dailey offered, seeming to appease Gary as he led the way into the kitchen. They sat at a gleaming formica table trimmed with chrome, reminding Gary of the atmosphere of a diner. Dona's father poured beer into heavy glass steins, decorated with a union logo.

"Are you a Democrat?" Mr. Dailey asked abruptly.

"Yes. I did some volunteer work for the Stevenson campaign this summer."

Gary wondered what was next in the Dailey catechism.

Mr. Dailey grunted. "Yeah, don't know if Stevenson was the best candidate."

He launched into his political views with gusto as Gary sipped his beer and listened. Hugh Dailey was a great supporter of Harry Truman, summing up the president's virtues with the words, "Truman is honest and loyal to working families. I probably won't live to see his equal as president."

"*Pop,* Gary and I need to talk alone." Dona spoke softly as she entered the kitchen a few minutes later. To Gary, she looked about seventeen years old, dressed in blue jeans, a loose sweater and sneakers. Then he noticed the dark circles under her eyes and her anxious expression as she led him back into the living room.

"I didn't know you were engaged until a couple of weeks ago," she began. "I heard Bob Wessell and Nick talking."

"I know, Dona." He embraced her, feeling her trembling.

"I've been so worried, so sick with dread." She wept as he moved away from her. "If we marry in a civil ceremony right away," she resumed, her face glistening with tears, "that would be best for the baby."

So that was the way it had to be, he thought. *She has it all figured out.*

"Sit down," he said woodenly. She rocked back and forth, confiding all her worries and then presenting her proposal. Gary noticed that she had worked out all the details. When he left the house half an hour later, he had agreed to her terms, holding firm on one condition only. He would tell his parents the news in person on Saturday, and Dona would withhold any announcements until they returned to the office on Monday.

CHAPTER 30

▼

He found his mother gardening along the side of the house.

"Hyacinths," she explained. "I hope I'm not too late in the season planting these bulbs." She was kneeling, smoothing the dirt with a trowel. "Pink and white hyacinths for spring. I wanted a change from tulips."

She extended her hand for Gary to help her rise. "What are you doing here?" she asked suddenly. "I thought you'd be on your way to Redding by now."

"Is Dad home? I need to talk to you and Dad," Gary replied. His mother dropped her gardening gloves in the breakfast nook as his father came inside, saying, "I saw your car in the driveway."

"I have some news that will upset you both." Gary faced his parents in the small room, gripping the back of a chair. "I've become involved with a secretary at the firm, Dona Dailey. She's pregnant and we've decided to be married very soon."

Gary looked closely at his father as he spoke.

"Why, that's the oldest trick in the world!" Lloyd Morgan snapped.

"It takes two to *tango*," his mother said so quickly that Gary, wondering if *she* had ever danced the tango either literally or figuratively, could not control an incipient smile.

She slapped him then with all the force she had, crying out, "Wipe that smirk off your face. You've hurt two *girls!* Oh, how could you?"

Her blue eyes blazed with a fierceness Gary had never seen. He could not remember her ever spanking him, or even slapping his hands when he was a child. His cheek stung from the shock. His mother began crying and his father drew her to his side.

"Now, Grace, let's sit down in the living room."

Holding his wife's hand as he continued questioning Gary, his father demanded, "Are you even sure the baby is yours?"

His mother flinched as if she herself had been struck.

"Yes, Dad. I'm responsible."

"Does Natalie know yet?" his mother asked in a flat tone unlike herself.

"I'm going to call her right now," Gary told them.

Natalie answered on the first ring. "I thought you'd be on your way by now. Where are you?"

"I'm at my parents' house. Natalie, I'm so sorry. You'll never know how sorry…"

"What's happened? You're frightening me." Her voice rose in intensity.

He repeated the formula he had used with his parents. "I've become involved with someone. I must beg you to break our engagement, Natalie. I'm committed to someone else."

"You *betrayed* me? Is that what you're telling me? Have you betrayed me? Who is this woman? Do you love her?"

Her cry of passion went unanswered.

Gary could not respond. As he put down the receiver, he could still hear Natalie's voice, stinging him over the wires: "Do you love her?"

He went upstairs to his old bedroom, overlooking the back yard. From his window he could see the small pond by the rock garden, filled with succulent plants his mother had cultivated. When he was four years old, his father had given him toy sailboats to float in the pond. One summer day his mother, always welcoming playmates for her only child, had observed him maneuvering his two sailboats without giving his friend a turn.

"Gary," his mother had said, "Remember that we always share toys."

But when Gary had ignored her, pushing the other boy aside, saying, "My boats! I get to sail them," she had taken him to his room.

"You stay here until you're ready to be a polite boy and play nicely. Jamie and I will play together."

And that had been his punishment—watching his mother and Jamie skimming the sailboats across the pond. He had choked back tears, finally running to the garden and burying his face in his mother's bosom, promising to "be good."

Later she told him, "I didn't want you to be a selfish, spoiled brat."

He grew up knowing that his mother disciplined with love. Now he smarted from her words as much as from the slap. But what caused him even more shame was the crucial question Natalie had demanded of him.

"Do you love her?"

CHAPTER 31

▼

Ralph Perrault was reading the newspaper in the living room when he heard Natalie's disturbing cries. He rushed to her, saying, "Your mother's resting. What's going on?"

"It's over. I've lost him, Daddy."

When her father just stood there looking puzzled and provoked, she lashed out at him.

"Are you satisfied? I've lost my love, my marriage is off. I'll be the one who *takes care of Mother,* the dutiful daughter who stays at home for the *rest of my life.*" Her voice loaded every word with sarcastic bitterness. Ralph placed his hands on her shoulders, but she wrenched away, wanting to hurt him. She ran into the bedroom, alarming Julie. At their chest of drawers, Natalie pushed her sister aside, grabbing the engagement photo of herself and Gary at the Claremont and ripping it to pieces. Her diamond ring, always loose, slid from her finger and rolled across the hardwood floor.

"Julie, go to your mother," Ralph ordered from the doorway.

Natalie's aunts, Isabelle and Corinne, had answered Ralph Perrault's call. On that Saturday evening they had cleared the dinner dishes and were sitting with their brother. Julie had stayed with her mother, explaining as simply as possible that Natalie was "unhappy and unwell" because she had broken off with Gary. Natalie had refused to come out of the bedroom except to go to the bathroom, ignoring a tray of food brought by Aunt Corinne, pleading to be left alone.

Now Ralph was saying, "I never should have allowed Natalie to postpone her wedding in June. We could have managed somehow."

"Don't blame yourself, Ralph," Isabelle said. "Nine daughters out of ten would have gone ahead with their marriage plans. You just happened to have a different sort of daughter."

"Better a broken engagement than a broken marriage, I always say," Corinne stated sanctimoniously, but Isabelle repeated to Ralph, "Nothing is your fault. Natalie is strong."

"She's lying on her bed, not even crying now," Ralph said. "My poor, dear girl." He covered his face with his hands.

When her aunts had gone home to their own families, Natalie went into her mother's room, recently brightened with comfortable pillows and new curtains.

"I'll stay with Mother now, Julie."

Sitting in her pretty chintz chair, her mother reached out, "Nathawie, oh, my…"

"Don't try to talk, Mama. I just want to be with you," Natalie sobbed.

Julie knelt behind the chest of drawers in the shared bedroom, feeling for her sister's engagement ring. *She'll want this someday as a keepsake*, Julie thought. Sighing, she picked up the larger fragments of the torn photo with the stiff cover of the Hotel Claremont. Ruined. She put the ring in a box with her own jewelry and stuffed the scraps of the photo deep in the trash bin outside. Stretched out on her twin bed, Julie began her weekly letter to Johnny Browne.

Saturday, November 8, 1952

Dear Johnny,

Something awful happened to my sister today.

Everyone in the Perrault household was quiet on Sunday. At lunch, Natalie joined her mother and father and Julie at the dining room table.

"Don't worry, I'm not about to turn into Miss Havisham," she told her family. When the threesome stared at her, uncomprehending, Natalie remembered that none of them had ever read Dickens.

"This is my last week teaching. Tuesday is a holiday: Armistice Day," she continued. "Mrs. Livingston will be back on Wednesday. I'll be home after that."

"Why don't you take a vacation, a trip someplace," her father suggested.

"Where would I go?" Natalie retorted.

Monday morning Natalie wrote on the blackboard in her firm script:
William Cullen Bryant (1794–1878) "Thanatopsis" written in 1811
Thanatos = Personification of Death (Greek myth)
"To him who in the love of Nature holds communion with her visible forms,
She speaks a various language."

As the students filed into the classroom, they glanced at the words curiously. Miss Perrault always wrote a daily quotation for them to ponder.

"What do you learn about Bryant?" she inquired in her clear voice. "Just from this information?"

Feet shuffled under desks, eyes looked up at her, and then back down. She had learned how to wait patiently. Finally one boy spoke. "From his dates, we know he wrote the poem when he was a teenager."

"Yes," she encouraged. "According to Bryant's diary, he wrote 'Thanatopsis' after wandering in the woods near his home in Massachusetts the summer he was sixteen. What would a teenage boy know about death?"

Now hands were raised.

"People didn't live long in those days," one girl ventured. "Babies often died."

"I think about death now that my brother's in Korea," another boy added.

"Listen to the poem," Natalie instructed, "and see if Bryant has anything to say to us in 1952. Ron, read up to the line 'Earth and her waters'."

Listening to the adolescent voice, Natalie experienced that self-forgetfulness she found in teaching. She became enthralled by the solemn poem and her concentration was transmitted to the students who were sitting before her.

CHAPTER 32

▼

When Eric answered his apartment buzzer, he heard Gary's voice sounding hoarse, saying, "I need to talk to you."

One look at his cousin's face told Eric that Gary was suffering from some turmoil.

"God, I've really screwed up." Confiding everything to his cousin, Gary was remorseful and self-mocking. "After months of the elaborate ritual of courtship with Natalie, I'm now caught, planning a quick marriage because of one night. Dona is making sure she and I get married in haste. If I hadn't been so damned *lonely...*"

Eric listened without interrupting, but now he burst out, "No, you had it right when you said you screwed up—literally—no matter who seduced whom. What about Natalie? Aren't you even going to Redding to see her?" Eric demanded angrily. *How could Gary be unfaithful to Natalie?*

Eric's words hit him like a dash of ice water, provoking Gary's reply. "You're quick to pass judgment! I should have known you wouldn't understand."

Eric relented his severity. "We've never been close until these past few months. I have no right to judge."

Gary headed toward the door, saying, "One last favor to ask. Will you stand by me?"

Eric patted Gary's shoulder, answering, "As Best Man? Sure, what are cousins for?"

"Mother is inviting Dona and her father to dinner next Sunday. I believe she can turn any crisis into a social event," Gary added ruefully.

Jean explained to her mother, "Eric called with shocking news. Gary Morgan had an affair with a secretary at his firm, Dona Dailey. The upshot is that Gary has put her in the club."

Her mother's violet-blue eyes widened. "You mean…"

"Yes, the lady is *enceinte*, if you prefer the French euphemism, or 'in the family way,' as the Irish say. Natalie was not wise in delaying so long." Jean continued, half to herself, "Gary was not honorable, but Eric has shown his mettle."

"His medal?" her mother questioned.

Jean spelled out her meaning, "Eric has character, that mettle."

"Oh, Eric is a *prince,*" her mother agreed.

Leo Murphy had not hidden his surprise when Dona announced that she was giving two weeks notice since she and Gary would be married soon. The senior partner's solemn eyes moved from one young face to the other as he offered his congratulations.

"I've been afraid of losing Dona to another firm, but at least we'll keep her in the family," Murphy said, turning to her. "How am I ever going to replace you? Share your news with Josephine, and ask Jack to come to my office."

At noon, Gary and Dona escaped the faltering good wishes from their colleagues to head for the Alameda County Courthouse, where the window for marriage licenses was open. As Dona filled out information, Gary learned her age—twenty-five—and her birthday—October sixth. *Funny what you find out when you apply for a license.* Somehow, the bureaucratic paperwork only added to his sense of unreality. Acting on impulse, Gary guided Dona to Dave Rosenthal's office, introducing her to his friend.

"Dona and I are going to be married on the twenty-eighth," Gary said.

Bewildered, Dave smiled lopsidedly.

Chapter 33

"The Daileys probably don't know Piedmont streets very well," Grace Morgan said. "They're already ten minutes late."

"Relax, Mother. I heard a car drive up."

Lloyd Morgan folded the Sunday newspaper, straightening his tie automatically, as Gary opened the door. Dona and her father exchanged greetings. During the introductions, Gary's parents glanced from Dona to each other, showing surprised approval.

They probably thought she'd be a brassy type, wearing too much make up. Interesting how every man always does a double take when he sees Dona.

Gary became aware anew of her loveliness. Dona wore a brown velvet dress, becoming to her golden blonde hair and peachy complexion. She sat quietly as Hugh Dailey spoke.

"Glad we had your directions, Gary. More traffic than we expected for a Sunday." Mr. Dailey hesitated fractionally before quizzing Lloyd Morgan. "Do you drive to work or take the bus?"

"I drive. The officers have permanent parking places at the Port."

Hugh Dailey looked quite presentable in his blue suit, although it was somewhat tight in the shoulders. He seated himself near Dona, perched forward as though he was ready to jump up at any moment. All through dinner Hugh Dailey leapfrogged over many topics, as if afraid to allow a moment's silence. He gestured with his hands, nearly toppling a crystal goblet of water, but he recovered it with the swiftness of a baseball short stop.

"Whooo. That was close! Caught that glass just in time."

He took the stem of the goblet firmly in hand, moving it further away.

When Dona offered to remove the dinner plates, Grace Morgan declined.

"Mrs. Morgan's probably afraid we'll break something," Dailey said loudly to Dona.

Lloyd Morgan gave him a sharp glance as he threw his napkin on the table, saying, "We'll have our coffee in the living room."

The others looked expectantly at Gary as he told them that Judge Oliver had agreed to perform the marriage on the Friday evening after Thanksgiving.

"The Judge was very gracious," Gary added, not alluding to the anguish it had cost him when Judge Oliver had expressed his pleasure at the prospect of uniting Gary to his "charming Natalie." Gary had cut in quickly, correcting that impression, giving Dona's name as though he picked a different bride for every season of the year.

"I'm glad our families will be with us," Dona said. "My sister-in-law, Ginny, will be my attendant and most of our friends from Murphy and Gallagher will be there."

"Where will the ceremony be?" Grace Morgan asked.

For the first time that afternoon, Dona seemed less diffident.

"I told Gary that I've always longed to go to the Claremont." She spoke assertively. "It will be perfect for our ceremony and a light wedding supper."

Mr. Dailey smiled broadly. "I paid the deposit for a private room for the ceremony."

"No, Mr. Dailey," Gary interrupted. "That's kind of you, but I must insist on paying for everything. The expenses at the Claremont will be to my account."

As Dona and her father were leaving, Grace Morgan impulsively kissed Dona's cheek.

Chapter 34

In a small dressing room of the Claremont, Virginia Dailey comforted Dona with compliments and dry soda crackers.

"You look just beautiful. What color would you call your suit? Heather? And your hat with the little veil is perfect."

"What time is it?" Dona asked, gazing unseeing at herself in the vanity mirror.

"It's early." Ginny adjusted her own black velvet beret, wondering if it was unlucky for the matron-of-honor to wear black at a wedding.

"I have the most awful feeling that Gary won't show. He'll call it off."

"Bridal nerves," Ginny said firmly. "I was sure Brian would leave me standing at the altar. How's your tummy?"

Dona shrugged. "You're a darling to stay with me, Ginny. Why is it called morning sickness?" She munched on a cracker. "I'm sick all the time."

"How far along are you now?" Ginny questioned.

"About eight weeks. Do you have a mint or some gum?"

Ginny fished in her purse. "Here…oh, the corsages," she said in answer to a knock on the door. Dona opened the Claremont florist box, revealing baby white orchids with her name on a card: "For Dona with love, Gary." Ginny pinned a second corsage of yellow roses on her charcoal gray suit, blotting her lipstick and saying brightly, "We're all ready."

"What time is it now?" Dona asked again.

In the vestibule, Hugh Dailey waited impatiently with his son, Brian. "You'd think the Morgans would be here by now."

"Relax, Pop. You'll work up a sweat jumping up and down."

Brian Dailey had slicked down his curly hair as much as possible. His resemblance to his father was obvious, the snub nose and strong jaw giving his face a pugnacious cast. Hearing voices, Hugh Dailey leaped to his feet. Not recognizing the foursome, he said, "Thought you folks might be the Morgans arriving. I'm Hugh Dailey. This is Dona's brother, Brian."

"We're the Lundgrens," the dignified man said, introducing his wife Elinor, and Eric with his fiancée, Jean Swithin, who gave Brian a cool, appraising look as she said, "We represent the groom's family."

Eric had been apprehensive that Jean would not attend the wedding out of loyalty to Natalie.

"I may just boycott this ceremony," she told Eric the week before.

Familiar voices heralded the arrival of the Murphy and Gallagher contingent.

"Sorry we're late," Marilyn Gallagher explained to the Dailey men. "Our baby-sitter canceled. We had to drive our kids to the Blacks' house, sharing their sitter."

"The Murphys are spending Thanksgiving in Seattle with their daughter's family," Sabina added. Jack Gallagher moved to a bench where the Lundgrens sat talking with Dave and Rhonda Rosenthal. Finally, Hugh Dailey scurried to tell Dona that the Morgans and Judge Oliver had just arrived.

Eric gestured toward the guests from the law firm. He said, "They outnumber us, Gary, but we'll be on your turf at the Hotel Claremont."

Grace Morgan heard the comment as she pinned a white carnation boutonniere on Gary's lapel and handed a bachelor button to Eric.

"You're both very handsome."

She kissed Gary's cheek, then laughing, rubbed off her lipstick with a tissue.

"Our institution of marriage is as old as the family itself…" Judge Oliver intoned as two dozen souls gathered in the private room for the brief ceremony. The only tears shed came from Grace Morgan, unobtrusively without spoiling her delicate face, and from Hugh Dailey, noisily, as he wiped his eyes with a billowing white handkerchief.

When it was all over, everyone surged forward to kiss Dona and congratulate Gary. Lloyd Morgan was the last person to greet the newlyweds. His lips grazed Dona's cheek as he whispered, "Welcome to the family."

Gary had reserved the honeymoon suite at the Claremont for their wedding night, granting Dona's request. He had arranged for them to spend the rest of their weekend in Sausalito before she could make any other suggestions. Gary recalled, all too well, Natalie saying as recently as October that she hoped their honeymoon site would be Monterey.

"Steinbeck country, fishing boats, darling," Natalie had persuaded him over the phone. "I think Monterey is the most romantic spot in all of California."

Gary could see the illuminated Berkeley Tennis Club court from the window of the suite. He pulled the drapes closed, shutting out his memories of the view, his thoughts of Natalie. Now he realized that Dona had said something. She was roaming around the elegant room, touching the furniture. He turned to her.

"I just said the room is lovely." She removed her corsage. "I think everybody enjoyed the supper, don't you? People stayed longer than I thought they would."

"Everything was fine," Gary cut in. "How're you feeling?" He cupped her chin, noticing the strain around her eyes. She tiptoed to kiss him.

"I never told you before when I fell in love with you," she said, trying to interpret his mood, unable to read his eyes in the dimness.

"It was one day in the law library," she continued. "Your head was bent over a book at a certain angle and I wanted more than anything to kiss the back of your neck. You didn't hear me come in. At that exact moment I stood there, knowing I was in love with you."

Without speaking, he kissed her mouth, cradling her to him. After his shower he walked into the suite with a towel wrapped around his waist. Dona was kneeling on the bed, wearing a white satin nightgown with puffed sleeves, appearing strangely virginal. As Gary moved toward the light of the lamp, Dona gave a sudden cry of alarm. She was staring at the scar on his leg. Then he realized that on their night in his apartment, it had been too dark for her to see him naked. Their lovemaking had all taken place in darkness.

"I'm afraid you didn't get much of a bargain in me," he told her. "Didn't mean to shock you."

He pulled on the bottom of his pajamas.

"I was just startled," Dona said, reaching out her arms.

About three-thirty in the morning he was awakened by a crack of light from the bathroom and the sound of a toilet flushing. He found Dona huddled over the basin, wiping her face with a wash cloth.

"Feeling woozy?"

She nodded. "Throwing up is not very sexy."

"Let's try to get some sleep," he said.

Dona lay awake, trying to recapture the scenes of their wedding. No one had remembered to bring a camera. She would not even have any snapshots to keep, and already everything was a blur: fleeting glimpses of the Gallaghers and the Rosenthals in lively conversation; Sabina, giving her a curious stare, saying, "Miles and I want to invite you and Gary to dinner soon."

Her father—emotional and exuberant; her brother—quiet and watchful; the Lundgrens mingling with Josephine, Mae, and the Wessells, making all the polite overtures; and Eric Lundgren's fiancée, Jean Swithin, off by herself smoking a cigarette, joining the reception line after Eric's tactful urging. Jean had been the only guest who had not hugged or kissed Dona, but had thrust out her hand instead, looking at Dona with her penetrating gray eyes before kissing Gary full on his mouth.

"I prefer kissing the groom," Jean had said, seeming to mock everyone else.

But Dona could see Jean was at ease with the Lundgrens and the Morgans. Despite her plain features and understated style, Jean Swithin was the one wearing the gorgeous diamond solitaire surrounded by sapphires. Jean belonged. Anyone could see that.

"I hope you're as happy as I am," Dona whispered, caressing Gary's arm.

But Gary was either asleep or pretending to be.

Chapter 35

▼

Frances Swithin turned the pages of Eric and Jean's wedding album as though she hadn't already seen all the pictures in the past three weeks. She enjoyed reading the article from *The San Francisco Chronicle's* society page, headlined:

> *Lundgren—Swithin Wedding Rites*
> *Held at St. Luke's Episcopal Church*

Frances knew anyone reading between the lines would realize that Jean's parents were divorced or separated. Still, Harry had conducted himself well, both at the rehearsal dinner hosted by the Lundgrens at the Fairmont Hotel and on the wedding day, December 26, escorting Jean down the aisle with dignity. In his boyhood, Harry had served as an acolyte at St. Luke's. He was touched that Jean and Eric had chosen that church for their marriage ceremony.

Jean's own attendance at church had been sporadic until the summer of her engagement, when she began worshiping regularly at the early service.

"We'll have to jump through all the hoops," Jean said to Eric, "but I've had a good talk with the rector, and he advises counseling for us."

Eric, a self-described lapsed Lutheran, agreed to attend the sessions with Jean through the autumn months. At first he was simply pleasing Jean, even teasing her about carrying her devotion to T. S. Eliot and that poet's adherence to the Anglican Church to extreme lengths. Then Eric warmed to the rector; he looked forward to their frank discussions on worldly topics, as well as on personal issues.

Jean had not been able to persuade Natalie Perrault to be her attendant or even to attend the wedding. Natalie had sent a wooden tray as a gift, with her note, promising to come for a visit in the spring. Frances was turning to the last photos in the album—candid shots taken at the reception held at the St. Francis Hotel.

"I never would have known Gary's bride was pregnant if you hadn't told me," she remarked to Jean. "She seemed so shy at your reception."

"Probably intimidated by the crowd," Jean agreed. "After all, she didn't know anyone there except the Morgans. We'd better hustle if we're going to pick out my silver pattern before we meet Eric for lunch. Daddy told me to send him the bill from Shreve's. Imagine! And here I was thinking that stainless steel flatware would be fine for us."

"Harry seems confident his California cuisine restaurant will catch on," her mother added. "I heard him telling your father-in-law that he's betting healthful salads, seafood, and Sonoma County wines will be the next trend in fine dining."

In the offices of Murphy and Gallagher, Leo Murphy was hosting a buffet spread out on the library table. Spouses had been invited. Dona entered, swinging Gary's hand in hers.

"We still haven't forgiven Gary for stealing you away from us," Jack Gallagher greeted Dona. A succession of temporary legal secretaries had failed to meet Josephine Pennington's high standards.

"If you ever return to M and G, we could put a play pen in the corner for your baby," Josephine joked. "I'm sure Mr. Murphy wouldn't mind, now that he's a grandfather."

"Little Mother," Sabina crooned to Dona as Miles Black stood in the background.

Leo Murphy announced, "I'm pleased to tell you that our firm will henceforth be known as Murphy, Gallagher and *Black* as of February first."

Cheers drowned out his words. The senior partner held up his palm.

"Furthermore, we are opening a branch office in San Francisco to be headed by Bob Wessell and Nick Nicharios. Marilyn, shall we unveil the cakes now?"

Marilyn Gallagher brought in two cakes; one was a chocolate confection decorated with the words, "Congratulations, Sabina."

'It's a tort *torte*," Marilyn announced to the groans of the lawyers.

"She's been waiting for years to use that line." Jack laughed.

A carrot cake pictured the Bay Bridge in golden frosting with the inscription, "Bob and Nick—Westward Expansion." To much applause and ribbing, the three honorees embraced Leo Murphy, as Gary called out, "Hear, hear!"

Back at their apartment, Dona said to Gary, "I thought I'd invite your parents to dinner tomorrow. Show off our wedding china and silver."

"Not a good idea. Put off hosting any parties until we find a house."

"But we've been to your folks' house so often, and we *owe* Sabina and Miles a dinner."

"Forget your social obligations. With Bob and Nick leaving the Oakland office, I have a big caseload now. You're going to have to get used to the idea that I have briefs to prepare over the weekend. Lawyers don't work nine-to-five. You know that!"

Gary had spoken more sharply than he intended to, but he was irritated that Dona was looking at him as though he was going to hit her.

For God's sake, why did he always feel he had to apologize to her?

For the next half hour Dona busied herself in the kitchen, washing and putting away the dishes with staged silence, while Gary wrote notes on a legal pad. When he took a break, he found Dona standing in front of a mirror in the bedroom. She was smoothing her hands over her flower-printed maternity smock, viewing herself in profile. Looking at him, she said, "I felt life! Just now, it was a fluttering, like a bird beating its wings."

He placed his hands over hers, smiling. "I don't feel it. Sorry for being such a bear, honey. Why don't you call that real estate agent and ask her to show us some houses tomorrow? I'll take us out to dinner," Gary offered.

"Pop's coming to dinner tonight."

This would be the third time since their marriage that Hugh Dailey had spent a Saturday evening with them, uninvited.

"Pop's lonely," Dona said, seeing Gary's grimace. "Ginny says he keeps showing up at their house, too."

"Call the agent. Here's her card. Living in this cramped apartment is getting on our nerves."

Chapter 36

▼

"Eureka…I have found it"
motto of California

    Two years after California was admitted to the Union as the thirty-first state, schools were established in Redding. Prospectors, speculators and adventurers of all breeds flocked to the Sacramento River. Lumber pioneers, railroad workers, schoolteachers and preachers soon followed the gold seekers. These families who settled in the valleys of the Cascade Range brought law and order, education, and religion to the emerging towns.

    A hundred years later, Shasta Union High School was a fine example of Spanish architectural style, located on the crest of Eureka Way. One February afternoon, Natalie stared east out of her classroom window toward the snowy shadow of Mount Lassen. Mrs. Livingston had retired at the end of the semester, persuading Natalie to replace her as a teacher.

    "The position is yours for the taking," Mrs. Livingston said. "I've decided to sell my little house and do some traveling. It's time for me to hang up my chalk."

    The superintendent hired Natalie without even interviewing anyone else. But it was a chance remark from her cousin, Louis Benson, that convinced Natalie to sign the teaching contract. Louie, one of Natalie's students in American Literature, told her, "The kids really like you. They say you're tough, but fair. But, *Jeez,* why do we have to read poetry?"

    Natalie placed her hands on her young cousin's shoulders, saying, "Because it is my mission in life to uplift your soul. No one can *live* without poetry."

"Don't get *weird* on me, Natalie."

She and Louie formed a pact. He stayed after school until four-thirty, giving Natalie time to grade papers and write lesson plans before Louie drove her home. In return, she tutored him with homework.

"It's starting to snow again. I'm ready to leave anytime," she suggested on this day.

Louie looked up from his book. "I'm caught up with all my homework except *yours*," he said, grinning. "I can't find a poem to read for tomorrow, so don't call on me. Okay?"

"Try this one by e. e. Cummings, 'Anyone lived in a pretty how town.'"

She handed Louie a poetry volume. Her cousin began reading the words aloud in a sing-song voice, sitting all scrunched up, then more expressively when he came to the stanza:

> *someones married their everyones*
> *laughed their cryings and did their dance*
> *(sleep wake hope and then) they*
> *said their nevers they slept their dream*

"It's funny and sad at the same time. Why did you think I'd like it?"

"Because I remember discovering that poem when I was your age. You told me you could hardly wait to leave Redding. You're so *bored*," Natalie exaggerated Louie's way of speaking as they left the classroom together.

"Can I borrow your book overnight?" Louie asked. "I'll read this poem tomorrow. How come he didn't capitalize words?"

"He was a poet who liked experimenting with his verses, ignoring conventional rules and rhyme schemes. I thought you might be interested in him because he volunteered as an ambulance driver in the First World War when he wasn't much older than you are now. His poems express how much he valued individual freedom."

As Louie drove his Chevy along the icy streets, he commented on the old-fashioned houses on their postage stamp lots with tiny garages.

"How does anyone park a car in one of those garages? No wonder Dad and Uncle Ralph built houses on the edge of town," Louie remarked to Natalie.

"I wouldn't mind living close to school. People can walk to town in good weather," Natalie mused.

"Yeah, to *a pretty how town*," Louie wisecracked.

"You'll probably be gone from Redding soon enough, Louie."

They passed Gil Sawyer's insurance office on California Street. Natalie said quietly, "One thing about living in a pretty how town, people know who you are. If we ran out of gas, we could go in that building right now and ask Mr. Sawyer for help."

"Yeah. When that cop stopped me for speeding, he read my name on my driver's license and asked right away if I was any relation to Benson Lumber Company," Louie interjected. "I got a warning instead of a ticket."

"Living in a town where your family is well known has its disadvantages, too," Natalie said, "but when Mother had her stroke, I learned how sympathetic friends could be."

Louie was quick to perceive that Natalie wasn't just thinking about her mother. He remembered how shocked everyone in the family had been when Natalie's fiancé married someone else. His sister, Edy, had told him, "That *creep* jilted Nat. Whatever you do, don't ever bring up Gary Morgan's name."

Louie never had mentioned Natalie's ruptured engagement, but the kids at Shasta High knew something sad had happened. All the girls noticed that Natalie was no longer wearing her ring. Sometimes she seemed absent-minded in class, as if she was listening for something.

"What do you hear about Wayne?" Natalie asked Louie suddenly. Wayne Benson had suffered frostbite in Korea.

"The doctors have to amputate two toes. Mom's going to Letterman Hospital to be with him."

"I'm so sorry."

"It's tough. But at least Wayne will be home soon. Home to our *pretty how town.*"

"See you tomorrow, Louie," Natalie said, opening the car door.

"Thanks for the book. I like the poem, but could you call on someone else to read it?"

"You're not getting off the hook. Nobody will think you're *weird.*" Natalie laughed.

Chapter 37

In April, Leo Murphy confronted Gary with his biggest legal challenge yet.

"I'm giving you the laborers' union case versus Bayshore Excavation," the senior partner told him.

"The asbestos case? I thought Jack was handling that."

"Jack is co-counsel with me on another case; we're going to court this week," Murphy explained. "I want you bird-dogging Bayshore." He dismissed Gary with the comment, "You can't spend your whole career counseling the Mrs. Raffertys of Oakland."

Gary began spending long sessions with the union members, digging out the facts surrounding the claim of workers who suffered from silicosis. The men had been exposed to asbestos during the excavation and demolition of tenements in Oakland. The clauses in the union contract with Bayshore were ambiguous enough to put the claim on shaky ground, but when Gary visited several sick workers in Kaiser Hospital and heard their rasping voices, he knew he had to give his all to the case.

"The bastards shoulda give us some protective gear, Mr. Morgan," one ailing worker wheezed. "By God, I been working at all kinds a jobs, includin' CCC work durin' the Depression, and I never got sick. But that damn punk supervisor from Bayshore was on our asses to hurry up." A coughing fit interrupted his speech.

One of his cohorts in the next bed continued. "That's right, Mr. Morgan. All that guy from Bayshore cared about was meeting a deadline. We didn't know till we started the demolition about asbestos in those apartment buildings and warehouses. We were breathing filth and contaminated dust, too. And that sonna bitch in his white shirt and tie coming at us every day…"

Gary was glad he was wearing a blue denim shirt, sleeves rolled up, instead of a business suit. He told the second man, Fergus, "We're going to win. I'll get the names of all the men who worked on the site. In the meantime, the union is paying for your medical care."

A pair of rheumy eyes met his as Fergus said, "You're all right, Morgan."

His fellow worker, still hacking, waved as Gary left Kaiser Hospital.

Gary barged into Sabina's office, saying, "I've got to win this case!"

As he described his visit with the afflicted men and the outrage he felt on their behalf, Gary said, "*Silicosis.* That's what the doctors are calling it, Sabina. *Black lung.* Same condition. That's why my Grandfather Morgan and Great Uncle Ivor migrated here from Wales—to escape from the mines."

Sabina gave her full attention as Gary uttered his emotions.

"It's a righteous cause," she said. Her intensity matched his as she added, "It's why we became lawyers, isn't it? A case like this redeems us, knowing we can make a difference. It makes up for the long struggle to put *Juris Doctor* after our names."

Later, as Gary was reading the list of the union workers, he focused on one name: *Fielding, Arthur.* He wondered why that name registered. Then he read the data: thirty-four years old, married, home address in San Leandro. Gary decided to call Fielding. He wanted one compelling witness to represent all the workers.

"You'll need to give me a full account of the daily routine on the work site," Gary told Arthur Fielding. "I want the jury to have a clear picture of what you men had to deal with day in and day out. Not just the dry facts, but the work environment."

"Even though I wasn't bothered as much as some of the men, I was choked up every day," Fielding said. "At first I tried to be reasonable with the supervisor from Bayshore. I told him we just wanted to get some protective clothing and masks. I made a formal written report, requesting a scientific analysis of the stuff we were breathing. Those guys from Bayshore wouldn't listen to any of our complaints."

His words convinced Gary of his intelligence.

Gary said, "Having your written report, the exact dates and details, will help us when we go to court. You'll be well-prepared for testimony, Mr. Fielding."

"I go by Art."

"We're in this together, Art. I don't want you coming off as *too* scripted, but you'll know what to expect." Gary set up a meeting with Art Fielding to prepare him for the case.

The hearing was set for the first Wednesday in April. That morning Gary reviewed the case with Sabina Black. Jack Gallagher gestured "thumbs up" as he said, "Go get 'em."

Even Mae Ryan was excited, checking Gary's briefcase. "Are you sure you have all your files, Mr. Morgan?" Mae asked.

"Yes, Mae. I packed my own chute." Seeing her puzzled expression, Gary said, "I read someplace that parachute jumpers always pack their own chutes."

Standing off to view him, Mae said, "You look fine, Mr. Morgan."

"Geronimo!" Gary exited the office with a shout.

Bayshore Excavation's attorney came across as supercilious and ill-prepared. He was a fiftyish lawyer who had acted mainly as the company's tax attorney. His voice was irritatingly nasal, and he had the habit of shuffling his papers as he talked, causing the judge to admonish him twice to speak up for the court recorder.

Gary kept his line of questioning crisp. When his star witness took the stand, Gary elicited Art Fielding's service record in the Navy as a signal corpsman on an aircraft carrier. He held his breath, expecting an objection from the defendant's lawyer on grounds of relevance, but none came. Fielding's employment evaluations were outstanding.

On cross examination, Bayshore's attorney asked, "Now, uh, Mr. Fielding, didn't you and other workers expect there to be a little dust on a demolition job of this size?"

But the attorney's sarcasm fell flat when Fielding answered. "We realized the first day that the friable asbestos was more than ordinary dust and debris. We improvised facemasks from handkerchiefs. I requested that work be halted long enough to determine..."

"You had no authorization to halt work," the lawyer interrupted. "You should have filed a report with your union."

"I wasn't worried about authorization," Fielding continued, still in a mild tone. "I was concerned about the men who were gasping for breath after a few hours of work. I did make a written report when our complaints were ignored."

At the break, Gary praised Art Fielding for his composure on the stand. "I was afraid for a minute you were going to volunteer *too* much information, but I didn't want to stem the flow of your narration. You were a strong witness, Art."

Fielding's eyes shone. He had a compact physique under his tweed coat and twill slacks. Gary had suggested that he not wear a business suit to court.

"Now, I have a question for you, Art," Gary said. "Do you have a sister named Agnes?"

"Yes, I do." Fielding looked surprised.

"Is she a nurse?"

"Say, what's this all about?"

"I once knew a nurse named Agnes Fielding in 1945," Gary explained. "She was a physical therapist who helped me recover."

Art Fielding's face broke into a wide smile. "That would have been Agnes. I just couldn't figure where you were going with the interrogation."

"Understood. I hope Agnes is well and happy."

"Agnes and her husband have two sons. They've lived in Walnut Creek about three years now. Her husband is a P.E. teacher. Agnes works sometimes at Kaiser Hospital on call for emergencies, but the kids keep her busy."

"Please give Agnes my best regards," Gary said, realizing that the court proceedings were about to resume.

"There's my wife," Art Fielding said. "She told me she was too nervous to attend." He waved to a petite woman sitting in the back row.

In the middle of Gary's summation, he saw two women enter the courtroom, seating themselves near Fielding's wife. Dona and Sabina were now part of his audience.

"...Justice will be served when these workers receive the medical care and compensation due them, not for their sake alone, but for all future workers whose health and well-being must be protected from deadly materials and noxious fumes," Gary concluded.

He packed his brief case, shaking Art's hand and praising him. "Let me introduce you to my wife and colleague," Gary said to the Fieldings.

Dona was already hurrying up the aisle, with Sabina following her.

"You were wonderful, darling! And I've found us the perfect house on Ashby Avenue. Wait till you see it," Dona exclaimed.

"A high stakes case gives you quite an adrenaline rush, hmm, Gary?" Sabina said. "We were trying to be unobtrusive so we wouldn't distract you."

"Sure, as unobtrusive as two beautiful women can be in a courtroom," Gary kidded them, "one of whom is seven months pregnant."

The legal victory exceeded Gary's expectations. Bayshore Excavation was fined over a million dollars punitive as well as compensatory damages, vindicating the workers.

"This was a ground breaking case," Leo Murphy announced. "Land prices in the East Bay are skyrocketing. Didn't Will Rogers advise, 'Buy land. They're not making any more of it'? Developers are eager to tear down these old tenements to make room for new construction. But now we know how hazardous these projects can be to the workers."

Glad as he was that his stock was rising in the firm, Gary's deepest satisfaction came from a telephone call from his father.

"I had to read about you in the newspaper. You didn't even tell me you had this important case coming up," Lloyd Morgan said. "I'm proud of you, Gary. You must be a hero down at Murphy and Gallagher."

"Murphy, Gallagher and *Black*. Sabina Black assisted me. But my reward came from the thanks expressed by those workers who are still gasping for air, literally. Some of them are close to your age, Dad, but at least their medical treatment will be paid for. I didn't alert you and Mother about this case because I didn't want to raise false expectations."

"I can appreciate your feelings, son. Your mother wants to know all about this house you and Dona have found. I'll put her on."

Only two families had occupied the house on Ashby Avenue—a Dutch Colonial built in the nineteen-twenties. The real estate agent pointed out some obvious flaws and deferred maintenance.

But Dona exclaimed, "I can just imagine how the rooms will look with fresh paint. I love the hardwood floors, don't you, Gary? And the wainscoting is beautiful."

"I used to think my wife was a good poker player," Gary had said to the agent in mock resignation.

"Don't you want to tour the new houses in Walnut Creek? I thought you'd want all the latest kitchen appliances."

Dona responded, "This house has personality, lots of real life and history. I saw pencil marks on the bedroom wall where the children's heights had been measured."

Gary laughed outright. "We'll make an offer this afternoon," he told the agent. "I assume pencil marks are included in the seller's price."

Dona had not confided to Gary that one of the main attractions of the house on Ashby Avenue was its proximity to the Hotel Claremont. True, it was located on the flat land, not on a curving hillside nearer the hotel, but it was the kind of neighborhood Dona had always visualized for her home.

While their house was being painted, Gary packed most of their belongings in boxes. As he was cleaning out one closet he had asked Dona, "What's in this bundle, wrapped in paper?"

"My tennis rackets and shoes."

"You're not planning on playing tennis any time soon, I trust."

"Next year. Our house is near the Berkeley Tennis Club."

She had looked at him defiantly, as if expecting Gary to comment sarcastically. Instead, he had kissed her, saying, "Ah, I understand. You're planning your life *A.B., after baby*."

Chapter 38

▼

One Sunday afternoon, as Gary finished writing a brief, he glanced around the Boalt Hall library. A smile of recognition crossed his face as Paul Sawyer gestured to him. They walked out of the quiet library to talk.

"I heard from Ed Tate that you've already passed the bar exam," Gary said, extending his hand. "Congratulations!"

"Thanks. As you can imagine, I'm eager to join Cobb and Fortis. But what are you doing in this academic setting? You're making your reputation in the real world. I read about the Bayshore case," Paul said.

"My wife and I are just one week away from moving into a house. Our apartment is a jumble of boxes. I can concentrate better here."

Outside, as they were about to part, Paul said, "I have some news you'll be sorry to hear."

Gary felt himself bracing as if for a blow. "From Redding?"

"Natalie's mother died in late March. I didn't think you knew."

"No, I didn't."

"She had a heart attack, died at home." Paul studied Gary's face as he spoke.

"Thank you for telling me. I'll write to Natalie."

"I attended the funeral," Paul continued. "I don't know if Natalie ever told you that her mother moved to Redding from San Francisco in 1919, following the flu epidemic."

"Yes, Natalie told me her mother's history. What about memorial gifts?"

"The family requested donations to Shasta Union School District," Paul answered.

Gary wrote the information on his legal pad.

"The Perraults received more sad news recently," Paul added. "Julie's boyfriend, Johnny Browne, was killed in action in Korea."

"Are we going to be out of that mess soon?" Gary asked, visualizing Julie's expressive young face, "or are we going to send kids off to war every five years?"

When she woke up from her nap, Dona sought something to do. On impulse, she opened the top drawer of Gary's bureau, intending to pack some of his things. As she lifted a pile of his handkerchiefs, she felt something stiff underneath. Curious, she pulled out a folder labeled *Hotel Claremont* with a photo of four people seated at a table: Eric Lundgren next to Jean; Gary with his arm around a girl with dark hair and light eyes. She read the date May 10, 1952, exactly a year ago.

So that was what she looked like. Natalie. Only once had Dona ever heard her name spoken inadvertently by Gary's mother. Grace Morgan had covered her mouth as though she had uttered a profanity.

Hearing Gary's footsteps in the apartment entry, Dona thrust the photograph back in the drawer, arranging the handkerchiefs on top. Furtive as a burglar caught in the act, she opened and shut her vanity drawer with a bang, calling out, "Hi, honey. Were you able to get much work done?"

"Yeah. Hope you had a rest."

He walked to his desk, checkbook in hand. Using his Murphy and Gallagher letterhead, he wrote:

> *Dear Natalie,*
>
> *Today I learned from Paul Sawyer of your mother's death. She was a lovely lady.*
>
> *I feel privileged to have known her. You are the daughter she deserved. Please convey my sincere sympathy for your loss to your father and to Julie.*
>
> *Fondly, Gary*

Referring to the address Paul had given him, Gary wrote to the Shasta Union School District, enclosing a check for one hundred dollars in memory of Marie Perrault. He covered his face with both hands, elbows on his desk.

"Something the matter?" Dona asked.

"No. Stuffy in here, isn't it?" He shoved the envelopes deep in his briefcase.

"I can hardly wait till we're in our own house," Dona said. "I just hope you and your father don't spend the whole evening talking about Senator McCarthy."

Gary grinned. "Or as Mother calls him, 'that *awful* man.' Joe McCarthy would not be a welcome guest in Mother's home, would he? Okay, honey. Dad and I won't talk politics. You can tell about the haul you made from the baby shower Sabina gave you."

Dona looked serious, saying, "Don't patronize me. McCarthy and his committee really are evil, ruining people's lives and reputations. You needn't treat me like a child."

"We're going around in circles. I'm simply agreeing with *you* that we won't waste our breath on Joe McCarthy tonight. He'll be exposed as the phony he is soon enough."

Gary walked into the bedroom to change his shirt and get a fresh handkerchief.

As they drove to Piedmont, Dona thought, *He still loves her. Natalie. Why else would he be so secretive about keeping her photograph hidden in his bureau?*

Early in their marriage Gary had expected Dona to be interested in his work, but as her morning sickness persisted, she had acted indifferent when he talked shop with her. Only during the Bayshore case did she respond more like the confident legal secretary he had known. The bright, sensual Dona who had so aroused him, had become this self-absorbed woman whose main topics were her visits to the obstetrician and her decorating plans for their house. To Gary's relief, however, his mother had warmed to Dona, sympathizing with her through each stage of pregnancy. Even his father greeted Dona affectionately every time they met.

At odd moments, Gary caught Dona looking at him inquisitively as though she, too, was wondering, *Is this all there is?* like the Peggy Lee song.

As he parked in his parents' driveway, he looked Dona full in the face. She drew back, asking, "What is it?"

Instead of intimacy, he saw anxiety in her eyes. But he said only, "It'll be better when we're in our own house, won't it?"

Chapter 39

Shasta High held commencement exercises in late May, a tradition from the nineteen-twenties and the Depression years when students went to work on farms immediately following graduation. Now most teenagers signed up for military duty or found jobs in town. Julie Perrault felt fortunate that Gil Sawyer had offered her full-time work in his insurance office again.

"Until you decide where you're going to college," Mr. Sawyer had advised her. Like almost everyone else, Paul's father was skirting around her grief over Johnny Browne's death. After the first expressions of sympathy to the Browne family and the public memorial service, people avoided mentioning Johnny's death. Julie would walk into a room and conversation would cease. Friends at school acted as though Julie should get over her mourning period, urging her to join in all the senior parties and festivities. Even her cousin, Jackie Munz, told her, "You ought to begin dating again, Julie."

Julie cut Jackie's suggestions short. Only her father and Natalie understood. Grief had bonded the family—first the sudden loss of Marie Perrault just when she seemed to be making gains in speech, and then the heartbreaking news of Johnny Browne being killed in action.

Julie told her father, "I feel better being around adults. All the kids seem so superficial. Working in Mr. Sawyer's office will be good for me."

Julie's dark auburn hair was cut very short, in a gamine style. Her father wished he could take away her pain as easily as he had bandaged her scraped knees and little hurts when she was a child. And Natalie was still more solemn than a twenty-four year old should be. Ralph admitted to himself that the girls cheered him more than he comforted them. Despite their losses, Natalie and Julie still had their hopes for the future, whereas he found himself hanging onto the past.

When the chairman of the high school board approached him about presenting the scholarship in Marie Perrault's name, Ralph suggested Natalie instead, since she had renewed her contract to teach. "Natalie knows the students," he explained.

On the evening of graduation, the Perraults sat together on the stage as Natalie rose to announce the first recipient of the one thousand dollar award. Many of Redding's leading business owners had contributed to the scholarship fund. Among the list of individual donors, Natalie saw Gary Morgan's name for the first time.

"My mother was a working woman her whole life," Natalie began her speech, "whose dignity is now measured by the affection and generosity of this community, the school, and the friends who knew her. She would have been overwhelmed by the tributes expressed."

Natalie's voice grew stronger as her eyes searched the audience and then focused on Paul Sawyer, sitting off to one side.

"But above all, Marie Perrault was a practical woman. She would be gratified to know that graduates of Shasta Union High School will have opportunities for higher education denied to her in her youth. My father, my sister, and I are delighted and proud to announce that the student chosen by the faculty to receive the 1953 Marie Perrault Scholarship is…"

Ralph Perrault shook hands with the red-faced boy who marched up to the stage as Julie wiped away her tears. The winner was a "grind"—a chemistry class whiz—aspiring to become a doctor.

At the reception following the ceremony, Paul Sawyer greeted Julie with a present. Natalie, serving punch to the graduates and their families, could see Julie exclaiming over the gift. Ralph Perrault joined Natalie at the punch table.

"I was surprised to see Paul here," Ralph said. "Thought he was already working at that law firm in Oakland."

"Cobb and Fortis. Paul told me Monday is his first official day on the job. He's visiting his parents, packing things for his move into an apartment in Oakland."

Julie said, "Look what Paul gave me; a bracelet with gold nuggets."

"I'm taking Natalie to dinner, Mr. Perrault," Paul explained a few minutes later. "We have some catching up to do."

"Now that we have flights from Redding to San Francisco, I've decided to visit Jean and Eric Lundgren next week," Natalie told Paul at the steak house. "My cousin, Louie Benson, is taking flying lessons from one of the pilots from World War II. Our airport needs commercial pilots, with so many men gone to Korea," she broke off, seeing the blank expression on Paul's face. "Well, my travel plans are of no interest to you."

"Not true. Your plans are always of interest to me. I was trying to think who Eric Lundgren was. Then I remembered. Gary Morgan's cousin, isn't he?"

"Yes. Jean Swithin was my best friend at Cal."

"If you're going to San Francisco, why don't we get together? You could help me celebrate my first week with Cobb and Fortis. Ed and Bev Tate would like to see you, too," Paul suggested.

Natalie looked down at her plate. "Not this time, but thanks anyway, Paul."

"*Thanks anyway?* What's that supposed to mean?" Paul asked. "You think I'm inviting you out as a favor?" His face reddened. "You imagine I'm just your hometown buddy. Does it never occur to you, Natalie, that I could have non-Platonic feelings for you? That I care about you more than anyone else I can think of!"

"Paul, don't. Just don't say anything more. I like you far too much to put you in a category. Besides, there are friends and then there are *best* friends. You're a rock."

Natalie was leaning forward, reaching across the table to him.

"You say that because you're still in love with him," Paul said, withdrawing his hand from her touch.

"Are you carrying the torch for Gary Morgan? Because if you are, you're an even bigger fool than he was for losing you!"

"Could we leave now?" Natalie asked as she stood up.

"No, we haven't finished our steaks, and I'm your best friend in the world, remember."

He still sounded bitter.

"You are, Paul. Let's not ruin a perfect friendship by becoming lovers." She tried to coax a smile from him.

"No sense wasting our dinners," he replied.

A few minutes later, she was persuading him to tell her about his work. What sort of cases would he handle? Was he dreading court appearances or eager to take on an active role?

That was the thing about Natalie, Paul reflected, she was a good conversationalist, but she was an even better listener. He opened up to her, flattered in spite of himself by her questions and the attentive expression in her green eyes.

Chapter 40

▼

Natalie was surprised to see that the DC-3 plane was nearly full when she boarded it, even though she was early. She took a window seat, staring out at the landscape around the Redding airport.

"Excuse me, Miss, is this seat taken?" A middle-aged man bent toward her.

"No," she answered.

"Your first time on this flight?"

"Yes. I didn't expect it to be so popular."

"This is my third trip," her traveling companion said. "It sure beats driving if you have business in San Francisco."

The pilot ambled up the narrow aisle, glancing at his passengers. "Natalie, hello! Welcome aboard. Enjoy your flight."

"I will as long as Louie isn't flying us today."

The seasoned pilot grinned. "Be a while before Louie earns his wings, but he's eager to be a sky jockey. You're gettin' to be a regular, Roy."

"The only way to travel, Bart." He shook the pilot's hand.

Turning to Natalie, the man introduced himself, "Roy Naylor."

"Natalie Perrault."

The name sounded familiar to her, but she couldn't place him. As the twenty-one seater plane lifted off, Natalie gripped the armrest tightly, sucking in her breath.

Roy Naylor said, "Take-offs and landings are always the most nerve-wracking, aren't they?"

"I guess," Natalie answered. "This is my first airplane ride ever."

Her seatmate passed a stick of gum to her. "Sometimes this helps".

He leaned back, relaxing. When the plane leveled off at a cruising altitude of five thousand feet, Roy Naylor began talking about the new housing complex he was building on the outskirts of Redding. Mountain Homesites. She remembered seeing the signs announcing the name. Then she also recalled the law firm Gary's fraternity brother, Reed Houghton, had joined.

"By any chance are you related to the lawyers, Houghton and Naylor?" she asked.

"My father's younger brother is the senior partner," Naylor explained. "The firm is drawing up legal documents for my Homesites. I expect to begin sales soon."

As they chatted easily, Naylor revealed that he had purchased timberland on the edge of the Forest Service boundary some years before.

"The land is scenic, near Mount Lassen. It was a bargain in '48. I'm expecting to sell lots for vacation homes," he said enthusiastically.

"You may have crossed paths with my father, Ralph Perrault. He's the ranger on the district," Natalie said.

"Tall, rugged-looking man?" Roy Naylor asked. "I think he's the one who gave me a forest map, told me I needed to check with county agencies." He shook his head. "So your father's the ranger. Small world, isn't it?"

"Tiny," Natalie agreed with a slight laugh. "Your conversation has helped me get over my fear of flying, Mr. Naylor."

"Roy, please."

As the plane began its final descent and the stewardess reminded passengers to buckle their seat belts, Roy Naylor said, "Pleasure to talk with you, Natalie. I've been rambling on about my business. What brings you to San Francisco?"

"I'm visiting a college friend. Her mother, Mrs. Swithin, invited me to stay with her."

Eric Lundgren met Natalie's plane. He bent to kiss her cheek. "I wasn't sure if I should wear a red carnation so you'd recognize me," he greeted her. "Jean's sorry she couldn't be here. Her last two days of teaching, you know."

"Hope it wasn't too inconvenient for you."

"No, the market's closed." Eric put his hand on her shoulder lightly, then lifted her small suitcase. "Your timing is perfect. We'll have dinner this evening at our place. I've really enjoyed reading the anecdotes of teaching you've sent our way."

Natalie noticed how thoughtful Eric was. The two of them chatted easily on the drive to Frances Swithin's apartment.

"It was my idea to have you stay with me. I'm glad to have company," Frances Swithin welcomed her. "This was Jean's room. Make yourself at home."

Remembering Jean's untidy dorm room with books open and term papers on every surface, Natalie appreciated the smart bedroom with its modern furnishings and sophisticated decor. She unpacked, calling out, "Your apartment is lovely."

During their afternoon conversation, Frances Swithin confided to Natalie, "Eric is such a considerate son-in-law. I'm spoiled, Natalie. Last month I asked him to advise me on putting my savings into investments. He and Jean want me to retire. I told him I wouldn't dream of giving up my job. What would I do all day? Get fat eating bonbons and watching television?"

"I can't imagine you being idle," Natalie replied, wondering at Jean's mother's candid comments to a relative stranger. Frances was curled up on the modular couch, wearing black Capri pants and a white rayon shirt, looking almost collegiate, despite her salt and pepper hair.

What must it be like to have a mother who was fun?

Changing the subject, Natalie asked, "Will Jean be teaching next year?"

"No. She found out that teaching was not her calling. She'll tell you her reasons tonight at dinner. What about you, Natalie?"

"Teaching has been my therapy, Mrs. Swithin," Natalie responded.

"Call me Frances, please. I feel as though we've known each other forever, even though Jean never could persuade you to visit us. Oh, there's Hal."

Soon Natalie was asking Hal about his courses, mentioning her cousin, Louie Benson.

"Louie wants to get away from Redding. I wonder how he'd like San Francisco State next year," Natalie explained.

"What's he interested in?" Hal asked.

"He's taking flying lessons. He spends most of his time working on his car."

"He has his own car!" Hal blurted out, casting a look at his mother.

"Our basement garage has only one space per apartment," Frances told Natalie. "Hal can get around the city on public transportation."

"Didn't mean to start something," Natalie said.

"You look like marriage agrees with you," Natalie said, hugging Jean that evening as she entered the foyer of the Lundgrens' apartment.

"It's been too long, Natalie. I've missed you." Jean studied Natalie's face.

"What a view!" Natalie walked over to the sliding doors onto the balcony as Eric handed round the wine glasses and Frances served the canapés she had brought.

"Mother still doesn't think I can cook, just because I don't meet her standards," Jean laughed. "But I've been trying all kinds of recipes lately, haven't I, Eric?"

"And I'm still alive and kicking," Eric said.

"I hope we're not having fish," Hal said. "Mom's cooked fish two times this week."

"Brain food, kid," Jean said. "You need it. But tonight we're having braised beef and noodles. Straight out of my *Joy of Cooking* book."

"I'm impressed," Natalie stated, thinking that Jean appeared very comfortable in her role as a San Francisco matron. Natalie's fingers trailed over the cherry-wood carved arms of her chair. Such elegance. Surely much of this furniture was antique, probably worth a small fortune. And Jean looked stylish in her turquoise linen dress with jet buttons and a high Chinese collar. She had a curly permanent now, making her seem more mature.

"No wonder you're giving up teaching," Natalie said suddenly.

"I'm too impatient with teenagers," Jean admitted. "And Eric's going to a conference in London in August; he invited me to tag along. We had to send our regrets to *Elizabeth R* because we missed her coronation, but we'll be in England for two full weeks. Can you blame me for not renewing my contract to teach at K. W. Academy?"

"Give my regards to T. S. Eliot," Natalie said. "I trust he'll invite you to tea."

"I'll need your car, Mom," Hal said as they finished dinner. "Double-date tonight. My turn to provide wheels."

"Just don't be late," Frances said, handing Hal her car keys.

"Tomorrow's Thursday," Eric said. "Be at the office when the opening bell rings."

As soon as Hal was out the door, Frances sighed. "What can you expect at Hal's age? Hormones raging."

Eric and Jean exchanged glances. "You're too good-natured, Frances," Eric stated. "Too easy on Hal. I'm here to back you up."

Jean began clearing the table, saying to Natalie, "Not an interesting topic for you, Nat. Let's visit in the kitchen while Eric chastises Mother for her leniency. He loves playing the role of male authority figure," Jean added. "Just tell Mother whatever you'd like to do tomorrow: shopping, museums or a matinee. My final obligation to K.W. Academy will be completed after the graduation tomorrow night. Eric's folks have invited us to come to Atherton on Saturday. You did bring your swimsuit, didn't you?"

Talking rapidly, Jean had kicked off her pumps while she rinsed plates, splashing water all over the counter—more like her former self.

"I don't expect to be entertained," Natalie remarked, stacking dishes.

"I'll get it, honey," Eric called out as the phone rang in a bedroom. Frances surveyed the living room, emptying ashtrays.

"I don't think Hal even used his napkin," she said as Jean and Natalie entered, "so this one doesn't need to go in the wash."

"Mother, I wish you'd stop acting like the maid around her."

Jean lit a cigarette, wiggling her stocking feet on the Persian rug.

Looking excited, Eric hurried into the living room. He removed his glasses, rubbing the bridge of his nose.

"Who called?" Jean asked.

"It was Gary." His eyes swept over Natalie and then back to Jean. "He wanted us to know, it's a girl! Dona went into labor suddenly this afternoon. Baby was born just two hours ago, ten days premature, but doing fine, he says. What's today? June tenth?"

Eric looked at Natalie very directly. He wasn't wearing his glasses and it seemed that his eyes held a tender expression meant for her alone. Then he glanced away as if Natalie had caught him at something very private. Until that moment, she had not believed in the reality of Gary's marriage. She could never picture him as married, never visualize his wife. But now this baby was a reality—the ultimate reality.

In a rush, Jean and Frances began asking Eric all the usual feminine questions: How much did the baby weigh? What was her name? And when Eric shrugged, lifting his palms, Jean burst out, "Why, you're no good. Just like a man not to get the details."

Chapter 41

"Her name is Grace Elizabeth," Dona said, "for both of our mothers."

"But she'll be called *Gracie*. She'll hate that," Gary's mother protested.

"No, Mother. Dona's decision on the name is final," Gary said. "I promised her she could name our baby."

Lloyd Morgan said, "You know you're flattered, Grandma!"

They were gathered around Dona's hospital bed, waiting for the nurse to bring in the baby. Dona was sitting up, her hazel eyes bright. Grace Morgan reached out to wipe her daughter-in-law's forehead with a cool cloth.

"It's really a blessing you had such a short labor," she murmured. "You don't look worn out."

Hugh Dailey shuffled from foot to foot, unable to be still. "Good thing you called Gary right away," he said, "so he could get you to the hospital in time."

"Here she is," the nurse bustled in, placing the infant in Dona's outstretched arms. "Too many people in here," the nurse scolded, shooing them out. "Only the new father may stay in the room."

Gary could see one tiny hand at the tip of the blanket. Curiously, he moved closer as Dona handed him the baby. The infant opened her deep blue eyes, staring steadily into Gary's face. His mind told him she couldn't focus yet, but already his newborn child appeared to study him.

"She's looking very judicious, very wise," Gary said. He kissed the baby's head and whispered to Dona, "I love you, darling."

Gary had never been around babies, never anticipated how he would feel when his own child arrived. For the past several months he had ignored the parenting articles Dona had placed before him. He had refused to attend Lamaze classes, pleading his heavy caseload. Whenever Dona and her sister-in-law Ginny had chatted about baby clothes and carriages and bathinettes, he had walked out of the room. The whole subject of infant care had bored him. Now, as he examined his daughter's delicate fingers and toes, stroked her cheek gently and held her close to him, he kept marveling at this baby. Flesh of his flesh.

"She's perfect, isn't she?" Gary's eyes met Dona's. "You're both quite remarkable. I'm in awe of you."

Chapter 42

Natalie had forgotten how windy San Francisco could be. Wearing her gray and white striped cotton dress and a cardigan sweater, she felt not only dowdy, but also downright cold. She had been shopping for gifts for Julie and her father.

"Mark Twain was right when he wrote that the coldest day of his life was one July in San Francisco," Natalie said. "It was already in the eighties yesterday in Redding."

Frances asked, "Any other place you'd like to go?"

"No, thanks so much for helping me find things. Julie will be thrilled when she sees a box from I. Magnin, even though it's just a scarf."

"You can find lovely things at Magnin's, not too costly if you shop carefully. But what about yourself, Natalie? Wouldn't you like to buy something new?"

"I brought my black suit with me."

"Why don't we pop into Ransohoff's? I saw some darling blouses there."

Frances persuaded Natalie to buy a magenta silk blouse for only five dollars more than she had planned to spend. Back at the apartment, when she tried on the blouse with its subtly plunging neckline under her severe black suit, Natalie had to admit she was pleased with her city look.

Frances admired her. "Few women can wear magenta, but it flatters your coloring, and your silver lapel pin is perfect."

"I'd like to take us out to dinner," Natalie offered.

"Since you treated me to lunch, I thought we'd just have soup and crackers here tonight," Frances suggested. "You'll be going out tomorrow with Jean and Eric."

Natalie headed for the bedroom to change her clothes. A moment later Frances knocked. "A phone call for you."

Puzzled, she answered the phone.

"Natalie? Roy Naylor here."

"Oh, hello."

"If you have no other plans, I wondered if I might take you to dinner tonight. My uncle recommended several good restaurants." Roy spoke as though they were longtime friends.

"All right, I'm free tonight," she heard herself say, giving him the address.

"I'll be by at six," Naylor said.

Only then did Natalie wonder how on earth he had got Frances Swithin's phone number. What exactly had she said to him on the plane?

"Who's your date, Natalie?" Frances asked.

"A friend of my father's," Natalie lied. "He's in San Francisco on business."

When Roy Naylor buzzed the apartment from the lobby, she said, "I'll be right down."

In response to Frances' questioning look, Natalie explained, "He has a taxi waiting."

Roy swept her into the cab, saying, "Great that you could make it. So many restaurants, so little time," he added with a smile. "Hope you like Italian food."

Seated by his side on the plane, she had not looked at him closely. He had been mainly a reassuring voice. Now she noticed that his eyes were brown, and his dark hair, flecked with gray, was trimmed short. He wore a charcoal gray suit, a white shirt with a maroon tie, and no wedding band.

Very conservative, Natalie thought, compared to his casual attire on the plane. How fortuitous that she had packed her good black suit, purchased for her mother's funeral and worn only a few times since then to church.

As Roy Naylor guided her into the restaurant, she realized he was just two inches taller than she was in her high heels. His broad shoulders and deep chest made him appear bigger when he was seated. The restaurant was dimly lighted, inconspicuous on the outside, but filled with stimulating foreign aromas as they entered. Passing a polished wooden bar with a brass railing and original paintings of early California scenes on the walls, Natalie remarked, "I almost expected a dance hall girl to greet us."

Roy laughed more than her small joke deserved. "This place does have a Barbary Coast look to it," he agreed.

"Straight out of the movies," Natalie said.

Roy ordered martinis for them, saying, "To San Francisco, long may she reign as a beautiful city."

As he related his session at Houghton and Naylor, Roy thought that Natalie Perrault, sitting across from him, appeared far more sophisticated than the anxious girl on her first flight. He explained that his uncle had turned him over to a young lawyer.

"At this point, it's just a matter of making sure all the *i*'s are dotted and *t*'s are crossed, I suppose," Roy said. "My job was mainly to read and sign everything put before me. Good Lord, must have been fifty pages! My business affairs are peanuts compared to most of the firm's clients."

He did not tell her what Reed Houghton had revealed to him. As he concluded their conference, Reed had remarked, "At Cal I met a girl from Redding. In fact, she became engaged to a fraternity brother of mine, a pal from Boalt Hall." Reed added, "A grand girl. I was set to be best man, then the wedding was postponed and I left on a trip to Europe. After I returned, I heard my friend had married someone else."

Roy Naylor had waited for Houghton to continue.

"Natalie Perrault was the girl's name," Reed concluded.

"The Perraults are an old family in Redding," Roy responded quickly, standing to shake hands with Reed. "Thanks for your help."

Now, as the waiter gave his recommendations with a flourish and the wine steward poured the *Chianti classico* for Roy to taste, Natalie's green eyes sparkled with merriment. Ray looked over the menu, giving their order for *agnello arrosto al rosmarino*, receiving nods of approval from the waiter who said, "An excellent choice, sir," and dashed off. Roy leaned closer to Natalie, whispering, "When I'm offered a wine to sample, I always want to say, 'unacceptable,' but I've never had the nerve! I'm no wine connoisseur."

"Neither am I," Natalie said, "so there's no reason for you to try to impress me."

But she felt flattered, nevertheless.

"Who are you when you're not a traveling lady visiting a friend?"

"I'm an English teacher. One of those dreadful creatures that assigns book reports and requires students to recite poetry. There! My guilty secret is out."

Natalie lifted her chin, expecting him to smile at her banter. Instead, he said quite seriously, "I wish I knew some poetry to recite. Maybe if I weren't such an illiterate guy, I'd stand a better chance with you."

She raised both hands in the air in a theatrical gesture, "Now I'm the one who's embarrassed, Roy. The minute I say I teach English, people seem to expect me to scold them for splitting infinitives or dangling participles. For tonight I'm a teacher *incognito.*"

He laughed, raising his glass of wine, "I salute you! Teaching is a noble profession."

She began tucking into her *entrée*. "Mmm, this is very good."

He pierced a chunk of lamb, then said in a businesslike tone as if he was in a hurry to get something off his chest, "Well, Natalie, I'm a free man. My divorce became final in March. I want you to know that."

"I see." She didn't know how else to respond. Both of them ate silently for several moments, then he added, "Don't worry, I'm not about to pour out a tale of my wife not understanding me, but I'd like to show you around the city. My uncle invited me to his house tomorrow evening, but you and I could..."

"I have plans with my friends for tomorrow," Natalie said.

"I'm taking the Saturday flight back to Redding. Are you?"

"No. I'm visiting for a week, leaving on the Wednesday plane."

"That's right, you told me. What about next week, after you get home? I'd like to show you the parcel of land I bought near Lassen."

"We'll probably run into each other. Redding's not a very big town," Natalie answered.

"Run into each other?" His brown eyes widened. "I'm asking you for a date."

"I'd like to see your property," she answered.

Roy began filling in the details of his Mountain Homesites grand opening scheduled for the first of July. When he took her back to Frances Swithin's apartment in a cab, he brushed her cheek with a kiss, saying, "I'll call you when you're back in Redding."

The next few days flew by. Jean and Natalie strolled through Golden Gate Park, comparing notes on teaching, but keeping their conversations light. At the Lundgren home in Atherton, Natalie felt like she was a tourist visiting an English estate until Elinor Lundgren put her at ease with the remark, "We're so glad when Jean and Eric bring someone here to swim and relax. No sense in having a pool if no one uses it. My bathing suit days are over!"

Somehow, the house was luxurious without being pretentious. The attractive furniture was comfortable, the curtains and drapery simple, letting in the sunshine through tall French doors. On the patio where they spent most of the day, the casual lounge chairs looked well-used and colorful pottery brightened the scene.

Only once did Natalie feel sadness sweep over her when Nelson Lundgren said to Eric, "Remember how we always thought we'd have Gary handle our legal matters? Since he's with that labor union firm, Gary's out of the picture. Our family lawyer died last month. Now Elinor thinks we should update our wills, so I've contacted a young man at Houghton and Naylor."

Natalie and Jean toweled their hair dry after their swim as the men talked.

"Who's this mystery man I heard about from Mother?" Jean interjected loudly. "Your date Thursday night."

"Friend of Dad's from Redding," Natalie fibbed. Jean looked at her quizzically.

"No need to shield me from hearing Gary's name," Natalie added.

Even after Jean changed the subject, Natalie pondered the irony of hearing passing references to Houghton and Naylor law firm, first from Roy Naylor, and now from Nelson Lundgren.

"Can I persuade you to attend Grace Cathedral with me tomorrow? Eric and I worship at St. Luke's, but the Cathedral is such a San Francisco landmark, you really should see it."

"Whatever you like, Jean." Natalie leaned back in the deck chair, closing her eyes. After a moment she asked, "Do you see him often?"

"Who? Oh, Gary, you mean? No, not very often. Eric and Gary talk on the phone. Last month the entire family, Morgans, Lundgrens, and Daileys went to a housewarming party for Gary and Dona. They bought a house on Ashby Avenue."

Natalie sat up. "Is he happy with her, Jean?"

Jean bent her head, lighting a cigarette.

"I don't know, Nat. How can I tell?"

Chapter 43

Natalie had agreed to meet Roy Naylor on the outskirts of Redding and follow him to his property near Mount Lassen. Recently she had bought herself a sporty Chevrolet from Johnny Browne's father's dealership at the urging of her cousin, Wayne Benson, who was working there. When Wayne returned home, missing three toes from frostbite in Korea, he could have had a position as a salesman at his father's lumber company, but A. C. Browne offered Wayne a job as a mechanic at his Chevrolet franchise. Following the small town custom of looking out for friends, Mr. Browne was training Wayne Benson as he might have prepared his own son to take over the business some day.

"You'll bring in young people to buy," A.C. Browne told Wayne. "You can earn commissions on any car sales you make."

Natalie had been Wayne's first customer. Louie Benson had accompanied Natalie.

"It's in great condition, a year-old trade-in," Louie told her.

"I'll probably be paying for it well into my old age," Natalie said, eying the bronze metallic model and getting out her checkbook.

Ralph objected, saying, "You know you can use my Ford anytime, Natalie."

She answered, "That's your car, Dad. I'm an independent woman now. Besides, I like the color of my car, and Wayne earned a commission on the sale!"

Ralph laughed. "Okay. Think I should give you refresher driving lessons?"

In reality, Natalie thought of the car as granting her freedom. She never would have told her father she was seeing Roy Naylor. Too many questions.

"Nice wheels," Roy said, bringing out a map. "Here's where we're going. Sure you don't want to ride with me? The road into my property is bumpy."

"I'll be fine," she said as he climbed into his station wagon

Half an hour later Roy was unloading a picnic basket, while she smoothed out a blanket on the ground, covered with pine needles.

"Not quite 'a jug of wine, a loaf of bread and thou,'" he said, "but I hope a six-pack of beer and ham sandwiches will do."

"This is peaceful, far away from traffic noises," Natalie said. "I can see why you chose this site."

He motioned toward stakes strung with tape, measuring plots of land. His log cabin was nearly finished.

"Electricity is hooked up and the plumber is due next week to install the pipes for the bathroom and kitchen," Roy explained. "I see you wore boots. We can hike after lunch."

He took her hand as he showed her a little stream running behind his lot. "There, in that thicket, you might see a deer. I saw a doe and her fawn a few days ago."

Just as Natalie turned to face him, he kissed her. Everything about him felt warm and strong. Her face was pressed against his flannel shirt as he murmured her name. She smelled his shaving soap and tasted beer on his mouth as he kissed her again.

When she returned home in the late afternoon, Natalie found her Aunt Corinne in conversation with Julie.

"How are you managing the cooking now?" Corinne asked.

Julie glanced toward Natalie, "I thought Nat would take over that job."

"Hold on, Julie. Just because I'm on summer vacation doesn't mean I'm chief cook. Dad's perfectly capable of fixing his own breakfast and lunches. And now that virtually every local widow or divorcée between thirty-five and fifty is inviting him for home-cooked dinners, he's guaranteed at least one or two meals a week."

Her last remark brought a smile to Corinne's face and a scowl to Julie's.

"Ralph has become Redding's most eligible bachelor lately," Corinne said.

"Dad wouldn't be disloyal to Mama's memory," Julie said.

"Now, honey, everyone knows how much your dad loved Marie, but he's bound to want female companionship."

Corinne looked at Natalie. For once Natalie and her aunt viewed things the same way, even though Natalie was irritated by her aunt's comments. Lately, meals were erratic. Laundry piled up and housework got slighted.

"Here's what I suggest," Corinne proposed. Half an hour later Julie and Natalie had agreed on a schedule for sharing duties.

"We can't count on women wooing Dad, inviting him for dinners every week," Julie said. "Besides, Dad will never re-marry."

"Don't be so sure of that, Julie. Usually when there's a death, women mourn, but men marry." Corinne had the final word.

Chapter 44

"Come in, Paul," Julie said, surprised to see him. "I don't know where Natalie is."

"I drove up for the Fourth of July. How about barbecue with my folks, then watch the fireworks tonight?" Paul suggested. He couldn't get used to Julie's cropped head. Standing there barefooted, wearing khaki shorts and a red bandana halter, she appeared younger than ever. Then, as her face brightened, she said, "Really? A date? Sure, I'd love to. Dad went to a picnic at the Bensons, but I didn't want to go. Too much family!"

"Maybe you're not in the mood for barbecue with the Sawyer clan then," Paul said. "My sister, brother-in-law, and their kids are here from Davis."

"Your family's different. They won't ask me a million questions about my future." Julie answered so eagerly that Paul laughed.

While Julie hurried to change her clothes, Paul leafed through a magazine, expecting Natalie to enter the house any moment. Since their conversation a month before, Paul had put aside any thoughts of romance with Natalie. She was as unattainable as ever. For Paul her elusive independence been the key to her appeal. He was not given to analyzing his feelings deeply, but he realized that the entire Perrault family had always attracted him. Vaguely, Paul recalled a character in classic literature who had fallen in love with two sisters sequentially. What was that novel? Something he had read as an undergraduate. Natalie would know the book.

"I'm ready," Julie said. She had dressed in a dark blue denim blouse and matching skirt, her strappy sandals adding two inches to her height. As she offered her hand to Paul, showing off the gold nugget bracelet he had given her for graduation, he whistled.

"I can't imagine where Natalie has gone," Julie said, locking the front door.

At that moment, Natalie was sitting on Roy Naylor's couch as he called to her from the kitchen of his apartment. "A beer? I've got ginger ale."

"Ginger ale sounds good."

A few days before, Roy had shown her the model homes of his Mountain Homesites, but until today she had not been to his apartment. Wisely, Natalie had parked some distance away. His house was for sale—the one he had occupied with his wife.

"The judge granted the house to Lucille in the settlement, but she moved to Sacramento with our daughter. Didn't want the house. Now I'm trying to get the best price for her," Roy explained. "Linda, my daughter, has health problems. Lu thinks the medical facilities in Sacramento are better than the local docs."

Although Natalie wondered if Roy's divorce had been as friendly as he implied, she had asked him no questions during the past three weeks. They met either at his cabin near Mount Lassen or for lunch on the outskirts of town. She liked him better each time they were together; his energy was infectious, drawing her out of her lassitude. Roy was a man who took charge. He knew everyone in town, and he made her smile with his verbal thumbnail sketches of various personalities around Redding. Once, after greeting a local businessman, Roy had remarked to Natalie, "I'd keep my hands in my pockets around that guy if I were you."

He was never mean-spirited in his gossip, simply alert about people and their motives.

Now she held the chilled glass of ginger ale against her forehead, saying, "It's going to be a scorcher."

Roy added, "Let's stay here till evening. Everybody's at the park all day. I have air conditioning."

Natalie settled back on the couch. "Your apartment is very attractive. Not what I'd expect the ordinary bachelor place to be. I like your maps on the wall and these comfy cushions."

Roy downed his beer, touching her throat and mouth with his forefinger.

"You're looking very sexy. Are we going to spend today discussing the weather and my furniture?"

Lounging in her pale yellow sundress with narrow shoulder straps, her tanned bare legs stretched out on his couch, Natalie murmured, "I guess not," then put her glass down. She and Roy exchanged a gaze of mutual understanding. He leaned toward her, kissing her neck and mouth. She lay back, feeling the nubby fabric of his sofa against her bare shoulders, responding to Roy's urgency with increasing desire. His breath was hot against her skin, his voice husky as he spoke her name. He pulled her up, leading her into his bedroom, lifting her cotton sundress over her head. She kissed him again and again, pressing her body into him until they clasped each other on top of his bed. For a fraction of time she wondered if she should resist. There was something she should tell him. *Too late.* It was too late for talk.

Then he was naked upon her, thrusting himself inside her as she cried out in sharp pain, mingled with an ever stronger desire as he brought her to orgasm, erupting with his own climactic peak. Sweating, he gasped out, "Baby, I didn't know…I was your first."

As she leaped up, she saw a bloodstain on his beige bedspread. Natalie returned from the bathroom with a towel, trying to rub out the stain. Roy held her tenderly.

"Do you hurt?" he asked. She let him hold her, not looking at him.

"Just a little," she whispered.

"But, are you all right, Natalie? I had no idea…" he left the phrase unfinished.

"I know," she answered calmly. She felt she had a certain advantage over him as she sat on the bed without meeting his eyes.

"Look at me," he demanded, lifting her face with his strong hands. "Next time will be better. For you, I mean. I was too quick."

He kissed her on the lips, holding her gently, and she knew there would be a next time. She felt a sudden sense of release, a lightness as though she might faint. As they both stared at the bloodstain, Roy threw the coverlet aside, laughing. "Let's take a shower together."

For the next week Natalie felt a heightened state of awareness. She was prompt to answer the telephone, wary of questions from her father or Julie about her comings and goings. She reproached herself for hanging around, always waiting for Roy's calls, but she couldn't concentrate on the simplest tasks. She would drive to the library, intending to spend an hour reading, then turn around and hurry back, afraid she had missed Roy's invitation to meet him in town. Roy Naylor had awakened her sexuality in a way she never could have anticipated.

Julie was too full of her own musings about Paul Sawyer to pay attention to Natalie's moods. Paul had written her a note from Oakland, facetiously pleading with her to come to his rescue and organize his files. The stern secretary he shared with another lawyer at Cobb and Fortis never seemed to be around when he needed her.

Having a muddled time. Wish you were here, Paul wrote to Julie. Two days later, when the office phone rang, Julie answered, "Western Casualty and Life Insurance."

"What kind of casualties are you offering today?" asked a teasing voice.

"Paul, hi. Would you like to speak to your father?"

"In a minute. How about a date the evening of the eighteenth? I've been assigned a compensation case in Shasta County."

"Sounds fine." Julie cupped the phone receiver to her ear.

That evening Ralph observed that Natalie barely touched her dinner and that Julie was daydreaming. He was sure that men must be occupying both of his daughters' thoughts.

Chapter 45

"Did you know everybody's talking about Natalie's boyfriend?" Corinne asked Ralph one afternoon at the Forest Service district office. "Jackie saw them necking at the Palladian theater last Friday," she emphasized.

Ralph had no idea who the "boyfriend" was, but he was sure if he kept quiet his sister would reveal all, so he simply responded, "Natalie leads her own life."

"Roy Naylor has a reputation as a womanizer."

Ralph yawned, pretending to be bored by Corinne's gossip. Just then the dispatcher entered the office with news of a brush fire. Corinne hurried off to her own desk.

"The trail crew foreman spotted the fire here," said the dispatcher, pointing to the map hanging on the wall. "If the trail boss gave the correct location, the fire is barely within our protection jurisdiction. This is private ownership, about a mile away."

"Any report from the lookout tower?" Ralph asked.

"I'll call the lookout right now, tell him the fix we have from the crew."

East of the river in his Mountain Homesites office, Roy Naylor was drawing up an earnest money agreement for the middle-aged couple, eager to buy a two-bedroom Chateau Model, his third sale of the week. Roy had expected newly marrieds with G.I. loans to be his principal clients, but he was pleasantly surprised to find his houses also had appeal for families from the Bay Area, as well as grandparents in their fifties seeking a second home.

Roy shook hands with the couple in front of him as he closed his latest sale, saying, "I'll speed up the paper work for you two. Expect to move in within a month."

Ten minutes later Roy telephoned Natalie. "Can you get away this afternoon? Meet me at my cabin. Let's play hooky."

As Natalie drove onto the rough road that led to Roy's land, she saw him motioning her to stop. "What's the matter?" she asked.

"Smoke! Don't you smell it?" Roy's blue chambray shirt was darkened with sweat. "Go home, honey. Fire's somewhere to the southwest."

"What about you?"

"I've got emergency equipment, a Pulaski. Just leave, Natalie. I've got to protect my property."

"I'm staying. I'll help you."

In frustration Roy yelled, "You'll just be in the way! I don't have time to argue."

He ran toward his cabin, Natalie stumbling after him in her light sandals. Roy handed her a hose.

"Douse the roof, all around the cabin. I'm checking on my lot farthest to the south." Carrying his Pulaski, a combination ax and mattock, Roy raced away, shouting, "This is no place for a school teacher!"

Once Ralph and the dispatcher had confirmation of the fire's location from their spotter in the lookout tower, Ralph called the Shasta-Trinity Forest supervisor to inform him. His communication was simply part of the chain of command. So far, it looked like the trail crew could control the fire, but as Ralph concentrated on writing reports, he found his mind wandering to Corinne's comments about Natalie's involvement with Roy Naylor. Judging from his own recent experience as a widower of four months, he could well imagine younger women in town being attracted to Naylor.

Last month one of Redding's divorcées, a neighbor in her forties, had invited Ralph to dinner. Arlene Steuben was a buyer for a chain of department stores. This neighbor had been genuinely kind when Marie Perrault died, bringing a casserole to the family and attending the funeral.

Ralph arrived at Arlene's home, expecting a quiet meal and some shared memories of Marie. He had prepared polite inquiries about her activities in the women's garden club. Ralph was surprised to find his hostess "all dolled up" (his expression) and the table set with candles, a vase of roses, and fine china. He realized he should have worn his sport coat with his best slacks; he was sans tie as well. Since both Julie and Natalie had been out that evening, he had lacked feminine advice. Embarrassed, Ralph quipped, "I'm not used to such fanciness, Arlene," as he handed her a bottle of wine.

Every time he turned the conversation to general topics, she interjected a remark about how much she had always admired him, thanking Ralph profusely for hanging her Christmas tree lights every year. Bending over her wine glass, she hung on Ralph's every word, her myopic pale gray eyes fixing on him. Dinner was excellent: Swiss steak, mashed potatoes and gravy, green beans, and for dessert, a strawberry-rhubarb pie.

"It's just a pleasure to cook for a man with an appetite," Arlene gushed. "I hardly ever bake a pie for myself. What's the point?"

"That was just delicious." Ralph patted his stomach for emphasis. "Whew, let me do these dishes for you to work off some calories."

"Oh, my, no!" Arlene exclaimed, taking him by the hand to the living room. "You sit right here; be comfy." Busily, she plumped the pillows on her couch. Then, to his bewilderment, she patted his thigh familiarly as she sat close to him. At eight-thirty he escaped as gracefully as he could.

Who knew what loneliness drove his nice neighbor to such tactics? Ralph tried to blot out the image of Arlene's rouged face, her pervasive cologne, and her toothy smiles at his perfunctory compliments. And yet he could imagine that another man in his place would have thrilled to her seductive overtures. He suspected many widowers were led into romantic entanglements because of isolation. Ralph now wore his own celibacy as a familiar garment, but he realized how much his sisters and his daughters comforted him. He would have missed their feminine society if he lived alone.

Shortly afterwards, Ralph asked Arlene if she would like to try out a new prime rib restaurant on the way to Mount Shasta. He made sure Julie and Natalie came along, and he left most of the conversation to his daughters. Arlene got the message. She and Ralph resumed their friendly waves across the fence, exchanging comments about the weather. But Ralph promised that he would help his neighbor with her Christmas tree lights as usual.

Corinne's voice interrupted Ralph's reverie. His sister stuck her head in his doorway, saying, "That's the second call I've had from a civilian wanting to know about the fire."

Ralph roused himself. "Yeah, don't say too much. Just thank people for their interest."

The fire boss phoned in an update, reporting that four men could literally encircle the fire about twenty-four feet in circumference, but they couldn't suppress it.

"The east wind's coming up. I'm calling the blister rust crew," the dispatcher said. Ralph noted how near the fire was to private property. Checking information on an area map, he learned that Roy Naylor had bought those lots bordering the fire protection district.

Ralph called out to his dispatcher, "I'm going to take a look at the fire for myself."

✳   ✳   ✳   ✳

"We've got more men on the way," the fire boss told his workers, exhausted from their hours of digging trenches and setting backfires. "Dispatcher is sending twelve guys from the blister rust crew."

Gusts of wind had blown up within the past hour, causing sparks to jump the fire line, igniting underbrush and pine trees at the southwest corner of the township bordering the Forest Service district. A creek, no more than a trickle about a yard wide, formed the boundary between Roy Naylor's property and the public land at that corner. Through the dense smoke and trees, the fire boss could barely catch glimpses of a man with a Pulaski, hacking at brush.

"Hey, there," the crew boss shouted.

Roy Naylor moved forward to the narrow creek. "Damn wind shifted," he called out to the man across from him.

"Yeah, but here comes the cavalry to the rescue," the fire boss yelled as a water tanker truck pulled up, unloading the driver and two firefighters. Within minutes, the fresh crew relieved the original four men, dousing the fire along the perimeter. Just then a Forest Service pickup arrived on the scene.

"Judas Priest," the fire boss muttered, "it's the ranger. What's *he* doing here?"

Ralph Perrault surveyed the scene, facing the man across from him along the creek.

"Naylor?" Ralph barked out the name. "Need any help?"

"No, thanks," Roy said hoarsely. "Everything's under control."

Natalie came running up the trail, her hair plastered to her head, her face smudged and her sandals muddy.

Ralph did a double-take in comic fashion. "*Natalie*! Get out of here."

Natalie laughed. "You sound like a father in a melodrama, Dad. I see you and Roy have met."

Roy said, "You have a stubborn daughter, Mr. Perrault."

"Go home, Natalie," her father repeated. "Right now".

"Judas Priest, is this a fire line or Grand Central Station?" the fire boss grumbled, shaking his head at the confrontation between the ranger and his daughter.

When Ralph reached home half an hour later, he saw Julie crouched near the radio.

"Eisenhower announced a cease fire in Korea. Mr. Sawyer let everyone at the office go home early."

Ralph sagged into his favorite chair, feeling suddenly bushed. "So it's over. I wonder how people are going to remember the Korean War years from now"

He knew Julie must be thinking about Johnny Browne, wondering why the truce couldn't have happened three months ago, but Ralph wasn't going to open that wound. Instead, he rose, saying, "Soon as I get cleaned up and your sister gets home I'm taking us out to dinner. I know it's Natalie's night to cook, but she's had quite a day."

"Where is Nat?" Julie asked.

"Natalie's been on the front lines of an honest-to-God forest fire. My turf."

Seeing Julie's anxious expression, Ralph added, gazing out the window, "She's fine, the fire's contained. Here comes your scorched sister now."

"What was the cause of the fire?" Roy Naylor asked several nights later.

"Campers," Ralph answered curtly. "No sign of arson, just carelessness. Remnants of a campfire. We're investigating. Trying to find the culprits."

Roy had accepted Natalie's invitation to the house reluctantly. He wished to avoid her father's scrutiny, but the ranger's manner had been civil.

"There's no reason for us to be secretive, is there?" Natalie asked Roy. "Tell Dad about your ideas for your property, your business deals. He'll probably welcome male companionship for a change."

Despite the late July heat, Natalie had cooked a pork roast for dinner, her father's favorite. The two men talked while she cleaned up. Roy was recounting his early years working at the lumber mill owned by his family when Natalie entered the living room. She knew Roy's history.

"I was class of '31 from Shasta High," Roy had told her. "Not a good year. Took off for Cal without a notion of what I wanted to study, joined a fraternity, damned near flunked out. Then my father died suddenly. Mother called me home to handle things. What did I know? A nineteen-year-old kid. But Mother didn't want to sell. We kept the mill going through the Depression. I learned a lot from the workers, but I never returned to Berkeley. Never got a college education. Then by the time we were at war, I was married with a child, got a military deferment."

Roy was skimming over these personal details as he talked to Ralph, but Natalie now realized the mill owned and operated by Roy's maternal grandfather was the same one where her father had worked part-time years ago to pay for Julie's appendectomy.

"…Anyway, after the war I gave up managing the mill, hired a guy with a business degree, and studied for my real estate exam. Didn't take any brains to see that land values were going sky high. That's when I used my inheritance to buy the lots bordering your forest, Mr. Perrault," Roy concluded.

"Sometimes I think a college degree is overrated," Ralph remarked. "Our crew foreman has fifteen years experience in the woods. We're hiring kids with bachelor of science degrees in forestry who think they are going on one long camping adventure."

"To Dad a 'kid' is anyone under forty," Natalie interjected.

"Good. I barely qualify," Roy said, winking at her.

Later, Ralph commented to Natalie, "I wouldn't have thought Roy Naylor would be your type. Paul Sawyer's coming here every weekend. Think he's stuck on Julie?"

"Oh, yes, Dad," Natalie laughed. "I think Paul's definitely smitten."

Chapter 46

"Do we have another typewriter in the house? The 'L' key is jammed," Gary called out one Saturday.

Dona, nursing the baby, shushed him. "My typewriter's in the closet. Top shelf," she whispered.

"Why are we whispering?" Gary asked. "Gracie won't know what normal speech sounds like. Look at her." He put the sleeping baby in her crib.

"What are you typing?" Dona asked a few minutes later.

"A summary of cases for the *California Law Review*. After my triumph over Bayshore Excavation, Jack Gallagher suggested we submit digests of key decisions. Guess who got picked to write the condensed versions."

"I could type them for you," Dona said eagerly.

"You're busy enough with Gracie. The *Review* pays for each case published. Also gives Murphy and Gallagher some prestige."

Dona bent over his shoulder, reading the typed sheet.

"I'm not as rusty as you," she said. "Strikeovers! Let me retype this."

He left her alone for twenty minutes. When he returned, she handed him the finished product with a flourish.

"I'm humbled," he grinned. "Would you really like to do this? The reports just have to be legible for the printer. But first you have to sit on my lap and give me a kiss."

That evening Dona said, "As a kid, when I went to the movies, I always wanted to be one of the career women. You know, the Katharine Hepburn, Roz Russell types. For my twelfth birthday I begged Mother for a real typewriter. She bought a used one and I taught myself to type. Hunt and peck style. I'd set myself up with paper and red pencils and pretend one corner of my bedroom was my office."

"Precocious kid," Gary said.

"I don't remember playing with dolls very much. Now look at me. Just a housewife and a mommy."

"Come here, honey," Gary motioned her to the couch. "You're much more than a housewife and mommy. But how about a bonus? If you really want to type these summaries, keep the earnings as fun money. Go on a shopping spree every month."

"What about Gracie's education?" Dona asked.

"I set up Gracie's trust fund the week after she was born."

Openmouthed, Dona said, "Really? But you never told me. You're always so secretive about money matters."

"Like my father, I suppose," Gary mused. "Guess I thought you never needed to worry about our finances, so why bore you with details. Dad invested wisely over the years. He's always been reticent about discussing finances, but he and Mother are well-off."

"Rich, you mean," Dona broke in. "I guess it's considered crass to talk about money if you're rich. Like taboos against talk of sex and politics at a dinner party. But I do resent being kept in the dark. I'll take you up on your offer of earning pin money."

"You'll be mistress of our household files. No secrets." Gary smiled. "I have a favor to ask in return. Now that we've resumed conjugal relations—isn't that what your gynecologist calls sex?—can you find a way to keep your father from dropping in on us every weekend?"

Dona said, "I told Pop bluntly I needed more rest."

"Any chance we can find Pop a girlfriend?" Gary asked.

"'Fraid not," Dona replied. "Pop's too set in his ways. His idea of a big weekend is a poker game with his union pals."

"I could invite Pop to Jack Gallagher's house for card games, I suppose," Gary joked.

"Do you realize this is the first time we've talked about anything except baby and household needs? *Ahh*, time for her eight o'clock nursing," Dona said, realizing her blouse was soaked. She headed upstairs, aware of the tenderness of her breasts.

I won't become one of those boring wives, Dona resolved. *Gary and I won't call each other "Mommy" and "Daddy" and become dull like other couples.*

As she rocked Gracie, wincing at the painful tugging at her nipples, Dona wondered if three months of nursing would be enough. She'd ask her obstetrician if she could put Gracie on the bottle soon. Her baby was blooming.

I'll join the Berkeley Tennis Club in September.

CHAPTER 47

"You mean there's a set price for a man's arm or whatever got chopped off in an accident?" Julie asked Paul.

He nodded. "Don't look so outraged. It's part of California's compensation code. I'm glad to see you taking such an interest in my field of law."

They were sitting on a bench in Redding's city park on the Sunday before Labor Day.

"I suppose there's a price on a human life, too," Julie persisted.

"Yes. To you, this sounds callous, but it's the only fair way to compensate workers for industrial accidents. Imagine the court time it would take for complex litigation arguing that this worker's loss was greater than someone else's. Families would be at the mercy of a particular judge or the cleverness of the lawyers representing the plaintiffs. Fixed benefits are the best we mere mortals can devise."

This serious mood of Julie's was not the atmosphere Paul had intended.

"You're right to raise questions. In fact, you'd probably make a good lawyer," he added lightly.

"Oh, sure," she smiled at him in a new way. When Paul had invited her out in the early summer, Julie had been flattered by his attentions. They had fallen into an easy friendship. Paul's embraces had been casual, his kisses almost perfunctory. He had warmed to her questions, her artless ways. One minute Julie would be earnest, her large slanted eyes focusing on him intently, then her mood would change to liveliness, and her teasing would charm him. Now, as he took her hand in his, kissing her palm, she stroked his curly blond hair. As desire swept over them, their mouths met and they clung together on the narrow park bench. Finally they broke apart.

"How would you like living in Oakland?" Paul asked.

"You mean as your secretary or something?"

"*No*, sweets, I mean as my wife. I'm asking you to marry me."

Julie drew back. "I wouldn't want to be second choice, Paul."

"You're not! How could you ever think that? I love you. I tried not to rush things this summer when I realized I loved you. Every time I drove back to Oakland, I kept looking forward to the next time I'd see you."

His face was close to hers. She noticed his freckles, the slight wrinkles around his blue-green eyes, a faint scar on his chin as though he had nicked himself shaving. She felt as though Paul was suddenly a stranger, not the friend she had known for so long. And this stranger was speaking to her of his love.

"I was never engaged to Johnny Browne. We were going steady in high school and then he was drafted," Julie began. "Sometimes I can hardly remember what Johnny looked like. He was gone so long, I even stopped writing for a while. Then he was killed, so nothing mattered any more. My last letters to him were returned. I couldn't bear to read them, so I tore them up, one by one, into little pieces, because he was never coming home."

Paul leaned away as Julie spoke, averting his eyes. Her voice sounded flat, then tremulous as she said the words "coming home."

"Julie, you don't need to tell me..."

She gestured dismissively. "I just wanted you to understand my feelings. I never talked to anyone else this way. I love you, Paul. We will be happy, won't we?"

He embraced her, saying, "I imagine we'll have the usual quota of life's troubles."

Julie burst out, "Don't say that. Promise me we'll be happy together."

Her expression was so intense that Paul didn't dare laugh.

"We'll be happy within my power to make us so."

They rose from the bench, holding hands as they walked out of the park. After a few minutes Julie asked, "Were you ever in love with Natalie?"

"No, I never loved Natalie," he lied. It was a deception, but Paul felt absolved of his falsehood by Julie's smile. He repeated, "We'll be happy. I promise."

Natalie was moving into an apartment near the high school. That evening she packed the last of her belongings, finishing the housework.

"Let that go, honey," her father said, seeing her using the vacuum cleaner. "I want to talk to you."

He rarely used endearments.

"Sounds serious, Dad," she said, sitting down.

"Well, serious news, but happy, too. At least I hope you'll think so. Paul wants to marry Julie and take her away from us soon."

"Really!"

"Julie's so young, I was reluctant to give my blessing. She wants a family wedding here in Redding in November."

Natalie kept an attentive look on her face.

"You know, honey, there was a time when I thought you and Paul would be just right for each other. He obviously cared for you, and right after your broken engagement…"

"No, Dad," Natalie interrupted. "Paul and I were never lovers. Besides, I never would have married him. Paul's a Republican!"

Ralph laughed. "I'm going to miss having you at home, talking politics."

Natalie convinced her father that she needed to live closer to the high school. Roy was delighted. Surrounded by his staff at the housing complex, he could break away now to meet Natalie at her place without calling attention to his whereabouts.

Natalie was an entirely new sort of woman for Roy. On their first date, he had wanted to impress her. Then he felt great tenderness toward her when they became lovers. Her warmth and sensuality continually surprised him, but often she would become a different person, very serious and erudite. She said things like, "So you attribute your homesite sales this month to the prevailing low interest rates?"

At first he thought she was deliberately putting him on, sprinkling their bedroom talk with references to financial news.

"Hey, Natalie, I don't have a Ph.D. in economics," he joked. "I'm a simple real estate salesman."

"You're no George Babbitt," she retorted.

"Don't know George," Roy replied. "Who's he?"

Natalie looked embarrassed. "A Sinclair Lewis character in a novel. *Babbitt*."

"Nobody real," Roy stated. Still, their affair endured.

Jean Lundgren had sent Natalie several post cards from England. Clearly she and Eric were enjoying a second honeymoon. In mid-October, Natalie opened a bulky letter from Jean which began:

Couldn't wait to tell you that I'm pregnant. Eric is so elated he's even given up smoking, trying to bribe me to do the same. We think our infant was conceived at the Dorchester Hotel or in our rented car near Thomas Hardy's stomping grounds in Wessex. (Just kidding!!)

When are you coming to visit us?

Chapter 48

Paul and Julie's wedding was held in Redding's Presbyterian church, where Natalie and Gary had planned to marry the year before.

"Should I invite Johnny Browne's parents to the wedding?" Julie asked her sister.

"It's always an honor to be invited to a wedding. The Brownes will know you are thinking of them," Natalie advised. All questions of etiquette Julie referred to Natalie, not realizing that the prenuptial bustle and excitement might be painful reminders.

At the reception, Ed Tate, Paul's best man, was sitting by Natalie. He kept up a forced heartiness that made her want to scream. Bev Tate relieved the tension, saying, "Julie is an Audrey Hepburn look-alike. Ed and I hope to know her better."

Natalie replied, "The actress who played a princess? I guess Julie's eyes are similar."

In her ivory satin gown with a fingertip veil over her cropped head, Julie appeared as radiant as every bride should look. Their reception at the historic hotel had a joyful family atmosphere. Uncle Will was busy as the photographer. Randy Munz and Louie Benson tied shoes and cans to Paul's car, while bridesmaid Jackie Munz, and CeeCee, the flower girl, distributed rice to guests. Paul's sister, Rebecca Worthington, remarked to Natalie, "Paul and Julie are so *comfortable* with each other."

Natalie agreed, adding, "Dad has always liked Paul so much." Privately she thought, *Would I ever want someone to say I looked 'comfortable' on my wedding day?*

As soon as Julie had thrown her bouquet, aiming at Natalie but reaching Edythe Benson instead, the guests dispersed to the entryway, pelting the newlyweds with rice.

Her father asked Natalie for one more dance around the floor.

"You're the handsomest man here in your tuxedo, Dad."

"And you should have a studio portrait taken in your green velvet gown," he replied.

An hour later, Natalie was in Roy's arms in her apartment. Julie had been apologetic about not inviting Roy to the wedding, wishing to keep the guest list limited to family and close friends. Natalie was just as glad Roy hadn't been there to raise questions and cause comments.

"Everything go according to plan?" Roy asked, removing her shoes.

"Yes, beautifully, thank goodness." Natalie yawned. "I'm suddenly tired."

He made a face. "Not *too* exhausted, I hope."

"No, never!" She pulled him toward her. "Stay with me tonight."

Chapter 49

The day after Thanksgiving, Roy asked Natalie to go with him to close his cabin for the winter. All was well when they entered, stamping their boots and pulling off their gloves.

"I hope I haven't waited too late in the year to shut off the water," he said. "Good. The pipes didn't freeze."

"No sign of mice or squirrels getting in," Natalie remarked. The secluded cabin was her favorite place to be with Roy. She poured coffee from the thermos as Roy checked the window locks and cleaned out the stone fireplace.

"Next summer I'll put in a shower," Roy said, waving toward the unfinished corner by the kitchen sink.

"Home sweet home," Natalie murmured. "Have a turkey sandwich. I brought pie, too."

"Every man needs a place to get away, I guess," Roy said, half to himself.

They lay on the narrow cot together, covered by a worn flannel sheet and a Pendleton blanket. Roy was wearing long underwear.

"Are you warm enough in your skivvies and tee shirt?" he asked.

"Yes, but we need a bigger bed," Natalie's voice was muffled. "We'll manage. We always do." She was thinking of how much they would miss their times together in the cabin this coming winter.

Two weeks later, the principal entered Natalie's classroom at the end of the day. He nodded at a line on the blackboard.

Tell all the truth, but tell it slant Emily Dickinson (1830–1886)

"I've heard you always have a quotation for students to explain," he remarked.

"To *ponder,*" Natalie said. "I'm not sure poetry can ever be explained."

"Please come to my office. I won't keep you long."

In his office, the principal cleared his throat several times, staring across his desk at her.

"You know we're very pleased with your teaching," he began. "Several parents have told me how glad they are to have you at Shasta High. Your family is so respected. Well, you know how our town is."

"What's this all about?" Natalie demanded.

"The chairman of the school board came to me with reports you've been seen around town with a divorced man, Roy Naylor. His car has been parked near your apartment. Folks are pretty conventional, you know."

Natalie felt her color rising, more in anger than in embarrassment.

"My personal life is none of the board's business."

"But it is. There's a clause in your teaching contract referring to high moral character," the principal said defensively. "Now Natalie, I know you're a fine person. The chairman of the school board is old-fashioned in his ideas. Why do you live in an apartment alone? I'd think you'd rather be at home with your father, a young unmarried woman like you."

"I can hardly believe this," Natalie answered slowly. "If I'm to be judged by some mid-Victorian code of conduct, I'll look for a position elsewhere. I'm surprised, Walter, that you would bow to the puritanical opinions of fuddy-duddies instead of defending your own teachers."

An hour later, she was relating the scene to Roy in his apartment with a wry humor she had not felt earlier. "So I walked out of the principal's office," she concluded.

"You don't think the school board would break your contract?" Roy asked seriously.

"No, I'm not afraid of losing my job or my reputation either. I'm not fired."

Driving over to Roy's place, Natalie had been sure that he would hug her at this point, laughing and saying, "We'd better make things legal to keep the school board jackals away from you. Let's set a wedding date pronto."

Natalie had anticipated Roy's proposal at any time. He always implied that they would be together. He told her he loved her, even though she had no illusions that theirs was a grand passion. Instead, she felt a profound release of everything pent up inside her whenever she was with him. He made her laugh. His self-confidence shielded her from all hurts.

Roy Naylor had no intention of marrying Natalie or anyone else. He had not forgotten the bitterness of his marriage. Even in their early years together, his wife Lucille had grown tepid toward him. After their daughter Linda was born, Lucille became increasingly fretful, exaggerating every ailment. Roy had tried to bring her out of her depression, but he had become exasperated with her complaints.

Linda was seven years old when she was diagnosed with rheumatic fever. Roy had turned Linda's care over to his wife. One evening he said, "Lu, we've had a rough patch. We need to get away from doctors for a while, just the two of us."

"I can't leave," she protested. "Who would take care of Linda?"

"My mother, or your mother could come up from Sacramento."

"No, Linda needs me. I can't leave her," his wife insisted.

"You mean you *won't* leave her. You'd rather turn Linda into a nervous hypochondriac like yourself. Don't, Lu. Don't do this to us."

"It's too late for us," his wife said with a bleakness he would not have believed possible from the healthy girl who had enjoyed throwing snowballs at him during their brief courtship.

Remembering all this and more, Roy now said to Natalie, "Maybe we should be more discreet, honey."

At that moment, Natalie not only knew that Roy was never going to marry her, she also realized that their love affair was dying. Her immediate reaction was an immense thankfulness that she had not given herself away. What if she had said aloud, as she almost *had* greeted him, "Now you'll have to make an honest woman of me"?

Involuntarily, she shuddered, as if she had stepped to the edge of a cliff and had almost lost her footing.

No more tender times in his cabin. No more loving in her apartment.

"I'm going to spend more time with my daughter," Roy said. "She got cheated these past two years. I'm taking Linda on a trip to L.A. right after Christmas."

Natalie wrapped herself in her winter coat as Roy kissed her, brushing her hair away from her forehead.

"I'll call you soon," he told her.

She drove a block away before she had to stop the car. Oblivious to anyone passing by who might glimpse her sobbing without restraint, she felt a catharsis. She would have breached her belief in true love quite willingly in exchange for something less with Roy Naylor, but now she realized that she had misjudged Roy as well. He was too honest for compromise.

Only when the chilly December air penetrated her car and the gathering dusk darkened the street did Natalie turn on the ignition, the lights, and head toward her father's house. As she opened the front door, she called out, "Dad. It's me."

His pickup truck was in the driveway. A lamp was lighted by his favorite chair. Where was he? Twenty minutes later he came striding into the house, appearing very happy.

"Where were you, Dad?"

"I was putting up Christmas lights for Arlene and we got to talking. I'm taking her out to dinner. Are you all right? You look done in, honey."

"I've had a bad day, a really rotten day, but I'll survive. You go on, Dad. May I sleep in my old room? I don't want to be alone tonight."

CHAPTER 50

▼

Hotel Claremont April, 1959

"Meeting adjourned," Gary Morgan said to the U.C. class reunion committee in a conference room at the Hotel Claremont. Why had he agreed to this role as chairman, he wondered, stuffing notes in his briefcase. Hurrying down the hallway, he glanced into an adjacent room. Gary saw a slim woman, dressed in jade green, standing alone, her face in three-quarters profile as he gave a quick intake of breath. Then, as if sensing his startled gaze, the woman turned.

"Gary!"

"Natalie, it *is* you!" He walked toward her quickly. "You haven't changed. You look just the same," he said. Even as he spoke, Gary took in a certain wistful expression in her eyes and the faint lines around her mouth. But that long neck, pointed chin, and silky dark hair were just as he remembered.

"How good to see you," Natalie began, instantly adding, "I was so sorry to hear of your father's death. Jean Lundgren wrote me."

"Yes, Dad died very suddenly," Gary said. "What are you doing at the Claremont?"

"Staying here a few days. I got put on a statewide curriculum commission," Natalie said. "I'm combining this meeting with visiting Julie and Paul and my three-year-old niece. How about you?"

"Class of '49 Reunion Committee, my B.A. year."

As they walked together, he said, "Let's go in the Terrace Room, catch up with each other."

She glanced at her watch. "Julie is expecting me."

"Later, then?" Gary persisted. "Paul and I cross swords in the courtroom occasionally or wave at each other at Boalt Hall functions, but we don't get much chance to talk. How's your father, Natalie?"

"Divorced." She paused, holding a notebook against her bosom. "Dad married a neighbor friend five years ago. It was a marriage of convenience that turned out to be unhappy."

"Sorry to hear that," Gary said.

Natalie gave Gary a certain confiding look. "I haven't told anyone yet, not even Julie, but I have another reason for being here."

He smiled, waiting for her to continue. "Well? I'm listening," he prompted.

"Oh, it would take too long to explain right now."

"May I call you this evening?"

She told him her hotel room number, adding, "Call me after eight, if you like."

"I will. Give my best to Julie," Gary said. "I liked your father immensely. Too bad his marriage didn't work out."

"He didn't really love his wife," Natalie said.

* * * *

That afternoon, at the Sawyers' Spanish-style home on a winding road near the Claremont, Natalie was reading to her niece Robin from a Dr. Seuss book she had brought as a gift. The child had Paul's fair hair, but Julie's dark eyes.

"I do *not* like green eggs and ham!" Robin repeated.

"Neither do I, sweetie," Natalie replied. "What's this? *Sleeping Beauty?*" She thumbed through a coloring book, commenting, "This story does have a better plot."

"Red-violet is my best crayon," Robin said, pointing to Sleeping Beauty's gown, colored in the vivid hue.

"Gorgeous," Natalie said.

"Give Aunt Natalie a rest," Julie said. "You need to take a nap if you're going to have dinner with us when Daddy gets home."

"That was Paul calling to say he'd be late," Julie told Natalie. "I'll never get used to his long hours. How about a glass of wine while Robin's napping?"

"Fine. You look terrific, Julie."

"*Salud,*" Julie said, raising her glass to Natalie. "You always look the same. Now tell me about Dad. How's he doing without Arlene?"

"Surprisingly, he's his usual steady self. Glad the legal stuff is settled. Dad was very generous to Arlene, even though theirs was what the law calls a 'short-term marriage.' Arlene wanted financial security, and Dad wanted a warm body in his bed and home-cooked meals," Natalie added. "By the way, Dad wants you and Paul to pick out whatever china and glassware of Mother's you wish to keep. You have the perfect home for entertaining."

Natalie gestured toward the arched doorway leading to the dining room, with its walnut trestle table and heavy chandelier. Privately, she thought the house was too grand for Julie and Paul.

"Remember all those extension classes I took to please Paul right after we were married?" Julie asked. "Political Science and Spanish. The only value I got from them was a few Spanish phrases to use with the gardener."

"If you and Paul take a trip to Mexico in the fall, I suggest you brush up on your Spanish," Natalie said. "You don't need to read *Don Quixote* in the original."

"Have a cheese puff." Julie offered the tray and refilled Natalie's glass of dry sherry. "No new man in your life? Dad told me at Christmas that you were dating a divorced man about town."

"You're as subtle as ever," Natalie said. "The man in question and I went out together a few times. His son was one of my students." She sipped her wine. "I'm a good listener. That seems to be my greatest attraction."

"Do you ever see Roy Naylor?" Julie asked.

"Roy is everywhere. It's hard to miss him in Redding. But no, I don't see him socially. He's become quite heavy in the last year. Never remarried."

"You're so casual about your affair with Roy," Julie persisted.

Natalie popped another cheese puff in her mouth.

"To satisfy your curiosity, I'll tell you that recently-divorced men are generally appreciative of female company with no strings."

Julie's eyes widened, making her look girlish, despite her sophisticated upswept hairstyle and filigree silver necklace.

"You sound bitter, Natalie."

Just then the front door opened and Paul walked into the living room, dropping his briefcase and bending to kiss Natalie.

"How's my favorite sister-in-law? What's this about you staying at the Claremont instead of with us? Look at all the room we have."

Paul was expansive over their dinner of grilled halibut and Spanish rice. Julie helped Robin spoon her food, saying, "Eat up so you can have dessert."

"Mommy makes *flan*," Robin told Natalie.

Paul asked Natalie questions about her teaching, arguing in favor of a statewide curriculum just to get Natalie's response.

"Surely you don't want every kid on the same lesson at the same hour, as I've heard the French school system works," Natalie protested.

"Perhaps not, but I don't respect teachers who have an 'anything goes' approach. We grew up learning our multiplication tables and reading from primers without serious damage to our psyches," Paul argued.

"Oh, I'm not in favor of throwing out the baby with the bath. Robin can learn phonetics from Dr. Seuss as readily as from *Dick and Jane*. My argument is that Robin should have Dr. Seuss and *Sleeping Beauty* and *Peanuts* comic strips read to her. She'll sort everything out in time," Natalie concluded.

Robin, who had perked up at the sound of her name, said "I like *Sleeping Beauty* best."

Now, Paul was telling Natalie all about Dave Rosenthal's prosecution of a kidnapper, the sensational trial in the headlines of the *Tribune*. Julie watched the two of them, wondering what her husband would think of Natalie's affairs. He always treated Natalie with such respect, exaggerating her high-minded independence. Julie felt an impulse to pull her sister down off her pedestal in front of Paul, to enlighten him about Natalie's cynical views, but as she served her special dessert, Julie knew she could never be disloyal. Natalie was her sister, and she did love her in spite of all their differences.

As Natalie was leaving, Paul told her, "Say, I heard from Ed Tate that Gary Morgan is now a full partner at Murphy, Gallagher and Black."

✶   ✶   ✶   ✶

Gary walked into a silent house at six o'clock. He found a note on the kitchen table.

> *Gracie is keeping your mother company at her house, staying overnight. I'm invited to dinner at a friend's house (you don't know her) in North Berkeley. We're on the Tennis Club Committee. Casserole is in the fridge.*
>
> Dona

Gary was not surprised to read that Dona was with a nameless friend. He didn't know her friends anymore. When he answered the phone these days, it was often an unfamiliar voice asking for her—somebody from the Berkeley Tennis Club or a member of a charity board. Dona had even broken off her friendship with Sabina Black for no reason that Gary could discern except that Sabina symbolized a tie to the firm that Dona now rejected.

Pulling the cold tuna fish casserole from the refrigerator, Gary reflected that today made the third time this month Dona had been absent when he arrived home. *But who's counting?* No longer hungry, he scraped the tuna and noodles into the sink, rinsing the bowl vigorously in hot water.

By degrees he and Dona had drifted apart. In the past year, Leo Murphy had called upon him to take on major work: a case representing the nurses' union, in addition to his handling of negotiations when the longshoremen threatened to strike. As the senior partner's declining health put more responsibility on him, Gary had expected Dona to understand. After explaining the significance of his cases, he had said, "I'm going to be working long hours, but I do appreciate Leo's trust in me."

Dona had answered coldly, "I suppose this means that we'll have no social life for months. Sometimes I wish you were with another law firm."

Her indifference chilled him. And once, when an old client from the builders' union stopped by the house to ask Gary for advice on a minor matter, Dona had reproached him, saying, "Please do not turn our home into a drop-in office for your poor souls."

Even when Gary's partnership in the firm was announced, Dona had responded, "Leo Murphy and Jack Gallagher will just pile more work on you."

Now he dialed his mother's number. "Hello, Mother. I hear Gracie's staying over night. Are you sure she isn't too much for you?"

"No, dear. We're having a fine time. We're just about to sit down for dinner."

"What about school in the morning?"

"Kindergarten? I'll drive her. She wants to talk to you."

"Hi, honey. Are you helping Grandma?"

"Yes. I set the table."

"Good girl. How was kindergarten today?"

"I did a finger-painting of a flower. Bye, Daddy."

Gary felt relieved that his mother was coping with his father's death fairly well after the initial shock. There had been no warning signs of Lloyd Morgan's condition. Gary had been completely absorbed in his cases. Several weeks had passed with only brief telephone conversations between Gary and his parents.

Then one afternoon in March, Lloyd Morgan's secretary had found him slumped over his desk at the Port of Oakland, dead from a heart attack at the age of fifty-nine.

Seeking to comfort his mother, Gary had said, "Dad must not have had a moment's anticipation of death. He must not have suffered, Mother."

"But I didn't get to tell him things," Grace Morgan had sobbed.

When Eric Lundgren suggested Reed Houghton of Houghton and Naylor to handle the estate, Gary had agreed readily. He had been shocked to learn that his father had been investing in high-risk stocks during the past few years.

"I turned over everything in my name to Lloyd to manage," Grace had confided to Reed. "He thought he could do better for our retirement than by following Nelson's conservative advice."

The stocks had taken a tumble in early March, the net asset value down sharply. Also, Lloyd Morgan had not qualified for full retirement benefits from the Port. Reed broke the news to Grace Morgan that the estate was worth considerably less than she had thought.

"Your house is free and clear," he reassured her. "You can live comfortably. Don't make any decisions in haste."

Gary conferred with Reed privately, explaining, "I believe Dad's pride caused him to take over Mother's investments from Uncle Nelson. Even though Dad earned a good salary, he was basically just a 'hired hand' at the Port."

Now, six weeks later, Grace Morgan was putting her house on the market, planning to move into a high-rise apartment near Lake Merritt. When Gary had broached Dona with a suggestion that his mother might like living with them for a while, she had rejected the idea.

"Your mother will want her own place," Dona had said sharply. "Besides, I'm in the midst of redecorating this spring."

On this April evening, Gary roamed the living room moodily, noticing the furniture covered with drop cloths that the painters had left behind.

At eight o'clock Gary was standing near the reception desk at the Claremont when he saw Natalie stopping to check for messages. She unfolded a paper with the words: "*Sir Gareth would like to meet you in the Terrace Bar.*"

As he approached her, Natalie laughed, saying, "Well, if it isn't Sir Gawain's brother!"

"In the flesh," Gary said, taking her arm, leading her to the windows facing the lights of the Bay Bridge. "This is still my favorite view from the Claremont," he remarked.

"Oh, yes. The glamour of this place hasn't faded," Natalie said.

Once they were seated, both of them simply looked at each other before Gary burst out, "You may not believe this, but I was thinking about you just before I saw you this afternoon. Being here in the Claremont brought back so many memories."

"I believe you," Natalie said. Then lightly, she added, "I hear you're a partner at Murphy and Gallagher. Congratulations."

"I've never regretted joining Murphy and Gallagher," Gary said, his deep blue eyes flashing. He went on eagerly as the waiter set down two Irish coffees, "Whether it's a big case or one of my long-time clients, I still get a charge out of the practice of labor law." He paused. "Are you going to satisfy my curiosity about why you're here in Berkeley?"

"I'm applying for a teaching position at Katherine Wylie Academy in San Francisco. The school where Jean Lundgren taught one year. Don't give me away, please, in case it doesn't work out. I'm scheduled for an interview tomorrow morning at ten."

Gary clasped her hand across the cocktail table, saying, "You'll get the job. I just know it."

She squeezed his hand gently, and for an instant time was suspended. Then they began speaking about their professions. Natalie said, "Even on days when I think the lesson is not going well or the students aren't responding, a kid will come up to me and share his ideas about something we're reading. That personal connection gives me such a lift."

Gary nodded, adding, "Sounds like satisfaction I feel in fighting the good fight for workers' protection." Natalie listened. Finally Gary rose, saying, "Call me tomorrow at the office. I'll be in all day, waiting to hear from you." He handed her his business card. She rubbed her thumb over his name. *Engraved, not printed,* she thought, watching him walk away with his long strides.

✳   ✳   ✳   ✳

When Gary entered his house, he could not see into the darkened living room, but he heard Dona call out, "Where have you been?" in a tone guaranteed to raise his hackles.

Angrily he confronted her. "I might ask you the same question."

Dona looked small, huddled on a love seat that was draped with a paint-spattered cloth.

"You never remember my schedule. I've told you I'm on the committee to arrange the dinner in May, the benefit sponsoring children's athletics in West Berkeley."

"How could I forget all your good works? I'm merely your husband, the guy who pays the bills around here."

He knew he sounded petty, but he couldn't stop himself from adding, "Does it ever occur to you, Dona, that you couldn't belong to all your worthy clubs and societies without my subsidizing you?"

He sank into a chair opposite her.

"Oh, so that's it?" She leaned forward, hurling out the words. "You resent my friends and my activities, don't you? You say I'm extravagant just because you aren't interested in the same things. Don't I deserve a life of my own?"

In their six and a half years of marriage, Gary now realized, he and Dona had seldom engaged in a real fight. They were not shouters. Both of them had resorted to avoidance tactics—prolonged silences instead of honest talk.

Gary turned on a lamp in order to study Dona's face.

"Is there someone else?" he asked.

Her shoulders slumped as she averted her head before answering very low, "No, but maybe there could be someone for me."

The light shone on her blonde hair as she fingered the sash of her ivory-colored satin robe.

"Dona, look at me," he said. "What do you mean?"

She raised her chin defiantly. "We're not together anymore. We're just two people sharing the same house, aren't we?"

A house that's in a constant state of redecorating and upheaval. He believed that his life had taken a new course in the past few hours. Seeing Natalie again had precipitated his need for a resolution to the stalemate of his marriage to Dona.

"I'll move out tomorrow, if that's what you wish," he said, standing up quickly.

Dona waited a full minute before asking, "Where will you go?"

"That's not your problem," he answered, thinking: *How detached she is. As though my leaving our home is merely a logistic concern. Dona must be feeling that every incident of our gradual estrangement has been leading up to this final rupture.*

But as she headed toward the hallway, Dona spoke huskily. "There is no other man, Gary, if that's what you're still thinking. There never has been anyone else for me."

Her high-heeled slippers clattered on the wooden stairs as she ran up to their bedroom.

He entered his den, the one room he had kept off-limits to painters and decorators. Stretched out on his couch, Gary felt conflicting emotions flowing through him—*relief that tonight's scene was over, worry about the future, but mostly a sense of release as though he was finally free of an onerous debt.*

Physical exhaustion overtook him. Soon he was sleeping dreamlessly.

Chapter 51

"Do you have any further questions about our school, Miss Perrault?" the principal of Katherine Wylie Academy asked.

"I've read your brochure," Natalie answered. "Your course offerings are impressive. I did wonder if you offer scholarships to deserving students."

"Indeed we do." The principal explained that since 1956, the scholarship program had enabled many qualified girls to attend the Academy. "Approximately one-third of our students are here on scholarships. We've become more diverse, too. Not the stereotypical enrollment people expect," she added. "As a new teacher at the Academy, you wouldn't have the salary you're now earning," the principal said, inviting Natalie's confidence.

"I've enjoyed my seven years at Shasta High, but I'm looking forward to new challenges," Natalie responded.

"Will you be at the Hotel Claremont this afternoon?" the principal asked. "I'll inform you as soon as we reach a final decision."

Two hours later, Natalie was phoning the law firm office, asking to speak to Gary.

"I got the job," she told him. "I'm very excited. I want to call Dad right away."

"Let's celebrate," Gary said, "but it may have to be late this evening."

"I'm driving back to San Francisco to visit with Jean this afternoon," Natalie explained. "I know you must be busy."

"I'm very busy, but I'll phone you later. You're still staying at the Claremont?"

"Yes," she answered, wondering at the urgent tone in his voice.

Jean welcomed Natalie to the apartment with the words, "Nels is napping. You could have given us some advance notice. How long are you in the Bay Area? Eric will be home soon."

Natalie grinned. "You'll be seeing me often." She told Jean about her teaching position at Katherine Wylie Academy.

"Nat, I'm so happy for you. Eric and I will help you find a place this summer. Rents are high, but we're keeping our apartment because Eric needs to be close to his office. So far it's working out." Jean spoke as rapidly as ever. After more questions from Natalie about housing in San Francisco, there was a lull in the conversation. Abruptly, Jean said, "We had hoped for more children, but I've suffered two miscarriages."

"Oh, I'm so sorry to hear that," Natalie said.

"I just brought it up to explain why this apartment is big enough for us. We're close to Mother, too." Jean smiled.

"You'll never guess who I saw last night," Natalie confided. "Gary Morgan. We had coffee together in the Terrace Bar."

Jean waited, carefully neutral in her expression.

"I'm seeing him again this evening at the Claremont. I couldn't tell anyone but you."

* * * *

Gary found a furnished apartment in Oakland near his office. He paid the first month's rent before driving to his mother's house that afternoon.

"Oh, it's you. Thank goodness. I heard a car drive up and I was afraid it was someone coming to look at the house. The agent promised me he'd phone first, but people just show up any time," his mother complained.

Gary hugged her, thinking that she seemed frail. "The house looks beautiful, Mother. I know it's upsetting for you to have people trooping through your home. Let's sit down. I need to talk."

"Would you like tea? A cup of coffee?" she offered.

He shook his head, leading his mother to the sofa by the window.

"Dona and I have separated. I'm moving into an apartment in Oakland today."

"I've sensed things were not going well for you and Dona this year," his mother said slowly. "What about Gracie?"

"I'm going to see her right after I leave you today. I'm sorry to burden you with my troubles at this time, but I'm so thankful Gracie has you for a grandmother."

She reached out to him, patting his arm.

"You've never interfered, Mother," Gary said suddenly. It was true. Once he had married, his mother had never passed judgment, given advice, or meddled in his life.

As he was leaving, Gary remarked, "You'll have a buyer soon, Mother. Your garden alone will guarantee the sale."

He walked the path to his house on Ashby Avenue as Gracie ran out to greet him.

"Daddy! Mommy says I can get roller skates."

He bent down to clasp his child close to him. "Won't that be fun, baby?"

"I'm not a baby!" Gracie said sternly.

"No, of course, you're not." He swung her hand in his.

Dona stood in the doorway, watching them. "We'd better go into the kitchen," she said. "The painters finished today, but it's still a mess downstairs."

In the old-fashioned kitchen, Gary told his daughter he was going to be living in Oakland.

"I have to be near my office," he explained, "but I'll see you almost every day."

"But when will you move back home?" Gracie asked logically.

Looking at Gary, Dona raised her eyebrows as if to say, *How are you going to answer that question, counselor?*

"It's best that I live in Oakland, honey." He stroked his daughter's tawny hair.

"But it won't be the same!" Gracie began to cry.

Dona reached out for Gracie. "Daddy loves you very much, darling. That won't ever change. Some things will be different, but everyone who loves you will be part of your life. You'll see."

Gracie squirmed away, running upstairs to her bedroom. Gary started to follow, but Dona said, "Let her go."

"It's your call, Dona," Gary said, studying his wife intently. "What happens to us?"

"You never really loved me as I loved you. And for the last two years everything has been dying between us," she said with a bitterness that saddened him. "Better to make a clean break."

"Let me say goodbye to Gracie," he pleaded, but she insisted, "I'll take care of her. Just go, Gary!"

"I never wanted you to be hurt." It was the most truthful thing he could say to her.

After unpacking, Gary looked closely at his furnished apartment for the first time.

He had been lucky to find the place. Three hundred dollars a month; garage an extra ten bucks. He peered through the flimsy curtains at the street, now at the height of the commuter traffic. Two rooms with a view of a working-class neighborhood. His kind of people.

I'm back where I was eight years ago. My apartment a block from North Gate. No, this is temporary. I don't even care where I live. I have my work. Oh, God, I hope I haven't lost Gracie. I'll do anything to keep her love. But Dona is a good mother. I should have told her so. Whatever Dona thinks of me, she'd never turn Gracie against me. We'll work it out. People will say, "The Morgans had an amicable divorce."
To think that it was just yesterday when I saw Natalie again.

In spite of everything, he could not deny a stirring of hope deep within himself

He dressed carefully in his best blue suit, white shirt, and a gold-colored silk tie. Gazing at his reflection in the spotted mirror in the bathroom, he marveled that he looked the same as ever. He needed a haircut. But nothing of the emotional upheaval of past twenty-four hours showed in his face. From a phone booth in the drug store on the street, Gary called the Claremont. When Natalie answered, he said, "How about dinner tonight in the Garden Room?"

Gary stopped at the hotel florist first. He spotted Natalie walking toward him, wearing a silvery gray dress of some flowing material, her smooth dark hair arranged in her classic page boy style. He offered her flowers, saying, "Congratulations on your teaching job."

"Oh, freesias and pink roses. How lovely," Natalie said, breathing the sweet fragrance.

At first, they acted almost shy with each other. Only after the attentive waiter brought the wine Gary had ordered, inquiring if everything was all right, did they relax.

Gary raised his glass to her, clearing his throat. "Natalie," he began, "Last night I wanted to tell you that if I were free, I would ask you all over again to be my love. Now, twenty-four hours later, I am free."

Natalie hesitated before saying, "I don't understand."

"Dona and I have separated. Emotionally I'm a free man, beginning today. Even the air smells fresher. When you told me you'd be teaching in San Francisco, my first thought was that I'd be able to see you often. I'd make excuses to visit Eric and Jean just to be near you. But now, there's no need for excuses," he told her in a rush as if afraid she would interrupt him.

"Yesterday you said I looked just the same, but inside I felt tired," Natalie said quietly. "Then when I was offered the teaching position, I felt young again. And now..."

"Every moment together is more than I dared hope for." Gary smiled in his self-mocking way that Natalie remembered from their past. "Listen to the two of us, analyzing everything."

She laughed. "It's because we don't have an orchestra playing in the background any longer. Years ago we didn't need to talk. Oh, Gary, I do miss the music."

She felt her tears welling up. He reached across the table, touching her cheek.

"I guess we'll just have to make our own music," he told her.

When Natalie checked out of the hotel, the clerk asked her, "Was everything satisfactory?"

"Everything was perfect," she replied.

"Was this your first visit to the Claremont?" the solicitous clerk continued.

"Oh, no. Seven years ago I danced in the ballroom, but I believe this will be my last stay at the Claremont."

CHAPTER 52

▼

Soon after their separation, Dona filed for divorce, uncontested by Gary, although her expenses on the house appalled him. He cared for Gracie every other weekend, with help from his mother, and from Eric and Jean at the senior Lundgrens' home in Atherton. Gracie was just a year older than Nels. Gary had nicknamed the two children *cousins squared*. Eric usually swam alongside as the kids dog-paddled in the pool. One day Gary heard Gracie tell Nels, "Daddy doesn't like to swim because his leg looks funny."

He hadn't realized until then that Gracie had noticed his scars.

When he received his copy of the petition for dissolution of marriage, Gary experienced an odd shock, seeing the words. *Petitioner: Dona Dailey Morgan v. Defendant: Gary L. Morgan.* He read the terms of the agreement, noting in particular the conditions for child support and visitation rights of the non-custodial parent. Remembering the adage—He who represents himself has a fool for a lawyer—Gary asked Reed Houghton to be his counsel. Dona's attorney had requested a meeting in the judge's chambers to negotiate an agreement between the parties. Gary and Reed arrived early.

"This is a tremendous favor you're doing me," Gary said to Reed. "I know you don't take on divorces as a rule."

Reed grinned. "Oh, I expect to be paid." More seriously, he added, "I've become a believer in fresh starts. For too long I avoided marriage because of my heart condition. Then I found my wonderful wife and regretted that I had wasted the past five years." He patted Gary on the shoulder as they saw Dona and her fatherly-looking attorney enter the chambers. Dona was wearing a royal blue suit

Gary had never seen before. She looked as attractive as ever, but already Dona seemed almost a stranger to him or someone he had known long ago.

The judge motioned everyone to be seated. At a certain point during the proceedings, Reed Houghton presented his argument to reduce the monthly alimony payments.

"Mr. Morgan's primary concern is the well-being of his daughter, Grace Elizabeth," Reed began earnestly. "Therefore, he has agreed to sign over the residence on Ashby Avenue to Mrs. Morgan, as well as waiving his claims to other community property. My client has established a trust fund for his daughter, which provides generous financial support. Mrs. Morgan has experience as a professional legal secretary. Therefore, she will have many opportunities for employment…"

That's what it means to have an advocate, Gary mused, observing his friend as one lawyer to another. After a brief huddle with her attorney, Dona agreed to the reduced alimony. At the end of the session, Gary walked over to Dona who said, "I simply want what's best for Gracie."

"We're in complete harmony as far as Gracie is concerned," Gary said, smiling.

The judge sighed. "No matter how amicable it is, there's always something sad about a divorce," he told the two lawyers representing the petitioner and the defendant.

*   *   *   *

In June, Gary had driven to Redding to be with Natalie. She had given up her apartment as soon as the school year ended, choosing to live with her father until she moved to San Francisco. Natalie was touched by Gary's thoughtfulness. He spent time with her father, hiking in Lassen Park. Ralph Perrault introduced Gary to his Forest Service colleagues, too.

One day Natalie invited Gary to accompany her to Shasta High.

"You can help me pack my books and clear out my classroom," she said. As Gary carried the last box out to her car, Natalie suggested, "Let's go around to the east side of the school. We might get a view of Mount Lassen. Too bad we can't see Mount Shasta from Eureka Way. That mountain is magnificent, snow-covered all year."

He embraced her from behind as they looked toward the forestland in the distance.

"Your country is grand and I love you so much," Gary said. "I should have driven without stopping to be with you seven summers ago," he added passionately. It was the only time he alluded to their past.

"You're here with me now," Natalie replied. "That's all that matters."

Natalie persuaded her father to accompany her when she moved to San Francisco in August. Jean and Eric Lundgren had advised her to lease an available apartment near Golden Gate Park. Although Ralph Perrault stayed with Julie and Paul and Robin in Berkeley, he roamed the streets of San Francisco like any tourist with Natalie acting as his guide.

"Dad is finally getting over his provincialism," Natalie told Gary after one venture to North Beach. "I could never persuade him to visit the Bay Area when I was a student at Cal."

After approving of Natalie's apartment—stocked with Grandmother Mirov's glassware, an eclectic assortment of family furniture, and bookshelves filled with poetry—her father returned to Redding, promising to visit Natalie often.

On this bright Friday in October, Natalie gathered her students' essays to take home to read over the weekend. After six weeks at K.W. Academy, her expectations were fulfilled. To think that she had worried that her students might be social butterflies! Instead, she had been delighted with their diversity and intellectual curiosity. The seniors had been reading *Le Morte D'Arthur* and many had engaged in lively debate about the chivalric code. Natalie had assigned the topic: Is Chivalry Dead in the Twentieth Century? She had a hunch the vote would be "Yes" in resounding numbers, but she was eager to read their arguments.

Her telephone was ringing when Natalie entered her apartment that afternoon.

"Hi, sweetheart. I'm just about to leave the office. I'll be at your pad in twenty minutes," Gary said.

"My *pad*!" Natalie laughed.

She changed from her school clothes to a full-skirted cotton dress and sandals, listening for Gary's knock on her door. She had given him an extra key to the building, but he always alerted her to his arrival.

"I have lots of news, all good," he said after kissing her several times. "Let's walk in the park. It's such a glorious day." Gary tossed his suit coat to one side, loosening his tie.

"I'll just get a sweater," Natalie said.

In Golden Gate Park, they strolled the paths, lined with Monterey pines and huge eucalyptus trees, partially shading them from the sunshine streaming down.

"I'm moving into an apartment in Piedmont next month," Gary said, "I think you'll like it. Mother is sure it's one of the buildings Grandfather Lundgren owned when she was a child."

"Good karma," Natalie suggested.

"And we have an invitation from Ed and Bev Tate to their party on Sunday of next week, celebrating Ed's being named partner at Cobb and Fortis. Julie and Paul are expected, too."

The Tates had bought Grace Morgan's home in May after the birth of their third son.

"Mother declined the Tates' invitation. She said going back to the house would make her miss Dad too much. But she's looking forward to seeing you soon. Let's sit down here."

Natalie glanced toward a family spreading a blanket in the open meadow. She turned to say something as Gary embraced her, kissing her deeply.

"I love you, Natalie. We waited too long once. Why should we wait any longer?"

"Oh, we won't waste another moment," she murmured, feeling light-hearted, as though their passage of time and trial had been something in a dream. He slipped a ring with a square-cut diamond on her finger, saying, "We can be married in the spring, sweetheart."

He held her tenderly against his chest, feeling her trembling in his arms.

It's not too late for us. He is my own true love.

Natalie looked into his eyes, brushing a shock of his hair back from his forehead. "We'll have our whole life ahead of us," she said softly.

Gary caressed her left hand, saying, "I took a chance on the size and guessed right. This ring isn't loose on your finger."

"It's beautiful. But then a crackerjack box ring would be beautiful to me."

He kissed her mouth, then her closed eyelids as her tears brimmed over.

Smiling in pure joy, anticipating what had nearly been lost forever, she confided, "I've fallen in love with you all over again."

As they rose from the bench, a brisk ocean breeze was blowing toward them. Gary put his arm around Natalie's shoulder. Together they faced west, walking through the sunshine and shadows of Golden Gate Park.

EPILOGUE

▼

From the *Berkeley Gazette*, June, 25, 1960   Society Section

St. John's Presbyterian Church was the setting for a pretty wedding last Saturday, uniting Miss Natalie Perrault of San Francisco and Mr. Gary Morgan of Piedmont. Given in marriage by her father, Mr. Ralph Perrault of Redding, the bride wore a pale blue taffeta gown with white lace bodice, complemented by a white satin Juliet cap, covered with seed pearls. She carried a bouquet of pink roses and white carnations. Sole attendant for the bride was Jean Lundgren, who donned a gray moiré taffeta dress with a corsage of pink carnations.

Both the benedict and the best man, his cousin Eric Lundgren, wore tuxedos with white ties for the afternoon ceremony. Mr. Morgan is a graduate of U.C. Berkeley, '49, and Boalt Hall Law School, '52. He is a partner with the firm Murphy, Gallagher, Black and Morgan of Oakland. The new Mrs. Morgan, also a U.C. alumna, M.A. '52, is a teacher at Katherine Wylie Academy of San Francisco. Following a reception in the Garden Room of the Hotel Claremont, the newlyweds left for a honeymoon in Carmel and Monterey.

Births: Week of July 10–16, 1960   Alta Bates Hospital
July 14: **Sawyer**, **Scott and Steven**, twin sons born to Mr. and Mrs. Paul Sawyer.

From the *Oakland Tribune*   June 20, 1961

David Rosenthal Named D.A. for Alameda County
Effective July 1, 1961 David Rosenthal will serve as District Attorney for Alameda County. Mr. Rosenthal, an alumnus of U.C. Berkeley, Boalt Hall, class of 1952, is a veteran of World War II, having served in the U.S. Army in the European theater. He and his wife, Rhonda, live with their children, Jacob and Rachel, in Oakland. Rosenthal gained prominence two years ago with his successful prosecution and conviction of a kidnapper.

Births: Week of August 24–30, 1961   Kaiser Hospital
August 30: **Morgan, David Griffith**, son born to Mr. and Mrs. Gary Morgan.

From the Redding *Record*, September 10, 1966

Community News:

A large turnout of U.S. Forest Service colleagues, family, and friends gathered for a retirement dinner last Saturday honoring District Ranger Ralph Perrault, who completed forty-five years of service with the U.S.F.S. High point of the celebration was the presentation of a pair of Danner boots. Perrault joked, "I must have worn out ten pairs of boots over the years. I don't need a watch."

From the Redding *Record* October 6, 1966

Obituaries:
Perrault, Ralph A. Born Sept. 22, 1899 in Lincoln, Nebraska
Citizens of Redding were saddened to learn of the sudden death of retired U.S.F.S. District Ranger Ralph Perrault from an apparent heart attack. Mr. Perrault had gone hiking in Lassen Park on Saturday. When he failed to return by evening, his sister, Ms. Corinne Munz, raised an alarm. Roy Naylor, who had joined the search, found his body on Mount Lassen.
"Mr. Perrault had almost reached the summit," commented a Park Ranger. "He literally died with his boots on."
Mr. Perrault's wife, Marie, died in 1953. He is survived by his daughters, Natalie Morgan and Julie Sawyer, one granddaughter, and three grandsons; his sisters, Mrs. Isabelle Benson and Ms. Corinne Munz. Funeral arrangements are pending.

From the San Francisco *Chronicle*   January 2, 1968

Obituaries:
Lundgren, Jean Swithin: born April 23, 1929 in San Francisco; beloved wife of Eric Lundgren; loving mother of Nelson Eric Lundgren. Mrs. Lundgren is survived by her mother, Mrs. Frances Swithin of the city; her father, Harry Swithin of Los Angeles; her brother, Hal Swithin, and two nieces. She earned her master's degree from U.C., Berkeley in 1952. Funeral services will be held at St. Luke's Episcopal Church on Van Ness Ave. at 11 a.m., January 5. The family suggests donations to the U.C. Doe Library or to the American Cancer Society.

From the *Berkeley Gazette* Sports Section   June 12, 1969

Berkeley Athlete Prepares for State Tennis Finals
   Sixteen-year old Grace Morgan, known as "Gracie," is seeded in the top ten for the amateur junior women's state tennis tournament. Like another Bay Area tennis legend, Helen Wills, Gracie learned the game at the Berkeley Tennis Club with encouragement from her mother, Dona Kiernan (Mrs. James Kiernan). Wearing her John Lennon-style glasses, Gracie looks studious, but once on the court she shows her competitive spirit and strength.

CNN   Breaking News: Fire Endangers Houses near Hotel Claremont October 21, 1991
Local reporters filed the following story from interviews:

Investigators now believe embers left from an illegal campfire ignited the catastrophic fire. Winds fanned the flames, spreading the conflagration over the grassy hillside. The burning eucalyptus trees intensified the heat of the blaze.

Paul Sawyer was just one of the citizen-heroes helping residents caught in the explosive fire that erupted in the Berkeley hills. After getting his wife, Julie, safely out of their home near the Hotel Claremont, Mr. Sawyer helped other neighbors evacuate as firefighters used every resource to protect the famous resort hotel.

ESPN Sunday Night Baseball   May, 2000   San Francisco, California

Announcer: Well, here we are in this beautiful ballpark overlooking newly named McCovey Cove in San Francisco Bay. What a great statue of the Giants' legendary player, Willie Mays! From our vantage point we have a clear view of the East Bay. That white building on the hillside with the blue sky in the background looks like a castle, doesn't it?

Commentator: Oh, yes, everybody from Berkeley and Oakland who's watching us today will recognize the Hotel Claremont.

From the *Berkeley Daily Planet*   August, 2001

Excerpts: The Oakland Landmarks Preservation Advisory Board voted unanimously to propose to the Planning Commission that the 86-year-old Claremont Hotel and surrounding 22-acre property be designated a historic landmark. The LPAB approved the tennis courts and grove of eucalyptus trees (reported to be the largest in the country), as well as the main building, designed by well-known East Bay architect Charles W. Dickey. A hearing will be held next month to formalize the Landmarks Board's recommendation.

0-595-32475-4

Printed in the United States
21821LVS00004B/268-276